# The Edge
# of the Gulf

## A Novel of Suspense

# The Edge of the Gulf

## A Novel of Suspense

## Hadley Hury

Poisoned Pen Press

*Poisoned*
*Pen*
*Press*

Copyright © 2003 by Hadley Hury

First Edition 2003

10 9 8 7 6 5 4 3 2 1

Library of Congress Catalog Card Number: 2003108660

ISBN: 1-59058-083-4

Poisoned Pen Press
6962 E. First Ave., Ste. 103
Scottsdale, AZ 85251
www.poisonedpenpress.com
info@poisonedpenpress.com

Printed in the United States of America

*For my parents,*
*and for*
*M —*
*my queen, my angel, my darling*

It stops old wounds from hurting.
It revives the spirit. It quickens
the passions of mind and body,
yet lends tranquility to the soul.
—*Celtic proverb*
*about the sea*

# Chapter 1

On a satisfying current of confidence, Charlie Brompton said his last goodnights and walked down the steps of his restaurant into the warm June evening. The food had been characteristically impeccable, he had seen a few good friends, but not so many that he'd felt obliged to converse more than he really wanted, and Camilla Stokes, his adroit and charming manager, and soon to be principal owner of the 26-A, had told him a raucous new joke.

His buoyant frame of mind arose from a pervasive sense of trust. After wavering for the better part of two years, Charlie had finally decided to pass on the 26-A, the elegant eatery he had established nearly twenty years ago in the early days of Seaside and had named for the stretch of scenic coastal highway on which it had grown to such preeminence, as well as the Blue Bar, its famously funky alter-ego a few miles west in Old Laurel Beach. He had nurtured the 26-A into what everyone who knew anything agreed was the best restaurant, both in terms of food and ambience, on the Gulf Coast. Some insisted it was the best in the southeast between New Orleans and Savannah. Over the years, Charlie had also worked his magic on the Blue Bar. He had enhanced its weird, cozy cachet and brought it to truly legendary status as the quintessential beach joint.

At sixty-six, Charlie was finally as ready as he was going to be to let go of his brilliant, renowned, and adored offspring—his only children: he had found the right people to whom he could entrust their life and future.

◇◇◇

An hour later, emerging from the Blue Bar, he decided to leave his car in an out-of-town friend's drive and walk home, to enjoy the still fresh and breezy air of early summer. With less than an hour now to closing, the band's old soft-rock favorites and jazz had given way to slow-dance nostalgia. Their range was one of the things Charlie liked best about this favorite tried-and-true group: like the eclecticism of the Blue Bar itself, they had something for everyone. As he walked the familiar path, at first treading on crushed shell, then hard-pressed sand, among the low dunes and sea oats, the music eddied behind him, swirling away beneath the light slaps of wind from the Gulf and then welling back up in the silences.

> *"Lovely—never, never change,*
> *Keep that breathless charm—*
> *Can't you please arrange it?—'cause*
> *I love you—just the way you look tonight."*

Charlie had reached a point a few years back when the poignant lyrics of all the great songs about love and moons and Junes, about all the pairings of life, as opposed to its solitudes, no longer caused much of a twinge. When they no longer evoked the many relationships of his life that had never quite made it, or the one that almost did—the one for which he had fought, suffered, nearly become a different person. He couldn't remember now exactly when he'd first noticed this not insignificant release from the potent effects of good music, or how or why it had happened. Was it happenstance? Sheer will? A certain maturity? Hardening of the arteries? He was simply grateful for it. He loved music, of all sorts, and he had never liked trying to hide his heart from its power, any more than he would allow himself to pretend that it didn't matter.

Context, a longer view, old age. Who knew? But, whatever it was, it was, like so much in his life, good.

◇◇◇

He was whistling softly as he finally approached his house through the overarching trees, breathing in deeply the outrageously synthesized headiness of magnolias, myrtle, and laurel, all, because of a cool, wet spring, still in late bloom. He decided to go in the front door, even though the path from the beach brought one first into the side yard and more closely to the back of the house. He often chose to do this, because he never tired of standing for a moment in the drive, before mounting the verandah steps, just taking in the house. It always seemed, on his returns, to be dreaming, in the moonlight, or in the soft rain, the sunset, or the wind, and then, slowly, to awaken, with something like a gentle smile, at his approaching footsteps.

What a corny old geezer, what an old homebody he was becoming.

He'd set out years ago to build a world on his terms. He'd done more than all right. It wasn't perfect. He wasn't completely successful. But, as he turned the key in the heavy oak door and stepped into the ocherish lamplight of the lower gallery, he felt pleased and content with life at large and with his corner of it.

And not a little sorry for all the human beings he knew, or had known—too, too many—who could not say the same.

◇◇◇

Charlie was tired; he was rarely up this late anymore. But with his days as a hands-on parent and host now numbered he found that he sometimes liked to linger even more than usual over dinner at the 26-A, or take his drink into the kitchen beforehand and watch the easy command of Victor's magic, staying well out of his way, of course, perched on a stool in a corner but enjoying snippets of conversation when opportunities arose on the fly, or, afterward, nurse a brandy or coffee in the roof garden or bar, allowing Fentry to regale him with the latest Seaside gossip. And, more often than he had done in quite some time, he would then sometimes cap the evening by stopping by the Blue Bar for a few minutes, simply to walk through its laid-back but boisterously joyful funkiness, its uniquely rich and teeming diversity of life.

On a recent visit, an old friend from New Orleans (a seminarian in his youth who had opted out for a career as a distinguished pediatrician primarily because of his passions for medical science, rich food, and grand opera) had irreverently nailed it one such evening with a fond smile: "Ah, we're doing the stations of the cross."

◇◇◇

The great house felt assured, comfortably self-possessed, a bit mysterious and full of thoughts. It was after one, and the clocks had taken up the hushed chorus of their nightly rule.

He had turned out all the lights except for a side-table lamp beneath the broad curving staircase when he noticed the mail. He hadn't looked at it earlier on his way out; it still lay in a neat stack at the end of the table: the usual assortment of bills, business, odds and ends. He was shuffling it back, to be dealt with in the morning, when he noticed a plain white envelope with crude block lettering, no return address, postmarked Panama City Beach.

He opened it. It didn't take long to read.

> WE KNOW ALL ABOUT YOU. YOU THINK
> YOU'RE SMART BUT WHAT YOU ARE IS A
> FRAUD. YOU THINK NOBODY KNOWS AND
> YOU CAN GET AWAY WITH ANYTHING. THAT
> REMAINS TO BE SEEN.

Charlie was, for a moment, slightly nonplussed. "Jesus," he breathed. But, within minutes, he had torn the note and envelope into countless pieces and, not wanting it to adulterate the small brass waste can nearby, had walked all the way back into the mudroom off the kitchen to throw it into the trash.

It was difficult to be seriously upset or offended by such aberrant foolishness. It was only his passionate regard for personal privacy, his or anyone else's, that made him angry. Certainly, in any public sense, he had never hidden anything, and people had, over the years, taken or left him as he was: one of the most successful and prominent businessmen along the coast, former three-term mayor of Old Laurel, twice a South Walton county commissioner, senior warden of St. John's-by-the-Sea, pragmatically rabid nature preservationist.

He decided to put it out of his mind, and, to some degree, did so.

Slowly climbing the broad, curved staircase, he sought to reenter his earlier mood of quiet satisfaction. As he ascended, he looked at the oils and watercolors that curved along the high walls, looked down at the softly gleaming koa-wood parquet, heard the measured pulse of the clocks.

He might not have everything, but he had so much. Safety. Security. Friends. A beautiful and much-loved place. Regrets? Well, the losses that any human life is heir to. But nothing catastrophic, no unhealable wounds.

But then he found himself thinking, as he so often did, of Hudson DeForest.

In his heart, he wondered if Hudson had forgiven life, had forgiven himself.

And somewhere in the back of his mind, he wondered if Hudson would be able to forgive him.

It was one thing, he thought, to have loved and lost. Certainly, loss could involve all sorts of violence. But Hudson's loss—that kind of blow, that kind of violence—was altogether something else. Had it created an alien universe for him, one where quite possibly everything, and everyone, was irredeemable?

Would Hudson ever be able to listen to the great songs again?

If only Hudson knew what he, Charlie, knew. That he had had to build a life on trying to survive, to be content and confident, by acting like a survivor, by telling himself that he could be confident, be content. *If I appear to be, maybe I'll seem that way to the world. Maybe I'll even seem that way to myself.*

For the thousandth time, he thought, I, of all people, should—might?—be the one to help Hudson.

But he also knew that he, of all people, was the one person from whom Hudson might least allow it.

# Chapter 2

Hudson DeForest had driven out of Memphis before dawn, with the heat from the previous day already gathering a torpid pulse in the dark. As he finished loading the Highlander, a sole cardinal, perched in the crape myrtle, floated a series of falling notes, a tired serenade with little variation, over and over again. There had been no rain for more than two weeks, just seamlessly sunstruck days and breathless nights, more characteristic of August than of early June. Hudson was eager—no, anxious—to get out of town, to be speeding south through the Delta so that at first light the sharp green of the undulating fields and occasional stands of old forest might afford at least the optical illusion of freshness.

He also wanted to get to the cottage by mid-afternoon so that he would have time to unpack and turn around a few times before the long Gulf twilight set in. To arrive at twilight, always his favorite, and, for the past two years, also the most fearful time of day, would not be the way to begin. He had made good time and, unless he ran into unexpected road repairs, would be at the cottage around two o'clock. The closer he got, the stronger the urgency. Nothing was more critical now than getting to the cottage, unless perhaps it was the constant realization that he must stop focusing on its importance.

He was still in pain. He was still angry.

He was ready as he would ever be.

At noon, he crossed the long bridge over Mobile Bay, the first sight of southern blue waters looming up all around him. The glittering expanse stung his eyes. Two, two and a half more hours, and he would be there. He would pull over onto the narrow, sandy shoulder, into the shade of the pines. Even before carrying a first load up the walk overhung by the magnolia, the scrub oaks, and the two giant lantanas, he would simply climb the two steps to the front porch, put the key in the lock, and step inside. For only a moment. Then he would begin the business of settling in. But it was that one moment that he needed to come to now as soon as he could possibly reach it. The moment he had approached over and over again, for months, both consciously and in dreams, the moment he had lived up to but not yet through, and which, until he knew he could, stood between him and what remained of his heart.

◇◇◇

"Kate," he said, once softly, and then, immediately, more loudly with a kind of fury.

From sound sleep on the cool plank floor at the end of the bed, the golden retriever thrust up on his front legs, barked once, low, almost silently, and stared questioningly at the figure now sitting up in the bed.

"Sorry, Moon. It's okay. Go back to sleep…"

But Moon, despite only one prior visit to the cottage three years ago as a puppy, recognized a pre-dawn routine he had not seen for some time at home, a tone in Hudson's voice, a tension in his shoulders, and did not lie down.

"The Return of the Bad Roommate. Four forty-eight. Almost six hours. God knows I've done worse." He disentangled himself from the sheet. "Since I've wrecked your well-earned beauty rest, may I offer a low-fat Milkbone?

With Moon uncharacteristically following at his heel, Hudson shuffled along the hall to the main room with its open kitchen in one corner. Across the long room, he had left a lamp on near the hearth, and it illuminated the area in which he had made his stand for a couple of hours after a long walk down the beach at last twilight: magazines, a book, a glass. The third scotch was probably the culprit. He might have slept another hour or so. It hadn't seemed particularly indulgent. He rarely overdid it and had weaned himself, though not easily, off the sleeping pills a year ago. The furniture had been fanatically rearranged, and some pieces might be moved yet again. And though most of the packing had been carefully put away in its places, some things had even more carefully been left as a possible planned activity for today.

"A guy with a plan, Moon, that's your old man." Moon contented himself with a Milkbone and was looking up for another when, instead, he rolled his head aside and stared at a point about four feet up in the floor-to-ceiling bookshelves that flanked the fireplace.

It was the tentative yet querulous sound of Hudson's tabby cat, Olive, who thus far could discern no reason for her recent upheaval. She stared down, appalled, at Moon and then up at Hudson.

"All present and accounted for."

He made coffee, and just as the windows began to grey up with morning, he finally allowed himself to sit down and cry. No racking sobs, only a quiet weeping that lasted two or three minutes. Though Moon came closer and sat at his feet, the beasts seemed not otherwise perturbed, and by six-thirty, when real sunlight finally worked its way through the trees and the fanlight above the front door, and Hudson was making toast, Olive leapt gently onto the pickled pine floor. Without looking at either Hudson or Moon, she stretched, nudged her way around the long trestle table, still unconvinced, then sauntered to the middle of the kitchen and sat, unmoving, her shoulders rigid, expecting someone to begin right then and there to ameliorate her lingering perplexity and abject, though artfully masked, terror.

# Chapter 3

When he returned from a run on the beach an hour later, Hudson listened, for the third time, to the voice mail message that had come in yesterday just before his arrival:

> "Hi, Hudson, it's Charlie. Just want to check in. I'm out and about this afternoon and then meeting some folks for dinner at the restaurant at eight. But I'll be free by ten, so please call if you'd like to get together for a nightcap. In the bar or at the house. Just let Camilla or Fentry know at 433-2705. Retired gentlemen don't use cellular phones, and isn't that civilized? I would guess you might want to…get squared away this evening. But let me hear from you, tomorrow if not this evening. It's been too long. I've really looked forward to your getting back down here and I'm eager to see you."

So easy. No importuning, no insistence. Just Charlie's understanding that Hudson's first night in the cottage must likely be handled alone.

Well, if he didn't understand it, who would?

With a queasy mixture of acceptance and anger, Hudson deleted the message and poured a last cup of coffee.

Charlie. Always in charge, every base covered.

No detail left to chance, as Kate had once observed.

◇◇◇

He decided to leave the screened windows open for awhile longer. The light breeze he'd had with him for his run was still kicking and the day's heat hadn't begun to bank. Two bicycles flitted behind the screen of leaves, an older voice, low and morning quiet, answering a younger one, high-pitched and already completely engaged with the day. He stood, looking around the cottage.

It faced east, the small front yard a half-wild, half-cultivated thicket, and it came alive in the mornings with the bright dappled movement of early light. Through the four tall windows that ran the width of the porch, he stared at the small magnolia that stood in the yard's one relatively clear space, up near the porch. It was taller now, and thickening up, but was still young enough for its leaves to take on a green iridescence in the sun. Two yuccas, one against the porch and the other over in a corner, seemed larger than he had remembered, and an old Spanish bandolier sustained an erect pride of position halfway down the short walk, though it looked hoarier than ever. Two stubby palmettoss leaned in slightly toward one another on either side of the end of the walk. Three old scrub oaks appeared healthy, bristling with new leaves. They splayed squatly, but managed nonetheless to writhe to eight or nine feet, enough to do their part in shade-bearing. The lion's share of this job fell to the unremarkable but reliable pines.

When they bought the house three years ago, Hudson had thought the pines looked wan and reedy, and he had insisted on putting in two new ones almost too large to transplant. But all of the pines, old and new, seemed to have made it well through last year's big storm and might even be bushing up a little. Reds and longleafs, all dozen or so of them, except for one burly, twenty-five foot loblolly, rather thin, but together sufficient to the yeoman's work in fending off the sometimes brutal sun of a Gulf summer. Except on the odd, truly oppressive, day, until they handed off guard-duty in the afternoon to the tall stand of old oaks and pines along the small ravine in back, they were just thick enough and tall enough to let the cottage, for a rare couple of hours, float in a dreamy refraction of cool emerald light.

Hudson did not float with it. But he stood quietly for a long time, looking. He let the dance of light and the occasional morning sounds drift through the windows and the fan lights, let them lap around him, and remembered what Alex had said about living in the moment. *Lots more folks talk about living in the moment than actually manage to do it. It's hard, even for people not dealing with grief. You're going to have to keep trading on that steely will of yours for a long time to come, I suspect, but I believe you can start just letting yourself be. It's one of the reasons you're going down this summer. Trying to plan every moment has been just fine and you've done a good job of it, Hudson. You have. But you know as well as I that you've got to move on. You have to loosen that white-knuckled grip, just a bit. What you have is so much a part of you that it isn't going anywhere, so that's one thing you can scratch right off your worry list, isn't it?*

Hudson put on some Fauré piano music and began storing the rest of his gear; he unpacked his laptop, and arranged his cache of accumulated magazines, papers, and his fall reading. "Beautiful morning," he said now and again, at times to Moon and Olive, at times to the bright, swimming air.

# Chapter 4

They had been married two years when they came down in the
spring to close on the house, an Old Laurel cottage that Hudson
had lusted after through a protracted estate settlement that had
dragged on for years. For Hudson, who had just gone back into
the classroom after years in not-for-profits management, it was
a leap of faith as well as a dream come true. But with escalating
rents, they felt reasonably assured that it could make real as well
as dream sense. With Kate's freelance interiors work, they might
have the place to themselves as many weeks as they chose in
summer, plus Hudson's breaks in fall, spring, and winter.

They spent a month that first summer doing some minor
renovation, painting, shingling, having some bookcases built,
odds and ends; and they made a start on furniture, pulling in
an eclectic range of old West Florida country things, cane and
wicker, cool stripes and bold '40s fabrics on stuffed sofas and
chairs.

When they had left one dawn in mid-August, Kate wept.
They stood with their arms around one another, at the end of
the walk, all loaded and ready for the return to their parallel
realms of clients and deadlines (hers) and hormones, braces and
*Beowulf* (his), and she had finally laughed: "Well, for someone
who was never really much of a beach person, I guess I've made
a decent start."

◇◇◇

All things considered, and weather foremost among them, summer is not the ideal season for Laurel Beach. But teachers, profoundly travel-impaired as they are by their school calendars, cannot be choosers. For the very real and innumerable joys of their profession they sometimes pay, particularly in the South, a penalty in too many people and too much humidity. Hudson and Kate had known when they bought the cottage that, aside from some weeks in summer and over Christmas vacation, they would have only two stakes in the real glory time, a week in October and one in March.

"But there *are* those two weeks of perfection," Kate said. "And there *is* the time in summer. And considering most people's schedules, wouldn't we be ungrateful to whine?"

Although Kate, after a nearly thirty-year residency, was considered a Memphian even by Memphis standards, she was, in fact, from Louisville, and from a family that had an even more northerly orientation. She told Hudson that the one time her family did head south to water was, for no one reason in particular and in every possible particular, a nightmare. In Kate's lore it lived on as an existential sojourn involving bad plumbing, roaches, sunburn, and near-blindness when she had gotten creosote from a pier in her eye. Instead of the typical Memphis tropism toward the Gulf watering holes, or perhaps the Eastern mountains, she had spent most of her summers visiting cousins in Minnesota and Michigan's lake resorts.

Of course, it had become inevitable after she settled in Memphis that she had reason from time to time to discover various spots along the Gulf. But until Hudson took her there for the first time a year before they married, she had never seen Laurel. On the first evening, the images of a heat-prickly ten-year-old girl with wet sand in her suit and a sweaty patch on one eye evaporated, never to return. She fell in love with Laurel first through his eyes and then, almost immediately as though in time-lapse, on her own. Seeing him there she understood what the place meant to him and saw him whole, really, for the first time—all of his dimensions became integrated.

He had said, "I can't imagine how I got by all those years with just the odd week or two down here, and all the years I never came at all." They completed the business, begun when they'd met four years before, of falling in love, and they had returned to Memphis talking, for the first time, of marriage and getting back to the Gulf.

◇◇◇

They had returned in mid-October and saw the world as if for the first time. Any landscape in the northern hemisphere can attain a certain state of grace in the month of October, but already remarkable places can become transcendent.

Every morning they jogged through colors of such intensity that they seemed to register in the pulse. "It almost makes you giddy," said Kate. The water, though still warm, was no longer the translucent celadon of summer, but a flatter, richer color, nearly sapphire out where it met the brilliant cerulean sky. The sea oats waved, luxuriant and bronze, and the long dunes were whiter than at any other time of the year, crisply pleated in the brisk southwest wind. The air was so clear that they imagined they could almost see Seaside, four miles down the beach to the east.

In the cool morning sunlight they daubed idly about the cottage. Kate lined the kitchen shelves and stitched some throw pillows, Hudson refinished the low table in their bedroom. But they held to their agreement not to watch their week race past as a compulsive checklist of chores and expeditions hither and yon for old furniture or kitchen gadgets or quaint hardware.

"There will always be something else we need to do, to fix, to have," said Hudson as they strolled one evening, scotch in hand, up the road toward sunset. "But all we need this week is each other, and our fine cottage, and time."

Kate nestled into his sweatshirt and they bobbed along, an awkward four-legged creature, through the loose sand. The air had begun to chill, but the west was molten with the sun. Enormous, red, it burgeoned on the azure horizon, serene, settling itself grandly, leaving behind, above in the greenish violet evening, reefs of filigreed cumulus clouds casually flung, dark wine and golden.

"How old were you when you first came here?" she asked.

"Two, I think."

"What do you remember?"

"I remember my father holding me and the waves breaking around us, and I believe I remember sitting up next to a big pail. Sitting up and falling over, and rolling around. Crawling around in the surf line. How cool the sand was, and the way it drizzled out through my fingers and around my knees."

"My little crab."

"What does that make me now?"

"My big crab."

"It was thrilling and dangerous. I couldn't see the horizon so I suppose I thought it was the edge of the world."

"You've always liked edges."

"I thought that was just because I'm a touch claustrophobic. But, yeah, maybe that's where that started. Feeling that tow, that sucking pull all around, that feeling of the world slipping through your fingers. But knowing you're on the shore, your mama and your daddy looming up against the sun and spray like gods, their legs right there to grab. Knowing you're safe, knowing you won't be pulled off that big windowsill of the world."

"Safe excitement."

"Exactly."

"It's the same thing as our fondness for lighted windows in the night, isn't it? Approaching a house when it's dark and cold and seeing a warm, cozy interior through paned windows, and a wisp of smoke curling from a chimney."

"Exactly. Safe excitement."

"That's what we have, isn't it?"

"Yes."

They sat against a dune half a mile west of Laurel's one brief, ragged row of beachfront houses and felt the last light, amber and deep rose, weep down the sky. Due south, on the inky horizon, a solitary thunderstorm flickered, and as they watched, the high silvery tops of the clouds began to blow over, detach from their sagging purple bottoms, and strafe further out to sea.

Hudson said, "I never expected to find you. I never expected to go back to teaching. I never expected to rediscover through you just how much I love this place."

He looked down the beach, where the village huddled in pearly angles against the darkening eastern sky and where, two right turns and another half-mile walk up Pendennis Street, the cottage waited in the fresh twilight among its tangle of scrub oak and pine, lamplight spilling onto the porch.

"I never expected to live a moment anything so wonderful as this one. This one. Right here." The splendors of the evening dropped away suddenly and he fell, all at once and never more deeply, all the way, into her eyes. He kissed her warm forehead that smelled of the day's sun, and salt, and the scent that was only hers and something like rain on clover.

# Chapter 5

In the small but almost overbearingly chic house she shared with Chaz Cullen in Atlanta's Peachtree Hills neighborhood, Sydney Baird sat gazing into the chartreuse dusk as the lingering June light evaporated from the room. Before her on the narrow teak table sat a glass, its dregs of iced Earl Grey forgotten and tepid. Beside it several files from the shop lay in neat, alphabetical order, untouched.

A few last sounds of Saturday domestic industry filtered through the French doors. When she had driven up the narrow, winding road earlier, after a stint at the shop, several people whose early summer determination had not yet wilted had been out mowing and mulching and raking. She had listened as the ancient widower next door zealously attacked their common border of ligustrum, which meant that the branches would be thick and waxily dark in three weeks. It also meant that until then they would have a more unobstructed view of his back yard than they wanted, with its boldly staked tomato plants, the old-fashioned crimped-aluminum bedding edgers, a legacy set forth by his wife no doubt in an effort to contain his energetic mowing technique, the homely garage, sagging clothesline, and a deployment of homemade birdhouses and feeders that looked, when Sydney was in an expansive mood, countryish, and, when she was not, downright tacky.

Last year, shortly after she had moved in with Chaz, she had witnessed the old man's ritual with the hope that perhaps he might be soon be ready for a change of life of some kind, and that the rough edges of his property, one of the last on the street in need of upscaling, might pass into more appropriate hands. They had noticed a middle-aged man, apparently a son, briefly visiting every few weeks; perhaps he would take his father in or find a nice nursing home for him when his health began to fail. The seasons had elapsed, however, with no visible abatement of the old man's hardihood, from his hectic spring weeding to a meticulous hour-by-hour watering system throughout the summer, and a mulching in the fall and a division of bulbs that, in Sydney's view, approached obsession.

It wasn't that she wished him ill. She simply had a passion for things looking their best.

Caught unaware by the stealth of the twilight, she rose suddenly, the letter still in her hand, and moved about the room turning on lamps and picture-lights. The paintings, kilims, and good simple antiques came quietly alive. She laid the letter on the mantle and went into the little bar just off the dining room and poured a scotch and water. She took her drink and stood for a moment at the doors, looking into the small garden which offered up its last vibration of intense green and immaculate bloom. Chaz's reformation from his misbegotten years of fast living and substance abuse did not preclude the odd joint now and again for a bit of Sunday afternoon yard work. The narrow length of lawn still glowed in the last light, its vivid fescue anchored to the small gravel patio just beyond the doors with three large urns of red geraniums, cascading purple verbena, and yellow-gold ranunculus. To the right, through the gathering darkness and over the newly lowered level of the ligustrum row, Sydney surveyed a majority of the widower's yard, unmanicured and eccentrically rural.

For a moment, she was a cosmically lonely ten-year-old, looking through a screen door at a similar, though even scraggier, backyard in Coweta County, some fifty miles, and what seemed a hundred years, from Atlanta.

She stared hard at the rear of the old man's faded blue Chevrolet. The way it protruded from its sagging frame garage annoyed her until, dismissing something so paltry and remembering that soon she would no longer have to look at it anyway, she returned to the mantle and picked up the letter that had repeatedly drawn her attention from the accounts files she had brought home. Reaching for it she looked into the eyes of a framed photograph, the eyes of her recently deceased father-in-law.

◇◇◇

"You really love him, don't you?" she could again hear Peter Cullen saying. "He's been putting his life together, and I can tell you're going to be good for him—help him keep it together."

Another woman might have found this well-intended expression of admiration more self-interested and utilitarian than respectful, but Sydney had understood what Peter meant and she had warmed to it. Indeed, she had warmed to him, and had been sorry when he'd died quite unexpectedly in late February of a massive coronary. She'd never had a father, and he had seemed a good one.

They had been standing in the side porch of the house in Peachtree Battle on a night not long before Christmas. Peter had given them a small dinner party in celebration of their engagement, and she stood with him while Chaz went to bring the car around. Behind Peter, she saw the glow of the library, the fire still radiating patterns across the bindings of a lifetime's cargo of books, the good paintings, the good fabrics, the poinsettias.

"I love him more than I ever knew I could love anyone," she said, and Peter had taken her into his arms for a hug and then kissed her on the forehead.

"I can see that, and I am happier about my son than I ever knew I could be. He's going to be *fine*. And *you two* are going to be fine."

On the drive home, Sydney had nestled deep into her new Vera Wang jacket, holding Chaz's right hand and feeling the sort of simultaneous rush of emotion and clarity of thought she had previously experienced only when a performance was going exceptionally well. An actor, by nature—and formerly by profession—she had never, like some, distinguished between her art and her life.

The life that had been handed to her would not have been worth living if she had not, early on, decided to take it in hand and transform it. She was grateful for her talent and saw little reason to be falsely modest with herself about it. She had long ago ceased to wonder whether her emotions, her motivations, or her desire to recognize and use an opportunity were what many people would call *true* or if they arose from her instincts for *acting*. The instinct for giving a truthful performance depended fundamentally on being able to believe its truth oneself. That was her constant guide. Some people might prefer to call their barometric readings on their motives and actions morality; she didn't begrudge them that. By the same token she expected no one to question the strength and confidence that had gotten her through, to question her own unique gifts and instincts for doing the right thing, her perspective on what was real. What was true.

# Chapter 6

Like so much else, sooner or later he had to do it. Hudson decided on sooner.

He reached Charlie at home and asked him over for a drink around seven.

"I won't promise much in the way of dinner, but how about shrimp and a salad?"

"Are you sure you even want to bother with that?" asked Charlie. "We can eat here or at the restaurant, or…"

"No bother. It sounds just about exactly the right level of commitment to break in the kitchen. Two weeks ago I was reviewing *The Scarlet Letter* and *Jude the Obscure* with fifty-some-odd adolescent girls. Cleaning off the grill and marinating a few shrimp does not sound like work."

"An 'at-home.' Sounds great. I've got a good white Bordeaux I'll bring along."

Hudson turned off the phone and, for several minutes, sat very still, looking at it.

He wrestled yet again with the fact that, despite their history—or, bizarrely, because of it—Charlie now posed such a threat.

It was early afternoon before he narrowed the wooden blinds, turned on the central air, and headed out on a foraging expedition.

As the heat of the day blossomed, Hudson made his more "local" local rounds: the shrimp and some start-up groceries at the good, but wildly overpriced, market in Seaside; then the old liquor store and a stop for gas on Highway 331. There was more traffic than Hudson remembered, enough traffic, even on Scenic 26 between Laurel Beach and Seaside, to make the going slow, though most of it was, mercifully, concentrated around Seaside. It also made Hudson wonder how often he would want to make the twenty-mile trek west, through the beach communities on 98. It would have to be done. Moon had his requirements and most of them came in the large economy size; and though he was, indeed, Olive's slave, Hudson balked at the notion of paying more for cat food at one pop in the Seaside Market than he had paid the Memphis Humane Society for the cat herself.

◇◇◇

"…and brought the urban livestock with you," Charlie mused, considering the paw that Moon had just laid across his bare foot. "You are, as they say, a handsome dog."

"Well, I considered leaving Olive. They abhor changing homes, you know. A friend was willing to come in three times a week, but that seemed like an awful lot of cat patrol. I'm sure that in another day or two, Olive will be delighted she came and will resume her usual role as life of the party."

Olive, who was having none of this, glided from under the kitchen butcher block where she had made short work of some shrimp bits. She looked up once, momentarily, at Charlie, as if perhaps he were a curious afterthought. Apparently the late-night tableau of Hudson sprawled in the big chair on one side of the hearth, Charlie in the other, and Moon splayed smilingly between them did not warm the cockles of Olive's heart, for with a dismissive shake of her head, as if coming to her senses and remembering something far more important in another room, she sidled slowly down the long, wide hallway.

Charlie sank back in his chair, laughing. "Well, you're not off the hook yet."

His own longtime companion, Maisie, a yellow lab, had died several months before, peacefully in her sleep at the age of seventeen.

"I have a friend in Dune Allen whose lab is due soon, so I'll have a new pup on my hands by the end of the summer."

Hudson got up to lower the CD volume a bit. They were listening, around the edges of their conversation, to the punchy elegance of Art Tatum. He poured a scotch for each of them.

"Well, I've probably told you more about the Elliott School and the education of adolescent girls than you wanted to know."

"Hudson, I am so, so pleased that you're doing what you're doing." He stared hard at Hudson, holding his gaze, and smiled. "It's where you need to be, isn't it?"

"Probably. I remember my whole first year I kept thinking it was such a gift. These past two, I'm sure it's been a necessity. I don't know...."

"How you would've done it?"

"Yes. I mean, I still don't know how I'm doing, or what I'm doing, or why, but it was pretty essential, I think, to have to show up somewhere every day at eight fifteen and be constantly 'on' in the way teaching demands, every minute of the day, with four classes of young faces scrutinizing every turn of every synapse. Waiting for you to talk. Waiting for you to listen. Even when they're kind, and they were, that age is relentless. About everything. I had no place to hide. There's nothing like—nothing could've been like that. I kept thinking I would implode, just go up in smoke some day standing in front of a class while hearing myself prattle on about the symbolism in *Huckleberry Finn* or Jane Austen's humor or something. But I didn't. In working with fifteen- to seventeen-year-olds, one day becomes the next, imperceptibly; there are no seams. There's no such thing as *time*. Especially with the ninth graders. These shrill, gawky creatures stumble into your classroom in September like newborn colts with mouths full of braces, and the roller coaster starts, and the next thing you know they're these young women, sauntering out in June, new bodies, low voices, good haircuts. God love 'em."

"They're very lucky."

"Maybe," Hudson said. "I know I am."

There had been scrutiny—that came with the age group—but there had also been the sweet, innocent, unguarded concern and affection that could leap out of the same girl who only moments before might have acted a brassy brat. They knew how to call it because they didn't, like adults, weigh their options as thoroughly. They just connected. Thank God the one time he had really lost it was in the ninth grade class. He had tried discreetly to maneuver toward the door and finish some sort of sentence, but hadn't succeeded on either count. He had come back almost immediately, after dashing some cold water on his eyes and wiping them with his handkerchief. "Excuse me…" he had begun, striding to the front of the class. "Now, we were just…" but before he could get any further, three girls near the front, and within seconds, the entire class of fifteen, had surrounded the lectern quietly, and, one by one, hugged him, some shyly, some crying, some reaching out from their own painful frames of reference, all of them murmuring "We're sorry, Mr. DeForest, we're sorry" and "It's okay, it's okay."

◇◇◇

Hudson had discovered real love late and, as is often true in such cases, found himself profoundly moved by the experience. It at once seemed the most natural thing that had ever happened to him, an unexpected stroke of providence, and, for a strong individualist fairly well set in his ways, surprisingly defining. He was himself, but more so. Life suddenly made much more sense, was so much richer. He bloomed. The world bloomed. Kate—their love—did that.

◇◇◇

"Tell me about you," Hudson said.

"Well. I've been trying to be a man of more leisure, but I wonder if I have the talent for it." Charlie chuckled. "Is that what you English teacher types call irony?"

Charlie's entire career and, more important, his life, had been about helping people enjoy themselves. Now he was approaching sixty-seven at his own elegant pace and Hudson found it hard to believe that he wouldn't know, as he seemed always to know, exactly how he wanted to go about it. His appearance seemed unchanged. A man of medium height, compact, muscular and trim, he lounged easily in the big chair, one leg hiked over the arm. Thick white hair fell in a mop to one side and sprouted from the neck of his polo shirt. And, what had always come to mind first whenever Hudson thought of him during their occasional phone conversations, the startlingly blue eyes, bright with alertness and humor. Perhaps just the faint tracery of a few new lines around them.

"I almost peeked into the Blue Bar last night, coming back from my walk," said Hudson. "Looked hopping, as usual."

Charlie smiled. "The nonstop local pageant of life in Old Laurel. Good drinks, fine family dining, old friends, and just enough pretty young people with the sense to get out of Destin and Santa Rosa for an evening."

"You're not planning on giving it up anytime soon, are you?"

"Sometime soon," he said. "But they may have to lay me up on the bar, torch the whole damn place, drag it across the beach, and set me out to drift."

"But other than the fact that you live about a five-minute walk away from it and consider it your personal vanity and the pub of your domain, you haven't been hands-on for awhile, have you? Your manager, Terry?—he's still with you?"

"Yes. Four years now." He hesitated, then added, "That's not bad for these parts. Terry does a good job."

Hudson remembered him, but only indistinctly, a stocky man, fortyish, with short sandy hair, beard, and wire-rim glasses, a shadow in a Hawaiian shirt against a still bright evening sky as he and Kate sat on stools along the back bar on the deck sipping ice cold beers.

"No, no. You've pretty well got it. I just like to drop in, hang out occasionally. Like you say, the phantom master of the tavern. Local eccentric."

"You are one of the least eccentric people I know. And 26-A? How much are you there?"

"Oh, that's still my main enterprise. I go in to my little office at least for awhile just about every day. But I've been cutting back. I'll let go soon. I finally have the manager I'd been looking for. You'll like her. Camilla Stokes. About your age, maybe a year or two younger. Divorced, kind, patient, a model of efficiency, attractive. Very good-humored. Old guard classy. Just the right air about her."

"Fentry?"

"Fentry holds forth in the bar. The volume of business is such that it really requires its own oversight. Camilla handles the restaurant. They're a match made in heaven and I just love them both. We just celebrated his sixth year, a Sunday evening about a month ago. Everyone who was anyone was there. He wore a tux and Victor did Barbadian dishes. You know, Victor's coming up on his fifth anniversary."

"How is big Vic?"

"Just the same. All six-foot-four of him right up to his pony-tail. Quiet, reserved, soft-spoken. That terrific Aussie accent. And as serious as ever. We've given up trying to change that, it's the way he is, and he's a sweetheart. He dated a girl in Pensacola last year for awhile but she went back to her former boyfriend. I can't imagine what that guy had that Victor doesn't except perhaps a sense of humor. Half the people in the restaurant on any given night would leap across their partners and blissfully offer themselves up to him on a bed of romaine. We worried about him there for awhile. Victor low key is *really* low key. But he seems to have retreated back into that great calm, that wonderful simplicity of his. When he's not having his culinary visions he's still surfing and playing tennis."

"Sounds like you've got it covered."

For a split second, Charlie looked down and slightly to one side, as if he'd heard or, perhaps, remembered something, but then he returned his gaze to Hudson and gave him his slow, trademark grin. "Yeah, I guess I do. I'm a very fortunate man,

Hudson. It's all pretty perfect, when you think about it. I've sold everything else except for a piece of land east of Seagrove. It's time for some new life, new projects…I've been keeping my hand in as much as I want but I think I'm ready now to move on."

Easy for you, thought Hudson. New life, indeed. All pretty perfect, indeed. On top of the world—this particular stretch of world, anyway. No looking back for you, Charlie.

Instead, with level coolness he said, "But nobody's had a hand like yours."

◇◇◇

Charlie was the only child of a longtime manager of the Louisville Country Club. He learned firsthand the practical operations of running an upscale establishment and, always a quick study in his observations of people, he learned the equally essential subtleties of elegance, charm, and genuine hospitality. Both his parents were of good middle-class stock and had a quiet but distinctive personal style of their own. Nevertheless, the lines of privilege were clearly drawn and, though most of the members treated the personable good-looking boy like part of the family, Charlie realized early and often that he was a poor relation.

Wisely, he refused to feel embarrassment. When he graduated from the University of Kentucky and left for a three-year stint in the Navy, he pragmatically decided that he would use to his advantage his master-level training in the ways and means of the very rich. He would draw on and indeed be grateful for what was, after all, valuable experience, not unlike, say, growing up on a successful farm, or going to law school, or being an artist's apprentice. He'd had years of it, nearly two decades that had shaped him and showed him that people with wealth and/or breeding enjoy having a good time *of a particular sort and in a particular style* and that it took a person of a particular sort and with a particular sense of style to make it happen.

In fact, he decided, there was no reason, after such a long period of breathing the atmosphere, minding the details, and enjoying both the technique and the spirit of the process, that he should settle merely for succeeding as a creator of elegant hospitality for wealthy people of taste. He would simply succeed at becoming a wealthy person of taste himself. From his parents he had learned how to manage details with seeming effortlessness, so that the old guard of Louisville would have the pleasures of the club while feeling they'd scarcely left home. He realized he had impeccable taste. With that and his skills he could attain wealth enough, he would do it in his own way, and he would enjoy it. Hence the natural evolution of his *joie de vivre* and his role as an intuitive host, in life and in business.

His eminent good sense and determination eventually extended to his sexuality as well. On the day he emerged from the Navy, at age twenty-five, he quit trying to mislead himself about his thoughts and desires. He called the phone number in New Orleans of a fellow who had passed briefly on assignment through the Pensacola base a few months before and who had since left the service. It was his first, a very happy and memorable, significant relationship

Having fallen deeply in love with the Gulf, not particularly wishing to return to Louisville, and having no other destination in mind, Charlie settled for a time in Pensacola. He was assistant manager and then co-owner and manager of the town's best restaurant. He celebrated his twenty-ninth birthday by closing on his first beach rental property out on Santa Rosa Island, and had another within a year. Soon, he turned a large profit on selling his interest in the restaurant, and turned his sights further east, living between his house in the regentrifying East Bay area of Pensacola and a condo in Destin, where he opened a restaurant. In 1970, at thirty-five, he did well on the sale of the restaurant and the two beach properties he'd restored, and left Pensacola, with Andrew, ten years his junior, for Laurel Beach, to make his first real home.

He had always had a deep respect and a zealous concern for those stretches of the Emerald Coast that had managed to escape the first big development boom, from the end of the War up through the late '50s, and as his real estate interests expanded they never included careless abuse or trashy exploitations of the landscape. He eschewed hotels and motels and concentrated on renovating and building discreetly superb houses, something of an indulgence which was paid for by small, exclusive enclaves of duplex or quadplex condominiums and a couple of small, charming inns, all of which were nearly as elegant as his houses.

When Seaside had begun to develop twenty years ago, Charlie dabbled a bit; it was to his great financial advantage as the village immediately apotheosized into an upscale Southern destination. Hudson didn't doubt for a moment that Charlie still loomed large as the guiding presence at 26-A, as the doting patriarch behind the Blue Bar, and, in other degrees and fashions, as a force to be reckoned with along a hundred miles of the coast. But in the fifteen years Hudson had known him, Charlie had always handled life, himself, with a lightness, a grace. He had exquisite taste and a generous, almost exhaustive, sense of hospitality that anticipated every detail. But never once had Hudson seen a wheel turning, a pinched face, the slightest betrayal of effort. The man had a finely tuned informality. He liked to smile and he liked to see other people smile. He had been raised to consider manners as real values, foremost among them that no effort should be spared but must never show. He worked all his life to erase the line between working and living and to make it all one, large, marvelous party, for those for whom he cared and for himself.

But now, of course, everything had altered.

◇◇◇

Hudson asked, "And what are you doing at home?"

Charlie laughed and shook his head. "I could do two days' work every morning before I leave the house. I swear I think that house grows in the night." He looked around. "I probably should have a beautiful cottage like *this*. Just the right size. Right now I'm hip-deep in painters. My young cousin's coming for a couple of weeks and I'm using that as an excuse to do the north guest suite." He paused. "But I do love my home. More than ever."

They talked on. About the cottage, about the weather, about who had moved in and who had moved out of Laurel Beach and who was renting what, about local politics, until the clock-barometer on the big pine desk in the hall whirred dully, clicked, and feebly bleated out midnight. Kate had found the clock, which she had dated around 1900, at a flea market in Fort Walton and had had everything done to it that could be done. But its creaky wheeze continued, and anything more than three or four o'clock drove him crazy. On the long hours he would look at her, roll his eyes and shake his head like a madman. "Oh, but think of all the stories it brings into our house," she would say, sometimes making a few little whirring noises of her own just for spite. "Think of all it's seen."

He suddenly realized they had, during his reverie, become mired in a long and awkward pause.

"Hudson."

He blinked hard as Charlie began to speak again, now in a low and very measured way.

"You know I would never presume on your loss. I think we're very private men, the two of us. But I want to say that I am so glad to see you sitting here in front of me. You look well. I can only say that I know what you've been through is all anybody ever needs to know about hell. I knew there was nothing I could do except call and write every now and then. That you'd have to find your way by yourself. I can't imagine that there's anything I can do even now. But if there is, if there ever is *anything*, please let me be your friend. I've always known you are a strong man and a good one. I guess I just needed to say, face to face, I'm so, so sorry. And that I hope, even through the pain, you can feel just a little bit like some part of you has come home."

Hudson walked to the hearth and looked down, tightening his jaw. When he spoke his voice sounded, even to himself, as cold as the empty grate. "Thank you."

"And just..." Charlie nodded, almost as if to himself. "Just keep going."

"That's what I do."

Another long pause.

Charlie rose and stretched. Moon did too, and yawned.

Charlie said, "I have to have a little business dinner Friday evening but other than that I'm free into next week. You let *me* know when you want to get together. If you don't," he winked, "I'll probably start bothering you."

Hudson took a grip on himself. "Saturday, then. I want to arrive at your home at six-thirty, in time just to sit around here and there in it because I always like being there so much, *and* for a complete tour of all new art, furnishings, and paint colors. By seven-thirty, I want to be standing on your deck in the sunset if its tolerable and there's a breeze, or ensconced in that long, cool solarium looking east over the lagoon if it's not, sipping one of those rum things you do with fresh guava. I want us to arrive at 26-A at eight-thirty or whatever the exact moment is that the evening reaches that ineffable *frisson* that only Charlie Brompton's restaurant, the best in west Florida and arguably the best this side of New Orleans, can attain."

"Can't wait."

"My shrink, Alex, would be disappointed at the continuing tendency to over plan every second of my days and nights, but pleased that I'm 'asking for what I need' as he puts it."

His hand on the door, Charlie grinned, his hair more tousled than usual and the beginning of sleep near his eyes. He hugged Hudson, a bit awkwardly, for a moment.

"Smart shrink."

"Not only that, he's an Episcopal priest. Fifteen years a parish rector, wanted a change. You'd like him. He comes at psychology and spirituality with enormous common sense. Very articulate, in a theological good-ol'-boy sort of way. I get my head shrunk and my soul shriven all on the same nickel."

◇◇◇

As soon as Charlie was out the door, Hudson felt a tremor rifle through his body. He was glad he was past the first encounter. But he had no idea whether, when, or if he'd ever be able to let go of the fact that Charlie knew so much. That Charlie, more than anyone else, knew him. Knew Kate. Knew the two of them in Laurel.

It wasn't helped by his noticing again, as he turned off the lights, the key to the cottage that Charlie had left on the small table by the door. *"You may need this other one for some reason this summer."*

Charlie had been too close. Known too much. And Hudson felt it like a powerful undertow, a hollowing drag at his guts that made him feel all too familiarly desperate.

And that desperation made him feel an all too familiar rage.

Much later, after tossing in the sheets like a banshee for more than an hour, he finally edged into a shaky sleep.

Just as his consciousness slipped into darkness, he saw the two of them. Charlie and Kate. She was looking at him, in her eyes a question, while Charlie's had a shrewd glint. He smiled his lopsided grin at her and said, "Don't let him blame me."

◇◇◇

It had been those six days, that glimpse of the world in October, that had hovered in front of Hudson ever since, an eidetic image always just beyond the immediate reality, a memory more palpable than his own flesh, a measure, a radiance, a torment.

They had wavered for weeks over whether to remain in Memphis for Christmas and the New Year. They were tired; each of them had skirmished for a month with a nastily prevailing flu bug; Hudson's semester, featuring two new class preparations, had been especially demanding; a huge project Kate had been orchestrating through the fall all needed to come together just after the first of the year; Hudson's mother, a feisty woman of seventy-five, was recuperating from minor surgery. They finally decided to accept a Canadian family's very attractive request for three weeks at the cottage, and to stay put and do as close to nothing as possible.

The two weeks passed in a gray blur of cold, slashing rains, clotted at times with sleet and snow. They talked incessantly of the cottage, of Laurel. "We did the right thing," first one and the other would say. "It would have felt crowded and rushed," said Hudson. "Yes. We mustn't be like children," said Kate. "It's *there*. We don't have to prove a point. There's March. There's summer. There's next Christmas if we want it." They congratulated themselves on the premium holiday rental income. By the fire in their best friends' living room one evening after dinner, Kate whispered to Hudson: "The porch chairs are being paid for even as we speak." Through the days and nights, in their shared imagination, in the shifting fragments of what was one long happy conversation, they decorated and redecorated the cottage and planned holiday meals, took long walks up the beach to Seaside in a brisk morning breeze, read in the sunlight near the windows, built fires.

Every night in bed, Hudson would interrupt his homework reading now and then to riffle among his maps. Kate read a local history of South Walton County. She had used a photo of the cottage as a bookmark; whenever she stopped reading, she'd look at the photo and say: "I still can't believe it." Before sleep they would turn to the Weather Channel to see what might be happening on the coast. Was their place in the throes of this cold rain as well? Would tomorrow be sunny and seventy? They dreamed of Christmases and New Years to come.

◇◇◇

It had been on a crystalline, cold morning in early March—only two weeks before they were to go down during Hudson's spring break—a morning when a thick late frost burned off quickly in the sun, and the surprised daffodils bounced back unscathed, that the world ended.

Unimaginably, without warning, without even time for goodbyes.

Kate was gone.

# Chapter 7

Sydney looked at the clock on the desk again. Chaz was returning from another quick trip down to the coast to spend a weekend with Uncle Charlie and was due into Hartsfield within the hour.

She weighed her own first impressions of Charlie, from their weekend visit in April. Actually, he was Chaz's cousin-once-removed: his father and Charlie had been first cousins. Particularly close, apparently, more like brothers.

She had found him charming, sincere, funny. And still attractive. What was not to like? She felt fairly certain he'd taken to her. Most men did. It wasn't a suit she played shamelessly; like so much in life, it was simply the cards one had been dealt. Just as she was a source of strength and focus for Chaz, she had imagined that she might shed some pleasant lights from time to time into Charlie's declining years. She was nothing if not adaptable. Perhaps, she had thought, she would simply transfer the emergent attentions she had begun directing to Peter, instead, to Charlie.

Of course, he was gay; that could potentially prove to be a problem. Not that she cared in the least about the variety of people's sexuality; she had, after all, spent years in the theater and known a number of strong, kind, attractive, witty, intelligent and talented gay folks. No, what niggled at her was something else she'd encountered from time to time in gay men. Would

Charlie either not notice her enough, or notice her too much? She wanted to have an effect that might be of practical benefit to her and to Chaz. And why should she not? But what if, on the other hand, Charlie was one of those gay men who seemed at times so astoundingly perceptive, capable almost of knowing what you felt and thought even before you did yourself? She'd known one or two like that and it made her uncomfortable. Given the men in her childhood and her former fiancé, she had few delusions left about the male animal, and she found it necessary, not to manipulate, but to be able to anticipate, and thus to keep a very firm grip on her relations with men.

Certainly there could be nothing wrong with that. And it was part of who she was, the person she'd made of herself. No one had needed her when she was young, indeed no one had particularly noticed she was alive. She liked having people, especially men, depend on her.

She'd earned the right to enjoy being strong.

To being needed.

Wasn't it, after all, a common, key aspect of being human?

# Chapter 8

For Hudson, the first year was sheer blind agony, the summer a freefall through hot days and nights of numb solitude in which he alternately tried to grapple with and avoid the constantly ungraspable nightmare, not sleeping, not remembering to eat and not wanting to when he did, crying jaggedly while he tried to make himself work in the garden, seeing only two or three worried family members and friends very briefly, drinking far too much, staring at unnoted hours of mindless television programming the only criteria for which seemed to be that it have no credible storyline and not the faintest whiff of real emotion.

He had managed a frail semblance of getting himself together in the fall. His mid-life career change back to teaching had been a transition, like his marriage, to gratitude and joy. He loved teaching literature and writing, and he loved the all-girl environment; he enjoyed his upper-level courses but was also especially fond of the ninth graders. His changelings, as he called them. His work saved him.

For what, he couldn't imagine.

◇◇◇

He woke in mid-sentence, trying to formulate an answer.

It hadn't happened in quite some time. For a moment, utterly lost as he looked around the room, he forgot the question. It was always a question, sometimes posed by Kate, sometimes by Alex, and usually unanswerable. In its most nightmarish manifestations, the voice was an unknown, disembodied, oracular echo, welling up loudly and then trailing away into utter darkness, pursuing him up and down the pews and aisles of some cavernous, deteriorating, medieval sanctuary.

Three-fifteen. He had fallen asleep over a magazine, although not before, apparently, turning off the reading lamp. In the pale wash from the porch light through the windows, the sofa and chairs, the tables, and the large expanse of rug were a black-and-white study of softened angles and planes. Insubstantial. He did what the harsh necessity of time had taught him to do. He roused himself from the chair and rubbed his hands over his face. Standing, facing the windows, he stared hard at objects, riveting them into concrete reality, attempting to ground himself in the mundane.

He went down the hall to the bathroom and turned on the light. The man he was so profoundly unsure of, unsettled by, loomed there in the mirror again; would he ever go away? The tall, lanky body, stiff and awkward with confused sleep; the features, startled, eyes wildly searching. What by day might be a pleasant, if serious, face, with a strong jaw and large eyes of an unusual green, came at him now like some mottled ghoul. The thick red-brown hair, longish and somewhat curling, was caught in crazed snarls and dully showed all of its grey under the harsh light. The green irises of his eyes squinted noxiously in their bloodshot whites, the pale skin around them looking thin and bruised.

He went to the kitchen, got out a tea bag and put on the kettle. In the four or five minutes it took to come to a boil, the question, and the voice, came back to him. *Are you angry because she's gone, or because she won't go away?*

It was the rumbling, faceless howl in the void, and the kitchen burgeoned with it, pinning him against the counter. Everything else was obliterated and Hudson, engulfed, sensed no borders between it and himself; he reverberated like a hollow reed. When the hiss of the steam became a low screech, he saw two hands come up, whitish anonymous things, seemingly detached. He made a cup of tea and then sat down at the long trestle table. He could not feel his body; the hot tea seemed to trace a path down his throat but to lose itself where his chest should be. He knew that the process of draining away into space, of evaporating, took no time at all. The reassembly was the hard, slow part.

Beginning with: why bother?

He'd gutted out many a night at home, and had been doing better over the past several months. Fatigue had gotten him fairly well through the night before, but now, in the empty hours, the newness of the cottage was depleted.

Of everything except Kate. It was like having a second skin; he could look nowhere, at nothing, without seeing it with her, without being with her.

He tried to calm himself. This was to be expected, he told himself. He would get through this. He got up from the table; he turned off the porch light and opened the front door. A bright half-moon, augmented only slightly by one of Pendennis Street's two streetlights, filtered through the tangle of the front yard, leaving small pools of white across the porch and steps and down along the walk. Hudson stared through the thicket of leaves to the two six-foot palmettos that leaned in, just slightly, from either side of the crushed shell walk, out where it ended in the road. They inclined toward one another as if sharing a juicy piece of gossip, and Kate, God only knows why, had named them Louie and Martine. *"She's the one with that ruff of fronds off on one side. She's just said something sly and he's throwing back his head. Laughing."*

He went back in and shut the door. Moon was waiting with a resigned look. He had stayed put where he lay near the sofa when Hudson first awoke; he, too, knew something about interrupted nights and had a refined instinct for discretion. He sat now on the cool plank floor of the broad hallway, offering a companionable way to the bedroom or a friendly ear. Hudson wasn't calm, despite what he kept telling himself. He felt the loss of control. His head filled with spoken words and images coming faster and faster, one crowding out the other; the movie had started and there was no stopping it and he wasn't just watching it, he was in it.

"Go on, boy. Go back to sleep. It's all right." Moon obeyed, returning with admirable nonchalance to the spot between the sofa and the hearth that he seemed to be breaking in. His eyes, however, did not, for quite a long time, completely close.

Hudson poured another mug of tea and then sat in the other chair of the matched pair, the one he knew, from a small tear under one arm a silver bracelet had made, to have been hers. That way he wouldn't have to look at it. Maybe he would make that a house rule. God knows he had made other rarefied and vastly detailed deals with himself in the house in Memphis.

Just now it didn't matter that much. He knew that a vigil had begun and there was nothing to do but see it out. He felt it before him, pulling him in. He sat comfortably, the mug of tea at hand on a small table, and leaned his head back against the cushion. He let go, and let it come, again. Not hot, fast tears. Those caught you by surprise; and he'd become fairly adept, the momentary bout that morning notwithstanding, at heading them off. No, this was the fond, familiar terror. The not knowing what to believe. Kate was not with him; Kate was with him. He was surviving; he would never really be alive again as long as he lived. They had only had a handful of years, but they had defined life for him and he would never be the same. They had only had a handful of years and they would, over more years and in life's great leveling irony, lose their life-defining meaning and fade away.

He sat back, at once watching and within the frame, as the film of his fear took him toward morning. He thought of the evening with Charlie. That had gone fairly well. But had it gone perhaps too well? Which was more real: a high-functioning will and an impulse to reach out, or the need to grapple with the spiritual world and one's own wearied self-consciousness? Part of him already needed to see Charlie again, and yet he knew too that he had hardly been able to wait for him to leave. So that he wouldn't have to see his satisfaction. So that he could do this.

Keep this appointment. That was it, that was the great impossibility: he wanted connectedness to Kate and he couldn't have it. He could never make it right. Whatever he did or didn't do, life would never be right.

Well, this is how it is now. This day. It may not be this way tomorrow. I didn't seek it, it sought me. I can't avoid it. Goddamn it, I can't. Even if I want to, I can't avoid it every time or forever. There are going to be times when it's best to give in.

He let it all come, a long hard review, the longest and hardest and sweetest he'd taken up in close to a year. One palpable word, scene, dream after another; everything but the touch. It was all he wanted to do and all he wanted not to do. It was all there was to do. It was like making love to oneself, but it was all he had.

◇◇◇

By the time dawn seeped up amid the trees out front, he was spent, and hovering just this side of madness. But he was also mildly irritated. I might actually try for a nap this afternoon, he thought. Why not? There's always a first time. He wanted a shower and coffee, and he was hungry.

Very chill comfort, but he could hear Kate say: *Good.* She was the strongest person he'd ever known and never one for drama. *Go on, now. Get on with it.* He reached down to the stack of papers tossed on the floor and pulled up a book review. There were a few fine points he still needed to get right.

### Thirty Years At The Movies. By Pauline Kael (Dutton, 1291 pp.)

Pauline Kael opens this extraordinary career-collection of her film reviews with characteristic accuracy: "I've been lucky. I wrote about movies during a great period, and I wrote about them for a great readership, at *The New Yorker*. It was the best job in the world."

*For Keeps* reminds us that we are even luckier.

Kael has done more to set the standard for film criticism than any other writer. Not many individuals have the opportunity of critically engaging a human endeavor that, in the course of less than ninety years, has become the most popular art form in western civilization. In her career, Kael raised film reviewing to an art form of its own, which is the unique and collaborative role great criticism should play in any of the arts. There seems little doubt that she could have trained her focus as compellingly on literature, theatre or other performance arts; and as a cultural essayist, her intellectual incisiveness and wit are far superior to a number of our current pundits. It is one of the great synchronicities of the 20th Century that this passionately inquisitive gadfly grew up with the new medium and became, for millions of readers, its most voracious eye and most knowledgeable and articulate critical voice—and that, moreover, she is a hell of a lot of fun to read.

No less remarkable is the fact that the opportunity was not handed to her; she created it. Kael's first review was published in a small San Francisco quarterly in 1953, she was already in her mid-thirties, and she was not paid. What she had, and what a majority of those who pass themselves off as "reviewers" today sorely lack, was: (1) a passion for film, (2) great talent as a writer, and (3) a wide-ranging curiosity and intelligence not only about the medium's technique and aesthetic but about the social, cultural, and economic contexts from which the art emerges. She helped us *see*, and she made it simultaneously important and fun to do so. By the time she was finally paid for being the best in the nation at this new and important "job description," which, even today, some editors still have difficulty valuing, she was in her forties.

For the last twenty-five years of her career, she was film critic for *The New Yorker*. Millions of readers anticipated her weekly column and discussed it as fervently as they did the films themselves. She was provocative and demanding. This is what great criticism about a society's most popular art form can and should do: make people want to react to film, feel about it, think about it, and talk about it. Pauline Kael performed brilliantly the role of critic for any medium: she encouraged informed and passionate dialogue. That she did so vis-à-vis a brand-new artistic tradition that quickly laid an unprecedented, almost inarticulably profound claim on our nation's psyche makes her contribution even more uniquely riveting.

When Kael retired, in fragile health, from *The New Yorker* in 1991, movie buffs could barely mention the short-notice printed announcement to one another without coming close to tears. It may have been a sort of film-follower equivalent to baseball fans watching the Babe finally doff his cap. None of Kael's previous collections so compellingly demonstrates, as does *For Keeps*, the depth and breadth of her contribution, her central role in our ongoing discussion of what movies are and how we see them.

Especially now, in the age of video, laser disc, and DVD, *For Keeps* is an indispensable resource. As the heart, mind, voice, and humor of film criticism by which all others will long be compared, it is also an indefatigable cause for celebration. And hope—for another Golden Age of Film Criticism.

It was sometimes a kind of reassurance to fall asleep reworking an article, the words stretching, rocking gently, like one of those fragile swinging rope bridges, over the darkness below. And so, for an hour or so, he did.

# Chapter 9

By eight-thirty, Hudson was strolling through Laurel, his ostensible destination the little general store which doubled as the post office. Because the entire village was served by just five irregular streets from east to west and four even more irregular streets rambling from the beach on the south to the intersection of 26-A to the north, Hudson decided on a general walkabout in order not to arrive at his destination in less than five minutes.

He felt light-headed from the lack of sleep. He felt eighty-six, not forty-six. His eyes were dry and tight and his balance seemed a little off; he walked slowly and, until he found a gait, he had to watch his step. He heard Alex saying: *This is a really hard passage, Hud, but you've already started doing it. This stringing together of moments. Even as you let go of that cold but fairly reliable comfort of your will, you're going to find yourself, well—melting, I think. It may be sloppy at times, but at least you're going to be back in the picture and not merely trying to draw it from the outside. You've been "being" in some moments for the past year, you've told me so. In the classroom, with a friend or two, just here and there, a moment in your yard, sometimes when your writing really kicks in. Even a few with your crazy old shrink on his better days. Now, start stringing them together. The more you can let go and the more moments you can simply be in, the more they're going to start moving again, running together. You say you like good watercolors. Well, buddy, you're at a point now where your life becomes one.*

Fat, cottony clouds bulked in the west. There might be a thunderstorm by late afternoon, but now the eastern sky pitched above the live oaks of Pendennis Street was a brilliant turquoise. Heading south, Moon trotted ahead on his soft leash, smiling at the world and looking back occasionally to confirm with Hudson the glory of this miraculously reincarnated memory. Ever the gentleman, Moon greeted with only a delicate, passing sniff the ancient, baleful-eyed bulldog waddling along with an equally ancient and baleful-eyed man. Hudson whispered when they were past: "Not really a proper beach dog, eh, Moon?"

They turned right on Eulalie, covered the short distance to Yaupon Lane and, instead of going left, south, toward the broad expanse of dunes and beach, went right again. Yaupon is the western boundary of old Laurel and separated from the houses on Pendennis by the tall screen of pines and oaks that rise behind the cottage. At a couple of spots along the road, between the houses facing Eulalie, Hudson could see the upper back porch of the cottage looking out into the trees. On the western side of the road was a long, slender lagoon, overhung on the west by a tall, impenetrable wall of trees. Bright birds swooped and sang in the sunlight; in the hot afternoon they would retreat into the shaded depths of the thicket and slumber until twilight. Two miles down the beach, on the other side of this old stand of scrub forest, out of sight and, for most Laurel folks, as out of mind as they could keep it, lay Greenside, one of the new breed of residential beach communities, with its gate, its developer landscaping, its enormous, suburban-looking manses.

After about a hundred yards, Yaupon Lane elbowed back into Pendennis. Hudson enjoyed passing the cottage again; Moon looked twice and seemed to find it odd, though not particularly vexing, that they didn't turn into the walk. "You're right, boy, but we'll be back." This time they went all the way down Pendennis, passing Eulalie to the right, and then, further along, crossing first Decatur and then, Hudson's favorite, Lantana Boulevard. No more than twelve feet wide, Lantana had apparently gained the distinction of being a boulevard by being the longest lane in the village, making a broken-field jog through the cottages of Old Laurel at its broadest point of perhaps a mile.

Along the way, Hudson nodded or spoke to the few early risers who were walking or leisurely cruising on bikes. At one cottage, a sleepy young man sipped coffee with one hand while with the other he held a hose, watering a valiant, non-native bit of lawn; at another, a white-haired woman, whose name Hudson did not know but whom he recognized as a year-round resident, tended hardier indigenous varieties of hibiscus and laurel. It was hard to keep up with who-was-here-when unless you were one of the fixtures, like Charlie, who knew most of the year-round residents and many of the long-term visitors of each season. A newcomer, and now out of pocket for almost three years, Hudson knew only a handful of his neighbors, of either variety, and that might be enough. The illusion of intimacy, floating on an undercurrent of anonymity, appealed to him. At least for now, he thought.

Pendennis Street, like the rest of Laurel's patchwork of wandery roads, was fronted by a hodgepodge of architecture, some only local-color quaint at best, but the majority, and the effect as a whole, unpretentiously picturesque. A few large, two-story houses of white-painted clapboard, with dark green or gray shutters, were set back in deep yards of tall oaks trailing Spanish moss. At the other end of the scale stood a do-it-yourself stucco horror from the early '60s, fortunately almost obscured by palmettos and banana plants, which Kate had said resembled a large bratwurst. A few Old West Florida bungalows sported tall narrow windows with plantation shutters. Out along the water, of course, were some newer, larger beach houses. But most common in the village were the typical Old Laurel cottages, small but comfortable structures in various shapes and sizes from the '20s, '30s and '40s, some a bit older, almost all of which, like Hudson's, had been respectfully restored or renovated. On small lots, the cottages were built primarily of weathered shingle with porches, screened or open, across the front or along one side.

Though some of Laurel's properties are owned by completely absentee landlords for whom they are nothing but prime sources of income, most of the cottages belong to people who enjoy them at least a few weeks of the year and, in many cases, as much as two or three months, or more. The year-round population is very small but, in recent years, steadily increasing. Except for the Canadian snowbirds who take places in the winter, apparently finding the sometimes chill weather a tropical paradise compared to Ottawa and Toronto, most people who live in or come to Laurel Beach are Southerners, either current or by consanguinity. Some have been returning for many years from as far away as up East, the Midwest, Texas—where parents or jobs or marriages have taken them—coming back, the Gulf still in their blood, annually calling them back from wherever the American economic diaspora has taken them. But most come from hometowns across the South, as close as Mobile and New Orleans, Tallahassee, Montgomery and Birmingham, and from farther afield: Mississippi, Memphis, St. Louis, Nashville, Louisville, Atlanta.

◇◇◇

They circled out onto the beach, long enough for Moon to get in a decent romp, and then came back in on the east end of the short, if slightly wider, street modestly called Beachside, which, for all intents and purposes, is Laurel's main street. What this means precisely is that on the north side stands the little general store and diagonally across, on the south side, the Blue Bar. The former was a rebuilt version of the one that the founding fathers had put up in 1890, the latter an amalgamated structure of varying ages that has been, at various times over the century, a restaurant, an inn, a store, and a dancehall. Under Charlie's tutelage it had developed and sustained a good kitchen, serving lunch and dinner in its three large rooms, and boasted two great bars, both curving and long-flung, one inside and one along the back, on the deck that looked out over the dunes to the sea. Low-key and funky, the place had an atmosphere that Charlie had casually but carefully cultivated and might best be described as that of an old roadhouse by the sea. Folks strayed in from Santa Rosa and Destin, and even on the slum from Seaside, but by and large the Blue Bar, like Old Laurel itself, is something of a cherished, insiders' hang-out.

The only other businesses on Beachside are Laurel's *other* restaurant, the Comber, a nondescript fern-bar sort of place featuring a roof deck and indifferent Italian food; a small ice-cream parlor and bakery; and a gift shop cum beach gear cum art gallery. The owners of the Comber, a bland but perfectly pleasant couple from Pensacola, abdicated the scene every winter, and seemed to manage well enough by the summer overflow from the Blue Bar. The other two shops were open year-round, although the owners' hours tended to become more and more vagrant as the winter wore on.

Hudson left Moon lolling by a tub of petunias and geraniums on the sunny porch and went into the cool shadows of the Laurel Beach Market, where a young woman stood behind the counter, leaning down onto a newspaper, a cup of coffee at hand.

"Good morning," she said, pleasantly but without smiling. She straightened up and took a sip of her coffee. She was attractive in a quiet, understated way, early twenties, with large, intelligent brown eyes and glossy dark blonde hair, its wavy bob tousled and still a bit damp from her morning shower. "May I help you find something?"

"I need you to put on your postal service hat, if you will, and see if I have a package."

"Sure. I haven't looked yet." She leaned over and pulled at an unwieldy bag under one end of the counter. "It usually comes in around three, but there're things here from yesterday." She knelt down beside the bag. "What's the name?"

"DeForest. Hudson DeForest. It'll be something the shape of a video cassette."

"Yes," she said, righting herself. "Here it is. I have to ask for an ID, please."

As Hudson fished out his driver's license, the girl glanced at the address on the mailing packet. DeForest House, 183 Pendennis. "Oh, the neat cottage with all the trees and those two big flowering..." she gestured.

"The lantanas that ate Cleveland, yes, that's it."

She looked at him intently, almost smiling now. "We're neighbors."

"Oh, yes?"

She extended her arm across the counter and Hudson shook her hand. "Hi. I'm Susie Cogswell. I'm spending the summer in the Sandiford place on Yaupon. It's sort of kitty-corner behind you. I see the top of your house through the trees, and I pass it when I walk."

Hudson wasn't sure if the sightlines worked both ways, but he knew the only even partially clear view through the trees from his little upper back porch. "The dark green clapboard bungalow with white trim?"

He suddenly felt Laurel shrinking around him.

She nodded and looked eager, as if she had been located by radar on a desert island. "Did you just arrive? Are you here for the summer?" There was something charming in her open-faced directness, her interest, that kept it from seeming like prying.

"I came in day before yesterday. I'll be here for six weeks, anyway."

"Ah. That's nice." She seemed momentarily unsure of what to say; she didn't take her eyes from Hudson, but she folded the newspaper, lay it to one side, and sipped her coffee. Lying on the counter, where the paper had been, were two books. Face-up was an old fat hardback collection, which Hudson recognized, of literary criticism; face-down beneath it and off to one side lay a paperback of O'Neill's *Long Day's Journey Into Night*. As she noticed his glance, he said: "And how will you follow these up for a *really* good time?"

Her face relaxed into a smile, for the first time, and it brought her lower face more into sync with the wide, bright eyes. She let out an involuntary little laugh. "I'm finishing up my master's degree. Writing my thesis this summer."

"O'Neill?"

"Carson McCullers. This is just..." she waved a hand over the formidable heap, "just something else...." She looked a bit like a child who'd been caught sneaking candy.

"Hmm. Thesis on McCullers, O'Neill and critical essays on the side. No moss growing under your beach umbrella."

They chatted for another five minutes or so and the world grew even smaller. He confessed his own English major's heart and that he was a teacher, she the fact that she was, before leaving for Tulane six years ago, a Memphian. In fact, she was an Elliott grad. ("I missed you by two years," he said.) Her family had a time-share condo over in Destin to which they'd been coming for years, but she wanted the space to be alone and work on her paper before finishing up in the fall semester. Her grandfather was giving her half the rental on the Sandiford house as a master's graduation gift and she was covering the rest with her part-time wages from the store. ("The Sandifords are here in the fall and spring and knew someone was needed. It's great: I work four days a week, usually from eight to two.") After the thesis and her orals, she planned to take one year off for "unstructured reading" and to decide if and where she wanted to go on for her doctorate.

Hudson finally said: "Susie, it's good to meet you. I have to go now to do, as a matter of fact, some homework." He wagged the brown mailer.

"A book?"

"Well, no. This is my other job. Considering what they pay me, you might almost say my avocation. I write about film for *The Buzz*, the weekly 'alternative' paper in Memphis. Well, you may know it. It had started before you left town. I enjoy it; and I alternate weeks with the editor, so the volume is manageable."

In fact, a small press in Oxford, Mississippi, was bringing out a collection of his reviews. Hudson had always taken his gig with the paper seriously; he loved film and he had been weaned on Pauline Kael. Hence, the book review.

But he had been leery when the editor, a friend of a friend, approached him. "Are you sure the world needs another book of film reviews?" But the editor, a great film buff, persisted: "They're more than just film reviews. They're very good essays, they have broader cultural context." His goal for the coming weeks—in addition to the new reviews every other week, and some reading and preparation for his fall classes—was to select, and in some cases re-edit or revise, his favorite columns, about two-thirds of the nearly three hundred from the past nine years. Hudson fully expected the proposed collection, an unglamorous, literary journal-sized paperback, to sell, perhaps, two dozen copies, but what the hell? His friends, his mother, his head of school, and the folks at *The Buzz* thought it was pretty exciting.

So, apparently, did Susie. "How *cool*. I pick *The Buzz* up when I visit my parents. I've probably read you. Will you be getting your films like this while you're here?"

"Actually this is one I wanted to see again before editing an old review. Usually I'll be going into Destin or Pensacola for Friday openings and then e-mailing in over the weekend."

He smiled and headed for the door. "See you soon. I enjoyed our chat."

◇◇◇

He and Moon loped across Cedar and Potero and up Pendennis. They came to the head of the walk, and he hesitated for a moment, letting Moon run on ahead to the porch. He looked up the walk, framed between Louie and Martine, at the cottage, still dappled under the rising sun with the shadows of the pine and scrub oak. *Our stake in the future,* she had said. Then he heard Alex again: *Go on, now. Go to the Gulf. Your place. The cottage. Go to the sunsets, the loneliness, the memories, the future, the shrimp, the hushpuppies, the mosquitoes, an old friend or two, new ones, boredom, new things you can't possibly know about, the whole damn mess of life. Your life has now got to let degrees of love be in it again without your thinking it'll destroy you. Your aim in loving now can be to let life come to you without your need to exert the self-control that's gotten you this far. You must become more accepting, more open, like an innocent, trusting child, or a very old person. Don't let yourself reach for more fear than you have naturally on your palette. It'll be really hard but you gotta do it. And you can. Go on, boy. Thaw. Let it all run together.*

He kept his eyes open wide. Looking. He stretched out his arms and brushed the leaves as he went. Not hurrying. At least not too quickly.

◇◇◇

By two o-clock he had watched the movie and edited his review.

## Robert Altman's *The Gingerbread Man* is a small but triumphant masterwork

To say that Robert Altman's *The Gingerbread Man* is a sensuous thriller would be absolutely accurate and rather uselessly trivializing. Sensuous thrillers have, after all, in recent years become a dime-a-dozen phenomenon. American filmmaking today represents a near-classic example of a decadent period in art, and the rush to re-mine the rich genres and styles of our cinematic past is one of its chief characteristics. Though there's nothing inherently wrong in that, it can prove a fatal formula for filmic imagination when coupled with the current lemming-like attention span of Hollywood commerce.

The revival of interest in *film noir*, which began to manifest onscreen during the 1980s and thus far shows no signs of abating, can be attributed, as much as anything, to this jejune copycatting. The really fine ones have been few and far between (*The Grifters*, arguably, first among them), but there have been just enough to fuel the retro-*noir* trend as one of the few low-budget, safe-bet alternatives to blockbusterdom. Most of our leading directors, even those with sensibilities fundamentally at odds with the genre, have, at least at least once during the past 15 years, tried their hand at it.

What an unexpected and satisfying pleasure then, late stage of an old game, to have an American master remind us that we have more interesting reasons than the current failure of imagination for enjoying these dark studies of people of low degree, reasons that have to do less with our cinema's self-cannibalization and more to do with who we are and how we live today. Adapting his screenplay (pseudonymously credited to Al Hayes) from an original screen story by John Grisham, Altman has fashioned a dark jewel of a film in which the use of *noir* elements is not the usual matter of a few stylistic (quite often, extraneous or misapplied) flourishes. Like the great, vertiginous post-WWII *noir*, *The Gingerbread Man* is a window on a seductive, unsettling, psychological state—the classic *noir* state of the center not holding, of the threat of disunity from within—a window which, though of no useful perspective to the threatened protagonist, provides the viewer the comfortable distance of framing. We are able to lose ourselves completely in the world of the film because Altman creates a complete world, one in which style and substance are indistinguishable. And yet—even as we identify with the *noir* characters' bad behavior, their brazen weaknesses, corruption, and the mess they make of things—we shadow their missteps without falling into the void with them. *The Gingerbread Man* is an authoritatively conducted walk on the dark side; it is moviemaking that leaves you with slime on your heels, some fine points of moral ambivalence to chew, and a grin on your face at Altman's still-developing capacities to entertain.

In this character-driven hejira through paranoia and human failing, Kenneth Branagh plays Rick Magruder, a self-indulgent but successful Savannah attorney. He has made a name for himself, unpopular with the local law enforcement, by defending cop killers and other dicey, high-profile cases. He seems something of a sexual addict. He loves his children but usually picks them up late at his ex-wife's home and never seems to have enough attention for them. He drinks a little too much. He's arrogant. He's charming. It's as hard to take a barometric reading of his moral center as it is for the meteorologists to gauge whether Geraldo, the offshore hurricane that threatens Savannah throughout the film, will indeed make landfall. In the end, both tensions break and some air gets cleared, but not before Altman has sucked us into his accelerating vortex of narrative and spiritual atmospherics. Branagh's casting is brilliant: he makes Magruder unsympathetic and attractive by turns: smart, passive aggressive, bad-boy likable, with self-doubt that verges on self-loathing, worthy both of our scorn and of saving. The performance, low-key, delicately observed and detailed, and featuring a superb low-country accent, is Branagh's best in quite awhile.

The most archetypal form in the story is the troubled and troubling *noir* female (Embeth Davidtz) who takes Magruder for the ultimate ride that will either take him to the just wages of sin or to their mutual redemption. Davidtz is good in the somewhat underdeveloped role; she keeps the viewer off-balance just as she does Magruder. Her Mallory Doss is not easy to like but she's had a hard time, so it may not be her fault that she has a look in her eye like that of a wet alley cat. (Robert Downey Jr., lending local color as a tipsy private dick, gets one of the movie's best lines when Magruder assigns him to watch Mallory for a night: "You got me here babysittin' Pandora…")

It's hard to know how much of Grisham's original story remains on screen; most of the brilliantly fluid cinematic narrative is clearly Robert Altman at the top of his mature game. One can't help but suspect that the subtle character-layering, the evocatively saturated mood, color and tone, and the edgy psychology derive from Altman's screenplay. One of the most satisfying aspects of *The Gingerbread Man* is its marriage of Altman's characteristic insistence on unrushed, character-driven storytelling with steadily mounting suspense.

The director is marvelously aided and abetted by cinematographer Chagwei Gu and by his son, Stephen Altman, whose Savannah production design—rain-slick wrought iron and cobblestones, candlelight, Spanish moss, and gleaming mahogany sideboards—is a central aspect of the overall design.

Noteworthy is the fact that an unusually high percentage of setups are middle-distance shots through paned windows; backlight frames the characters, frequently in handsome 18th and 19th century interiors, against the night and the coming storm. We see the paneled libraries, antique furniture, exquisite fabrics, flowers, and silver cigarette boxes glow in lamplight, the stuff of civilization. But the characters inside these rain-streaked windows become increasingly anxious, their movements jerky and unsure, like spoiling watercolors. Altman masterfully builds a dissonant tension as the material world of old Savannah reassures us and suggests the protagonist is relatively untouchable, even as we sense his world unraveling. As the tale twists to its hairpin conclusion, the hurricane flings itself onshore, and Magruder's amoral self-absorption pulls a noose around his neck, we realize that *The Gingerbread Man* is, quite specifically, *noir* for the '90s. Instead of the psychologically and economically displaced anti-heroes of the genre in its late-'40s heyday, the outsider here is an articulate, well-dressed, sardonically witty attorney; instead of being outside by virtue of post-war urban anomie, the crisis he must finally confront is that he is standing outside his own life. Instead of being led astray into a life of crime through a real but misguided love for an evil, scheming woman, he is less sympathetically corrupted by insular sensuality and boredom. Magruder, like society at large, confuses data and real information; he is often on his cell phone but rarely in the conversation that most matters. In the postmodern colors, tone, and temperament of our era, Robert Altman recreates in *The Gingerbread Man* the *noir* narrative as a quest for authenticity, and posits a hero whose fragmented values and attention span seem maddeningly familiar.

Several lines of squalls, like gray armadas with tall ragged thunderheads for topsails, advanced in the afternoon and, with the thunder rumbling and the rain slashing down the windows behind the half-closed louvers of the bedroom shutters, Hudson slept.

# Chapter 10

Sitting on one arm of the brocaded chesterfield Sydney drew a deep swallow of scotch and read the letter. Again.

Chaz had brought the letter along on the first Sunday in March to the Buckhead restaurant where he was meeting her after an afternoon of sorting through his father's papers. She had known something was wrong immediately. He was breathing heavily, his eyes first darting nervously around the restaurant and then riveting expectantly on her. When their wine arrived, he had produced the letter from his pants pocket.

"Something with the inheritance?" Sydney asked, even before looking at the thick letter that had been folded back into its envelope. She had passed the last several days in increasing irritation over the new knowledge that although Chaz would be inheriting a little more than a million dollars, a bit more than she'd guessed, his father had stipulated, in his parsimonious Presbyterian wisdom, that it be doled out as a trust until Chaz reached the age of forty. To distract herself, she had focused instead on the matter of the unremarkable but spacious house off Blacklands Road. It wasn't the best end of the street but it was still good. They could live there, mortgage-free at least, or realize perhaps six or eight hundred thousand on it.

"No, not exactly," said Chaz. He had stared fixedly at the small bowl of freesias in the middle of the table. "Just read it."

◇◇◇

Sydney would always remember exactly what she felt on reading, that first time, the letter that Chaz had discovered in his father's desk. Always a quick study, she had, indistinctly but with instinctive certainty, seen her life rearrange itself before her eyes. Before she had finished reading the letter, she had known that her life was changing or, to put it more accurately, that her life was suddenly taking on its inevitable shape.

Now she laid the letter on the table and paced the room slowly, trying with the adjustment of a frame here and the smoothing of a rug there to enforce the sense of calm that she had learned to muster in any situation. For someone who had never really known a moment of internal peace in thirty-three years, and who had of necessity thrived more in a realm of anticipation than in the present tense, it was a useful tool, and had enabled her to become a perspicacious strategist in setting and attaining goals. If it might be said that some people were goal-oriented, Sydney was goal-driven. But this rapacious need to get to the next place often did its best work when she tempered it with a cool and critical stillness. Indeed, this combination of living with a mind in overdrive and one foot on the emotional brakes had, over the years, become instinctive. Where once, for a period in her twenties, her dreams and plans and frustrations sometimes kept her awake long hours of the night, she now could summon a remarkable objectivity that helped her channel her energies more usefully. It had certainly served her well as an actor, and now that she had left that career behind it served her well as she moved forward in her new life. And though this capacity for self-preserving poise perhaps did not engender any real serenity or relaxation of her constant vigilance, it at least produced some semblance of regenerative rest occasionally, and, here and there, for scattered moments anyway, an approximation of contentment.

As she wandered idly now about the room, placing the files back into her leather brief, sitting in the club chair and leafing through an auction catalogue, going for another ice cube for her drink, Sydney realized that until she had read the letter for the first time, that evening three months ago, she had actually been allowing herself to toy with the notion that her life was sufficient. That a handsome man who adored her and sizeable bucks and a house on a leafy street in Peachtree Battle were enough. Halfway through the letter, however, she realized that she had, uncharacteristically, been fooling herself, and Sydney did not suffer fools kindly, especially when the foolishness was her own. And so, less than five minutes later when she had handed the letter back across the table to him, she was back on track, in a whole new world of possibility, one that she recognized as truly worth her aspirations, effort, and skill. She had lifted her glass and smiled until he returned the toast, and she had spoken in a subdued but encouraging tone.

"You should go down and visit him, shouldn't you?"

And later, as the Porsche had swept through the pristine, fragrant air of Atlanta in early spring, around the curve past St. Philip's Cathedral, she had said, "And, in answer to your charmingly persistent question of these last several months, I *am* ready to marry you now. I had been thinking late summer, but now, I think, the sooner the better." She reached over and he gave her his hand. She held it tightly, and as they turned into Peachtree Hills, she laid her head back.

He needed her.

Despite the intermittent slashes of discreetly pale streetlight through the barely leafing tree branches overhead, the face that he saw was, as usual, radiant, constant, and sure.

◇◇◇

Sydney paced and sipped the last of her scotch, and waited for her knight errant to return. It seemed reasonable to assume that before they slept that night she would know more about how she should help, take charge. Organize possibilities. Her questions were ready, as were a subsequent array of responses and next-step options. She was prepared, she imagined, for anything Chaz might say and, of course, she was perfectly prepared to interpret *how* he said it. She had never intended to be in a position in which she would have so much riding on him. She loved him, she knew, and she loved his ravishing, slightly dissipated good looks, his sexiness, the way his desire for and trust in her shone from his eyes unguardedly, but she had never been blind to his weaknesses. But she drew courage and a quiet excitement from knowing that she had never once in her life taken an uncalculated risk. Although not perhaps in the way he had once said, Chaz's father had been right about one thing: *He'll be fine.*

She would see to it.

# Chapter 11

Charlie brought the drinks out onto the upper gallery, following Hudson's gaze toward the sunset, southwest over the Gulf.

"It's yours in a way, isn't it." It wasn't a question. He handed Hudson his drink. "That's how *I've* always felt."

"I guess you're right. I never articulated it that way but, yes, you're absolutely right. Just like people have their own river or lake or pond. This is *our* ocean."

"Well, for you Memphis folks, it really is. The Mississippi River feeds it, connects you to it." He gestured over the railing of the gallery. "Your blood's out there."

Hudson smiled. They had been having parts of this conversation for many years. He had always known that one reason Charlie took a shine to him was that he'd recognized Hudson's passion for the Gulf. "Well, you grew up on the Ohio, which leads *into* the Mississippi."

"Not the same. We seemed a little more removed in Louisville. When I was a boy we vacationed in Virginia, where both my parents had family, usually the mountains. Once or twice the beach, such as it is, Virginia Beach. Didn't know what real sand was till I got down here in the Navy. The Gulf and I adopted each other."

"Forty years?"

"Forty. My God." He squinted into the sunset, sipping his drink. Standing straight, with his white hair whipping in the wind and his other hand on the railing, he looked like a captain at sea. Or the benevolent lord of a great estate, which, it occurred to Hudson, he no doubt was. He looked like a man who had been in this place not four decades, but always, a man in whom place and soul have become inseparable.

"I remember," said Hudson, "when I was a kid, waking up in the middle of winters in Memphis, from dreams about Fort Walton and Destin—that's where my family used to come—and being completely wrecked that I wasn't really here, but *there*, with my third or fourth grade class to walk to in a cold rain. The dreams were so vivid, so real. I couldn't believe the cruel joke. It was devastating."

"Poor little guy."

"For a lot of years I think I fairly well lived for those two or three weeks in summer. I was always the navigator, in charge of the map, for the family car trip. I had everyone scouring the shoulders of the highway for the first trace of sand like prospectors for gold. We always had a contest as to who first smelled the ocean. When we hit the coast, before we got to wherever we were staying that year, my sister and I made my poor father pull over and let us out. We ran up the dunes and just stood for a minute or two. I guess that first sight of the Gulf was the purest joy I knew."

Hudson had been looking out to sea, but turned now to Charlie. "I wondered what it would be like now. If I'd feel either the excitement or that in some way I was coming home. The summer's something of a test flight. I've been on automatic pilot for quite awhile."

"And?"

"Nothing, here, there, or anywhere, is the same." He paused. But it's...good.... It's good."

"God, I hope so. Maybe not pure joy, oh no. But something that's always been here for you, something real." He grasped Hudson's arm. "Something."

Hudson nodded. They took in the magnificent view for another minute or so, framed by the tall old trees, the broad beach at Laurel white in the distance against a tangerine sky and the water going cobalt. "Let's go in," Hudson said. "Probably not for an old salt like you, but it's still pretty warm for a hot-natured, air-conditioning addicted city slicker like myself."

"Did you notice how I whisked you up here through the sunroom? I'll show you why, now. I have a surprise I'm pretty happy about and want to share with you in the living room."

◇◇◇

"It's a Walter Anderson. I've had it about a year now and I've never had a picture mean so much to me. It's Western Lake at sunrise."

Charlie sat in his favorite chair in the long, handsome room, facing the large oil over the mantel. "I can sit here for hours, perfectly content, usually reading or doing a crossword puzzle, but sometimes just listening to music and looking at it. Great company."

Hudson could understand. The landscape, some five feet wide and four feet tall, was at once imposing and retiring; it drew you into its rich color treatment of the lagoon that lay just to the east beyond the side porch of Charlie's house.

"It's *so* fine."

"Apparently it was one of the last things he did and someone got hold of it and had it in their home in D.C. for years, and then a dealer in Palm Beach got it who'd been over this way once or twice and knew what the inscription on the back meant. She called and made me an offer—an arm and a leg—but, of course, I had to have it. It was meant to be in this house. Right up there."

"I'd say so. Charlie, it really is magnificent. So, now that you're divesting yourself of your real estate, is this what you'll be doing?"

"No, no. I had to have this. But no, I don't plan to get any more serious about collecting. Don't need any more. This is the crowning jewel." Charlie modestly overlooked the fact that here and there, on walls throughout the house, along with a lot of excellent watercolors, oils, graphics and photos by local artists, hung small works and sketches by the likes of Homer, Roualt, Dufy, O'Keeffe, Gorey, Stuart Davis, and Marsden Hartley.

They had gone from room to room, sipping the Brompton house special Hudson had requested, some dark variant of mai tai, visiting the old pictures like friends, inspecting the new paint job upstairs, a few new pieces of furniture here and there, an old pine table that Charlie had just refinished, looking into the many bedrooms, sitting for awhile in the sunroom that opened onto the east porch and the lagoon beyond as Charlie brought out some photos from a recent party or two that had included a few people of Hudson's acquaintance.

At a little after eight, they stood again in the elegantly understated living room, its old mahogany and walnut pieces interspersed with bentwood cane chairs, the broad plank floors dark and lustrous, enlivened by gorgeous kilims. Charlie said: "Shall we freshen these here or have a second one there."

"There. You know," Hudson mused, looking at Charlie's new painting from yards away at the other end of the room, "it's odd, but its presence is so strong, it just seems so inevitably *there,* that I can't even remember what you had there before."

"That portrait of Andrew."

Charlie took the glasses to the small bar just inside the door of the library. "I always liked it there. That's all. Even my more vocal friends who have questioned the taste or sanity of my keeping it there know I'm not a torch carrier. It just worked there, and it was a good painting. We passed by it in the hall upstairs."

"Oh, of course." Andrew had been the great love of Charlie's life. Hudson had met him only once or twice before his final exit. There had apparently been three during the course of the relationship's sixteen-year span.

"But twelve years is long enough. And now I have this, this *miracle* painting." He laughed, but Hudson thought perhaps he had detected, in the laugh and somewhere deep in the lively blue eyes, a shadow of uncertainty.

He wondered why Charlie might feel vulnerable.

To the past, to Andrew? He thought not.

But if not that, what?

# Chapter 12

"Nothing has changed." Chaz luxuriated in the large chair by the hearth, looking at Sydney, who had nestled into one end of the sofa with her legs tucked up.

"He didn't say a word about his will, the land, anything. Zip. It was all very *en famille*, long walks on the beach, long talks about my father. Long talks about you. He can't wait for us to come down. But last night over dinner at 26-A, he did say that he had 'begun to reach some decisions about his life' that would 'affect' me, and that he'd let me know more about it soon."

"So we have absolutely no reason to think he knows anything about your father's unmailed letter, and, therefore, no reason to think that he thinks you suspect anything."

"None. Why would he? He knows we were never *that* close. It was my father he loved and I'm sure he heard for a lot of years what a source of anguish I was to him. Charlie may have felt sorry for me from time to time, but we were never tight. It wouldn't occur to him that I *expected* anything much from his will, especially since he's certain that my father never even let me in on the fact that he was Charlie's heir…"

Sydney interrupted smoothly, "…or thought you might possibly be interested in or capable of responsibly disposing of sixty to a hundred million dollars in prime real estate. With advocates like dear old dad, who needs enemies?"

Chaz looked away, out into the garden, his large, bright eyes haunted for a moment, even glum. His dramatic pale complexion, framed by dark, loose ringlets, looked to Sydney more than ever like the face of a beautiful, slightly dissolute lost boy.

"It's amazing what people can do in what they mistakenly assume are someone's 'best interests,'" she said. "My mother and that hideous stepfather, for instance. She thought she was doing it for me. That it was in my best interest." She paused. "I've told you how that worked out. And then of course there is my ace former fiancé." She paused again and then went on, quietly. "You know I had really begun to like your father. We seemed to be getting along so well. It never occurred to me that beneath that elegant exterior and the impeccable manners was a fearful, rather selfish old man, who had not a shred of faith in you. No real feeling for you, no knowledge even of who you really are and what you can really do. Well, my darling, we are looking out for our own best interests now."

"Charlie says he's proud of me."

"So did your father. And look what they've done, the two of them, to you. Is he proud enough of you to reconsider?"

"Well, there *is* some ambivalence there. I think dad's death has left him feeling older, more vulnerable. I got the feeling he really wants us to be closer. But, no.... He may feel warmly disposed to me now, but I don't think that's made him stupid. He knows there are precious few folks around who would hold that land in reserve or only allow a couple of tasteful houses to be built there. He may believe I've cleaned up my act and he may be growing sentimental, but he doesn't mistake me for his more-like-a-brother-than-a-cousin, my sainted father.

"But I do know that we've at least bought some time. His attorney is on some exchange program with a firm in London and he hasn't told him anything about his intentions. He says he needs to 'get completely settled in his mind' about the changes and isn't going to rush into handling it by phone, fax, and mail. He said that by the time the guy gets back in August, he'll be certain about 'all the pieces' and will sit down with him then.

I have the definite impression, though, that he plans to tell us about the house before then."

"A wedding gift," mused Sydney. "So as a public relations venture, an insurance policy, your junket was a success? You left Charlie even more convinced of your respectability and stable course in life."

"Right. The house is in the bag, maybe some cash."

Sydney smiled. "That's sweet. Of course, he might live another twenty years. What about the restaurant and the bar? They're worth another—what?—three or four million? If he's getting close to really retiring, couldn't we have a chance at convincing him that his own flesh and blood might want to take them on?"

"He knows that's not my thing and that although I think the coast is fine, I don't love it like he does."

"Who *does*?"

"The staff he's gotten into place at 26-A over the past few years. I met them all at the restaurant. They're confirmed year-rounders, they're hospitality people just like he is, and they're hands-on. That's the *real* flesh and blood as far as he's concerned. Except one guy, named Main. He's manager at the Blue Bar but apparently wasn't asked into the buyers' group with the others."

Sydney rose from the sofa, stretched, and headed toward the kitchen. "We need to think about all this. But right now we're going to sit down to the lovely pesto tortellini I picked up at Ciarazzi's and a good bottle of wine. You're tired. But I want to revive you enough for us to have wild and imaginative sex. I've missed you."

◇ ◇ ◇

Just before drifting into sleep, two hours later, she nuzzled into his neck, saying, "We need to get on down there, and for more than just a few days."

Chaz shifted under the crook of her arm and cupped his hand under her breast. "Okay."

Sydney did not so much sink into slumber that night as she was buoyed into it, aloft, as on a gentle but insistent wave. She reached for sleep as if with open arms, desiring rest so that she would be at her best for whatever lay ahead now. Beneath her she felt an unaccustomed swell of security in the shape of an annual trust and a house with a market value of more than a half-million.

But a siren song beckoned to her, drawing her out, out to a wider shining horizon, beyond the shallows of cranking out corporate training videos half the week and keeping the shop accounts for Chaz the other, beyond the endless schmoozing with pretentious clients, be they Atlanta's clamorous legions of nouveau riche or its disdainfully paranoid old guard, out beyond caring whether she could, indeed, beat the system at its own game.

Instead of the tiny hotel where they had once stayed in Venice, she saw Chaz in a gracefully cavernous palazzo, padding toward her in pale peach pajama bottoms across pools of summer moonlight. She saw not the frowsy flat in Notting Hill that an acquaintance had condescended to let them have for a few days, but a large house with a garden in a mews in Kensington. She saw the two of them, refining an A-list guest list by the fire as an autumn sunset emblazed their library overlooking Central Park.

She saw freedom and travel and laughter and great sex and people who came and went as you chose and who were not small and provincial and prosaic and lacking in the sorts of mystery that made life interesting.

And even with her eyes closed, she could see Chaz, lying close beside her. She saw that, until someone altered a piece of paper a few weeks from now, he was the heir to a fortune that would once and for all allow her to create the only role, in a life of performance, that she had never really played as fully as she would have liked.

The one role created not as a means of escape, created to satisfy no one's purposes but her own, no one's criteria but her own.

Herself.

It was the only one now that intrigued and challenged her. She saw this not as a dream, but as a fact, a truth that she could ensure would unfold. She slept soundly, gathering in the darkness her certainty of purpose, her focus and strength for the weeks ahead.

# Chapter 13

The next morning, Saturday, Hudson walked the four miles up the beach to Seaside. It would be hot again by mid-afternoon, but for now the humidity was still low and the sky and sea were dazzling. Moon ran ahead, bobbing back and forth between the sand and the surf, and bounding back to Hudson now and again to make sure everyone was having a good time. He knew not to run up to the other people they occasionally passed, and when another largish dog was in accompaniment, Hudson put the leash on to discourage any potential rowdiness.

They crossed Laurel's beach, one of the widest in west Florida, and headed east. Just beyond the village, Hudson could just glimpse, through the scrub forest, one corner of the upper gallery of Charlie's house. It angled toward the southwest, facing the Gulf and, for many months of the year, the sunsets, a discreet distance of some three hundred yards, across Laurel's broadest expanse of dunes, from the sea, nestled among a thick stand of tall pine, oak, and hickory, its east side porch looking across the long lagoon. The original house had been a big old barny thing, built in the '30s, for many years a rental property, and in dire need of work, when Charlie bought in 1970. Over the years, with restoration, renovation, additions, and much loving care, it had become exquisitely comfortable and graciously grand. A wonderful home.

Large as it was, there were certainly larger houses to be found along the coast, among the nouveau riche enclaves of Destin, Dune Allen, and Santa Rosa, and in the two or three even newer, planned residential communities like Greenway. And, quite probably, somewhere in the neo-quaint homogeneity of Seaside's closely controlled architecture, there might possibly be a couple of houses with higher market value. But few homes anywhere in the hundred-and-fifty-mile stretch between the 1920s Italianate Deco mansions of Pensacola's old East Bay neighborhood and the pretty little 19th-Century restorations in the old cotton port of Apalachicola could touch Brompton House, the name Charlie allowed only a few close friends—and not a single sign—to use.

He had met Charlie fifteen years ago, when some mutual friends in Memphis had suggested that he call him up during a visit to the coast. In those days, Hudson had been partial to a little rental house over in Navarre Beach. He had driven over one evening, thinking that he would simply have a drink and then stop for oysters or shrimp at one of the good places back along Highway 98. Instead, they became fast friends almost immediately, talking for three hours and drinking nearly two bottles of a very nice Pouilly Fuissé. Charlie had fixed omelets and salad, and, just before midnight, Hudson had been sent off to sleep in one of the guest rooms upstairs.

The same fondness at first sight struck again when Charlie had met Kate six years ago. After they spent an evening trading bits of Louisville lore, Charlie had drawled, smiling, "Well, *now* we know what the boy's been waiting for."

◇◇◇

Seaside is nothing if not self-contained. Many of the families with vacation homes there tend not to sojourn on the Gulf for any experience of otherness it may offer them, any influence of place. Solid burghers or striving wannabes, they come, instead—from Memphis and Atlanta and Birmingham—for the low-risk opportunity of extending themselves, only slightly, by means of another highly acceptable address. They tend to bring their own well-marshaled domesticity with them, many of them almost like 19th-Century travelers whose first priority was to carry as much a sense of home as possible to wherever in the world they went.

Seaside has its share, certainly, of simple middle-class vacationers, who have saved strenuously for a week or two in one of its uniformly cute, vastly overpriced dollhouses, or in one of the two inns. There are some year-rounders, and inevitably a contingent of recently divorced geezers down for their part of the time-share with the much-younger trophy wife or girlfriend. But more often one found on the beach at Seaside the beautifully maintained, youthfully middle-aged mother, passing time with a book until her next tennis game; the father doing business with his cell phone in one hand and, with the other, vigorously playing Frisbee with some combination of children and dogs; nearby, the nanny, either building sandcastles with the younger offspring or trying to pacify them with something from a wicker hamper laid out as if for a *Town and Country* shoot. Or, at least, that's the way some of its denizens *liked* to see themselves.

The beach to Seaside is not, as it were, "a two-way street," a cause for rejoicing among Laurel folk. A few people were, like Hudson, walking or jogging *east* in the brilliant morning, sunglassed, hatted, or capped against the climbing sun. But over the course of the entire three miles he passed only three or four individuals headed west. Aside from a few young bicyclists, only the most adventuresome of Seasiders ever left its tidy environs, for dinner at Criolla's or a casual meal or drinks at the Blue Bar, perhaps, or a quick poke around the shops just north of the 26-A intersection. When they did sally forth, it was usually by car, more likely than not a BMW, Jag, or Land Rover.

Of course, Laurel Beach had been *discovered*. Old Laurel cottages were at a premium and even undistinguished little structures on or near the beach sold for small fortunes. There was no place left on the Emerald Coast to hide, certainly not the oldest beach settlement for almost two hundred miles around. Hudson had already seen, cruising slowly up and down the village streets, often at dusk, the svelte vehicles with dark-tinted windows and out-of-state license plates, slowing or stopping to examine properties and lots for sale. Anybody with cash could build a big, new house, and, fortunately, that's exactly what a lot of folks wanted to do, but people always want what's hard to get, and more than a few potential buyers now found a cachet in Laurel's very limitedness and out-of-the-wayness—not a tennis court or golf course for miles—as well as the patina that only comes with age.

But there were only so many houses and cottages in Laurel and, through the grace of God and the persistence of a few good citizens, it was surrounded by National Park Seashore, wilderness areas, and state land preserves. Greenway was the closest any new community would ever be. And to the east, Seaside, monolithic and insular as it might be, was, nonetheless, an attractive, stable buffer against any further incursions from the tacky development, uncharitably known as the Redneck Riviera, that spewed up 98 from Panama City.

◇◇◇

Seaside is twenty years old, the admirable brainchild of a man who had inherited eighty acres on the edge of Seagrove Beach from his grandfather and didn't want to do just anything with it. With a team of urban designers and architects, he planned a neo-traditional seaside community no point of which is more than a half-mile from any other. To the great surprise of almost everyone, it had caught on. People liked the explicit building codes, which insisted that all Seaside cottages be designed within a set of traditional criteria indigenous to old West Florida: wood frames adapted to the climate, built off the ground with ample windows and cross ventilation, overhangs and porches to hold the shade and breezes in summer. Upper middle-class Southerners, especially, were drawn by the opportunity of creating something in their own desired image. Many, including a number of Memphians, abandoned Destin and Santa Rosa, the tradition of generations, for the new, more upscale architectural fantasy. The goal was instant tradition, a seaside community that would be to the Emerald Coast what Nantucket and Charleston, Savannah, Lewes, and Cape May were to the East. If the result necessarily fell short of those lofty aims, and sometimes resembled a movie set, as, indeed, it had served for one major studio film, it nonetheless carried a charm of its own.

Having Moon along for the outing, Hudson made fairly quick work of their destination: a look along the newer shops behind the town green, a quick peer into the Sundog bookstore, a hot dog from the take-out window of one of the little sandwich shops in the open-air market along with two large cups of water for Moon, some people-watching from the main pergola overlooking the center of the beach at the end of Tupelo Street.

Everything, the cottages, in shades of white and pastels, tightly stacked along the narrow lanes lined with hawthorn, flowering succulents, and palmetto, and the beach with its manicured sand and regimentally placed azure umbrellas, everything, and everyone, looked healthy and confident and well turned-out.

In order to catch some occasional shade, Hudson and Moon walked back to Laurel along 26-A.

Forty minutes later they turned south, at the Hibiscus Bed & Breakfast, into the village, passing the V intersection of Potero Street which angled off due south. With its old weather-shingled cottages and clapboard bungalows, intermittently canopied by oaks and Spanish moss, Pendennis Street beckoned like a dream, wiggling slightly in the radiant heat and smelling of hot pine and gardenia.

# Chapter 14

Twilight found Hudson sitting on the porch reading over his work. Three reviews he'd pulled up to consider: he had lightly edited one, decided to keep one exactly as it was, and substantially revised the other.

Moon lay at his feet, in the shade, sliding into an early evening nap, and even Olive had deigned to come out for a sniff of the cooling air. Both by Hudson's choosing and her own clear preference an indoor cat, Olive nonetheless, occasionally and only in his presence, toured the perimeters of the porch of the house in Memphis, and now had similarly extended her cautious range to the cottage. There had never been a danger of Olive's running away. She liked to look around a bit but was fundamentally uncurious about the world beyond the comforts of her own domain. She disdained it as a world of dirt and dogs and things like cars and planes and lawnmowers that made more noise than any civilized creature needed to endure. Her universe stopped at the edge of the porch and she always kept the door close to her back. She had been outside once, long ago, and like a hideous nightmare that's precisely where she wanted to keep it. She had been brought to the humane society by some good soul, unweaned, lost from her mother and siblings at only a few weeks and found cowering in a rainstorm under a mailbox alongside a busy street. She now sat in the last narrow slant of sun near the steps, engrossed in a pedicure of balletic invention.

## Death in Venice

Following on the heels of *The Portrait of a Lady* and the recently released *Washington Square*, American audiences now have their third chance in less than 18 months to respond to the rather quixotic challenge of translating Henry James to film. A writer perhaps best known for the "interiorization" of his novels, in which only the barely registered twist of a synapse or the smallest inaudible gasp may indicate cataclysmic psychological or emotional upheavals or some life-altering spiritual revelation, James's filmability suffers in direct proportion to the success with which he achieved his artistic purposes. If in the past few years Edith Wharton's works have met with better treatment at the hands of filmmakers, it may well be because her novels of manners tend to indicate the more obvious ironies of the manners themselves. James used the novel of manners to indicate large ideas and passions; they open outward as if from a great precipice, providing a dimensionally complex vision beyond the surface observation. As his view of the human comedy matured, taking on wider and more deeply felt concerns, he became a master of indirection, and his goal of seamlessly blending character, action, and theme fairly well displaced omniscient narrative.

By the time of *The Wings of the Dove* (1902), James was using brilliantly intricate stylistic effects to create (ironically enough) a new kind of realism, melding his theatrical sense of dialogue as narrative, multiple viewpoints, and dramatic ellipsis. A master of subtlety, he asks his readers to accept the responsibility of ferreting out for themselves what is happening in the story. Going even farther, James places many key moments "off-stage," as in classical tragedy: expected scenes never materialize; the reader is excluded from certain encounters. At the core of his later novels is James' belief that life is a process of *seeing* "the great things," through awareness attaining understanding and, thereby, achieving, if not freedom, the illusion of freedom. Through his masterfully controlled obliquities he sought to force the reader to *see* for himself. He wanted his art to provoke life, not talk about it. If this demand has caused more than a few 20th-Century readers to pass over James in favor of lighter or more explicit fare, it makes filming his major works an even thornier proposition.

Iain Softley's version of *The Wings of the Dove*, like Jane Campion's *The Portrait of a Lady*, isn't shy about taking liberties. For one thing, it is palpably condensed; and while at ninety-nine minutes it is a welcome relief from recent period pieces which, wanting in accuracy of detail or spirit, seek to impress with sheer length, there's an apologetic, Cliff Notes feel to the undertaking. Softley dares to distill the essence of James' novel rather than try to hoodwink us with an overstuffed Edwardian waxworks, and we can admire the effort even as we find it lacking. The foreshortening is also felt in how and when the primary characters meet one another: Softley's shortcuts and compressions make narrative filmic sense; they just don't happen, rather crucially, to be how James intended us to discover and come to know the relationships. And, finally, the key events of the denouement have been altered with cheapening, though not fatal, effects.

The plot is a melodrama ("vulgar" by James' own description). It's what he does with it, and what he would have us make of it, that pries open the big questions about human love and spiritual possibilities. Kate Croy (Helena Bonham Carter) is a pretty and penniless young woman taken in by her rich and scheming aunt (Charlotte Rampling), who seeks to marry her off suitably. But Kate is in love with the equally penniless and charming Merton Denscher (Linus Roache), a journalist. Kate's aunt will cut her off unless she drops Merton. Kate and Merton happen to befriend an orphaned American heiress, Millie Theale (Alison Elliott), who is terminally ill. Kate asks Merton to marry Millie, who is in love with him, knowing that she will leave her fortune to him and that after her imminent death, Kate and Merton can marry.

Though despicable, the couple's plan unfurls with James' ironic sympathy for the economic deter-minism that entraps Kate. What they do not bargain for is the Jamesian "great thing" that Millie's love for both of them evokes: her generosity of spirit and her capacity for love live on after her death, with profound consequences.

Much of the film takes place in Venice, where Millie goes when she hears the prognosis for her illness, and this is where Softley's film has its greatest success. It captures James' almost excruciatingly delicate tug-of-war between good and evil, life and death, spirit and flesh. Kate accompanies Millie and, soon, Merton joins them.

This brief season of glamour and tenderness, of duplicity and forgiveness, is mesmerizing. Softley's graceful pacing and his use of revelatory close-ups feel exactly right, Sandy Powell's costumes are very fine, and the cinematography of Eduardo Sera brings the golden light and rain-dappled shadows of Venice to ethereal life.

Helena Bonham Carter is more interesting here than ever before. She lets her voice nestle in a lower range and projects a canny maturity that is more watchable than the line-up of strident ingénues in which she has heretofore been stuck. Roache (who did a fine job in the title role in *Priest*) is perfect as Merton, intelligently sexy, at first cynical, ultimately vulnerable to the large lessons with which life engulfs him. As Millie, Elliott is pictorially correct, American as apple pie, with a sweet, fun-loving smile. The actress doesn't exude the magnanimity or spiritual grace necessary for us to see fully "the greatness" of which James provides such haunting intimations; on the other hand, her self-effacing rendition of simplicity does remind us that another of James' key points is that life, and one's sense of mortality, can have a way of creating unlikely heroes and alchemize even a perfunctory existence into a numinous life.

For all its presumptions and faux pas, Softley's essay of *The Wings of the Dove* is a fairly honorable defeat. At times, hovering around certain frames of the film, just off-camera and if only obliquely (discretions of which James might approve), we sense the mourning dove murmur of a sort of falling greatness. The film gives a richly visual life to the central poignancy of James' novel: in one of the most significant of its multiple, quiet epiphany scenes, Kate admonishes Merton about Millie: "She didn't come here to die, she came here to *live*."

Occasionally Hudson looked up from his reading and stared at the quiet street through the shrubs and trees. It seemed, at certain moments, almost a mirage. A piece of a conversation with Alex floated to him. *This is about your relationship to her. She believes in God and you believe in God. We can't know what she's doing about the relationship now. And, frankly, neither you nor I can make that our job. Yours is to change your relationship with her. It seems unspeakable, I'm sure, not only to feel the one thing you thought was forever unchangeable changing but to be called upon to be the agent of that change. But, Hud my man, you're the only one who can find those new places, or at least help those new degrees and qualities of loving find their own places to exist.*

He thought about Kate because it was unavoidable to do otherwise. She was—*is* the strongest person he knew. He would probably trade on her strength always. He had in the past two years and he really couldn't imagine letting go of that. It was one thing he felt he could keep and about which he could feel okay, and know that she would approve. He used it as a sort of inner barometer. Her example. To try to be strong himself.

# Chapter 15

As Sydney strolled through Neiman's looking for a few choice summer beach things, she recalled and reexamined a mild day in late March, one of those dazzlers that brought Atlantans out after their brief winter with a sense of ruffled entitlement, as if—instead of what really amounts to a few weeks of moderate chill—they were emerging from a protracted season of sunless hyperborean permafrost.

At one of the tables that had been insouciantly laid in the sun of the upper terrace at a small restaurant overlooking the river, Sydney and her old chum Daphne Kerrigan had chatted across a bowl of exquisite white and yellow tulips. They were finishing their lunch amid a merry Friday throng of executives and tennis matrons in sunglasses.

Although Sydney had more acquaintances than she could keep, despite her superb organizational skills, in strict Filofax order, she had never had many friends. The concept, especially, of "girlfriends" had always seemed repugnant to her.

◇◇◇

There had been one girl she had cultivated in junior high school in Coweta County. The girl had been a grade ahead of her and Sydney sensed that they might strike some sort of delicate balance that did not characterize most of the juvenile clan-building she saw around her, defined so unabashedly by the Southern rural rubric of family financial status for girls and sheer alpha-animal brawn for boys. The two of them had bonded with rage over their outsider status and their disdain for their families' severe financial and social limitations.

Her friend's father worked for the railroad and seemed alternately away for long stretches or asleep in a back bedroom; her mother grew irregular lines of vegetables in their scraggy backyard and, very peaceably, drank. Sydney's mother, a sad-faced wraith who managed day to day on religious fundamentalism, cigarettes, and misspent nervous energy, owned the two-chair beauty shop cum drug store in the neighboring burg of Moreland. Sydney's father had left them when she was not quite two and her mother had desperately married a widower from the small church. Though he was grossly fat and rather slow-witted, he had inherited a small but still viable farm machinery franchise. He seemed mostly to sit around in his underwear, his pink flesh burgeoning out of his big chair as he slumbered intermittently in the window unit air conditioning, watching, when he roused himself with a series of ragged snorts, a mélange of CNN, soap operas, and television preachers. Sydney, early on, had trained herself not to look at him when he was thus enthroned. Though she suspected nothing dangerous from him, she did not even want to see him watching her pass quickly through the room. And she had noticed one too many times, as a small girl, some aspect or other of his squished scrotum oozing from his shorts.

She and her friend had shared a mutually nurturing belief in their unrecognized natural gifts. They were excellent students, already bored with the mediocre scope and pace of education at the small-town school; they devoured great literature, celebrity magazines, and trashy paperbacks with equal voracity. Physically, her friend was more precocious, and she experimented knowingly with cosmetics and hairstyles. Even so, it was she who eventually became something of an acolyte to her younger friend's will and imagination. "You could be an actress, someday," she said. "I already am," said Sydney. And to prove it, she would enact scenes from favorite films they had seen at the theatre in Newnan or watched late at night on television or had read in books in her companion's bedroom. Even more than the actresses or characters she evoked in these impromptu reinterpretations, it was Sydney herself her friend had found compelling. Not picture-pretty by regional prevailing standards, she seemed original in her good looks, with her dramatic, searching, yet oddly self-collected eyes, her glossy chestnut hair tailored in a Peter Pan bob to flout the big-hair fashion of the day. One day she might be the young Audrey Hepburn in capri pants, shirt tied at the waist, and a pencil behind her ear; the next an approximation of Bette Midler's Rose, swathed in Joplinesque glad rags, rings, and beads. But never, thought her friend, was Sydney more infinitely watchable yet somehow unknowable than when she was herself.

The girl's father was transferred to Indiana; they moved away during her junior year. Sydney finished high school without taking the effort to make a new friend. She had a few dates her senior year with a wealthy peanut farmer's son who had some intelligence and, when they were alone and he felt less threatened by certain social stigma, sensitivity. But he was going to Charlottesville as a legacy, and she had been lucky to get a scholarship to little north Georgia college up in hill country. Already adept in picking her battles, Sydney saw insufficient reason to fight a four-year campaign for the relationship. They talked about movies, politics, music, who they were, what their futures might hold, took long drives in the country, passed a few Saturday afternoons in Atlanta, and had four stilted bouts of sex.

Unable to handle more than two years at the small backwoods college where she'd earned a free ride, Sydney escaped to the city, where she lived in a vile little studio, worked as a restaurant hostess and completed her degree in theatre and communication at Georgia State. She had done only a few shows at a couple of the better community theatres when she decided to go up for an audition for the Alliance Theatre Company. To the consternation of several more experienced actors with degrees from prestigious graduate programs at Vanderbilt or Northwestern, and pedigreed apprenticeships at the Arena, the Alley, or Actors' Theatre, she was offered a contract.

It was during her six years as a member of the repertory company that Sydney struck up a friendship with Daphne. Three years older, Daphne had been with the Alliance for two years when Sydney arrived and seemed already, with her feisty irreverence, an old hand. Because they were different types—Daphne was a petite Irish redhead from New Orleans—their fondness for one another was never clouded by competitiveness. Their common ground was the lack of pretension with which they practiced their craft and for which they secretly reviled their peers. Not that they didn't take the work seriously; they were dedicated. They simply could not abide the intellectual stuffiness and "furrowed-brow-late-night-high-art gobbledegook-chat," as Daphne called it, in which most of the company engaged. They were just good. Better, by their estimation, than anyone else in the group, and quite probably, they thought, because they did most of what they did onstage without so much pale cast of thought and more through instinct. Instead of being self-absorbed, they were indefatigably outward-directed. It was as if they breathed life in with hungry scrutiny and reproduced it on the exhale. They did not so much act as channel, effortlessly and at will, human behavior.

This ability to participate almost borderlessly in, even to anticipate, life, had served both of them well when they set their professional sights beyond the footlights. Daphne's impatience with her fellow thespians finally led her to pronounce that she would rather sell encyclopedias than have to sit backstage between scenes and hear one more conversation about Chekhovian subtext, and Sydney's coolly realistic assessment of a professional population in which at any given moment only five percent are employed was that she simply couldn't face the scenario that fifteen and twenty years from now she would be pacing a grungy flat in the East Village hoping desperately for a commercial or two each year. Sydney also, as the initial aura of glamour evaporated, increasingly found the idea of acting onstage a useless, rather arcane, confinement. The world loomed, and seemed more her size. In her years with the company, she carefully parlayed her currency as a big-actress-fish-in-the-small-Atlanta-pond into minor socialite, albeit bohemian, status. Her greatest performances took place nowhere near the Alliance stage. She was more focused on mastering the art of using the conventions of society in order to get what she wanted.

Far from selling encyclopedias, Daphne had in two short career steps become director of corporate communications for a new and rapidly expanding high tech firm. Sydney had signed on with a video production company as actor, producer, director, writer and talent recruiter, and, within a year, had also signed on as fiancée to one of her clients, Broward Boule Landerswaite IV, forty-eight, a perpetually tanned and twice-divorced son-in-waiting to a large agronomics corporation. Just in time, she came to realize that there was even more than met the eye to his fondness for bourbon, a variety of pills, mordant sense of humor, and other effete eccentricities, and to understand why one of her betrothed's previous marriages had lasted three years, the other not quite as many months, and why daddy, at seventy-three, was still president and CEO and probably looking around hard for a good deal. Sydney certainly considered going through the motions and then getting out as soon as possible with a good settlement, but had to overrule herself in the early morning hours after the Swan Ball. Staying overnight, she had wakened to find "Bouley" standing beside the massive 18th-Century bed, two feet from her face, wiping his behind with a silk handkerchief. Nodding to the side of the bed where he had lain, the sheet and coverlet thrown back, he said: "I left you a little gift." The worst of it was that he was giggling and held in his shaking hand, unknowingly it seemed, a heavy gold eight-inch letter-opener.

Four months after breaking the engagement and returning her full attention to her work, Sydney had met Charles Douglas Cullen at a festive opening in the Tula arts complex. Chaz was charming and handsome, and, though he was not apparently a weak man, a slightly haunted look behind his large, languid brown eyes told her that, despite his easy wit and physical confidence, he was looking for a kind of guidance. They sat at the far end of the parking lot, listening to WSB under an overhang of hackberries, and he talked freely about his wastrel phase, the boozing and hard drugs, even as they traded a few brief draws on a discreet cocktail-sized joint he had pulled from his jacket.

She joked about being an actress who was in flight from the stage but who kept being trapped in nightmarish training films not wholly of her devising. She acted out a particularly tedious passage a megalomaniacal manufacturer had not let her revise in his firm's human resources video. He talked rather off-handedly about his little business and she guessed that perhaps he was trying hard to make himself believe he liked it more than he actually did, that perhaps it was a vanity venture, a passing thing.

"I'm really happy these days," he said. Sydney thought that this, too, might be overstatement. But she thought that he could, indeed, be happier.

With her.

They made a stunning pair. She knew almost at once that she would never meet anyone who needed her as much and yet would manage to wear that need with such light, ironic grace. Chaz might not be perfect but she felt that she could optimize his assets. He was a gentleman with, though of course nothing like the Landerswaite fortune, some prospects and talents, he was sexy and fun and he had a good background and he absolutely adored her, and so she allowed herself, in so far as it seemed she ever might, to be in love.

◇◇◇

Daphne's idea of Friday expansiveness was to take fifty minutes for lunch, and even then she had used her cell phone twice. As Daphne talked, Sydney had looked down now and then, with a bemused smile, away, into the willows and oaks and beyond to the river, less from discretion than to indicate to her fellow diners that she bore in mortified silence her tablemate's lapse in etiquette. They had not gotten together in three or four months, but had nevertheless managed quickly to dispense with Sydney's engagement, Daphne's Christmas escape to Barbados with a divorce attorney she'd been dating, and her impending promotion to vice-president. Also, a bit about Sydney splitting her time between the videos and Chaz's business. And, finally, Chaz's father's death.

"Well, is Chaz, I mean, okay or whatever? Were they close?"

Sydney hesitated for a second. Instead of saying, "If you only knew how little love was lost there," she said, "They were as close, I think, as most fathers and sons. He'll miss him, but he's all right." It was not for nothing that Daphne was about to be made a VP for communications. She was a talker. And although most of her realm of influence lay outside the Perimeter, in the boardrooms, media outlets, and cocktail parties of the exurban counties, Sydney was nonetheless on guard.

It was over coffee, as Daphne looked at her watch for the third time, that she picked up Sydney's earlier mention of Chaz's recent visit to Old Laurel.

"Who is it, now, a brother?"

"No, his father's cousin. I've never met him. He was apparently quite close to Chaz's father. I'm eager to see his home in Laurel. Chaz says it's really wonderful."

"Old Laurel? Never been there. Near Destin?"

"Well, sort of, but it's closer to Seaside, just three or four miles down the beach."

"Oh, yeah. I've never been. When I was growing up we'd go over to Pensacola and Destin, but I haven't been in years. I admit it: I've become a Hilton Head kinda girl. At least those crackers know how to dress."

She paused. "You know, it may be Laurel Beach. I don't know, one of those, Santa Rosa, Seagrove, Laurel, Something Beach, where that sleazebag ex-husband of my cousin's ended up."

"Sounds like a story."

"A dirty little one. It *is* Laurel. Yeah, that's it. I think he's a bartender at some restaurant or bar that's some sort of a local big deal."

Sydney never forgot a name, and although she had only heard Chaz mention once or twice the one that now leapt to her mind, she said: "Terry Main?"

"My God, I think that's it! Martha and I weren't especially close, she's a second cousin, and I never met him, but, yeah, I believe that's it. How in the world do you know him?"

Sydney didn't miss a beat. "Never met him. But you know me and names, and I think Chaz just mentioned it in passing. His uncle..." she was editing herself as she went, "...lives near that place, I think, so they've been there. Laurel's really just a village. The Green House? or the Blue Bar, or..."

"I think that's it, the Blue Bar."

"So what's his crime?"

"Well, that he was a smarmy, scheming asshole, at least as that wing of the family's legend has it. This was eight or nine years ago and I was already up here and missed a lot of the juicier details. But apparently there actually *was* a crime. At least a sort of small-scale, tawdry one. Word had it later that he'd never really cared about Martha, that he'd only married her to promote himself. He'd worked his way up from the Ninth Ward and finished Loyola law school at night."

"After the wedding, he became corporate attorney for Martha's father's firm. After several years he apparently started embezzling money from the firm. Nothing dramatic. I think I remember my mom saying it was something like two hundred thousand eked out over three or four years. The marriage had been on the decline anyway, but Martha and her folks didn't want to bring charges. There was a small daughter, seven or eight. So there was a quick divorce and Susie father told him to leave town, not to apply to the Bar in any other state and or ever come back, or they would prosecute with the evidence they'd put together. A couple of years ago, someone from New Orleans who was staying in Destin mentioned to my brother that they'd seen the guy behind the bar at some place they went to in Laurel."

Sydney smiled and shook her head gently, looking as dismissive as possible. "Small world."

Now it was she who looked at her watch, counted out a tip, and moved her chair back. Daphne followed suit. When they hugged briefly beside her Mercedes, she laughed and said: "You'll have a wonderful time whenever you get around to going down there—but watch out for pirates and criminals and all those other local-color Gulf Coast characters."

"Oh, we will. Chaz'll be going down for another weekend sometime in the next few weeks, and we'll get down there together before long. We want some time away from here. From business. Eat shrimp. Swim. Be naughty."

"Now, let me know what you decide about a wedding."

"Okay." Sydney waved her off and got into her own car. She would leave a voice mail message letting Daphne know about a sudden decision to elope, just as they would, in some more sentimental manner, let Uncle Charlie know. That was of little consequence.

But what she had just heard about Terry Main *could* be, she felt sure, of consequence. As she drove back to town, oblivious to the brilliant sun dappling down through the hills and trees of Ashford-Dunwoody, Sydney began sorting out the hows and whys.

Terry Main. The only other member of Charlie's little clan who seemed, like his beloved cousin's son, not to have made the cut.

# Chapter 16

"How nice to meet you. Charlie's spoken of you often," said Camilla Stokes.

*My friend the poor widower*, no doubt, thought Hudson.

"Are you settling into your house?" She smiled up at him, peering over tortoise half-glasses. She checked some detail in the reservations list, then removed the glasses, patted the arm of the very tall, striking, young redheaded woman who had materialized at her elbow, and murmured, "The Georges want to come at nine instead of nine-thirty. Seven or eighteen should be free, I think." She came from behind the narrow mahogany table with its small reading stand, offered her hand, and gracefully edged Hudson toward the least crowded corner of the large foyer. "Laurel's so wonderful…."

She was a slender woman of medium height and wore a long, pale pistachio shift and plain gold earrings that set off her eyes and hair. Her eyes were hazel and revealed a certain calm, almost a languidity, and her slightly graying brown hair, parted in something like an old-fashioned page boy, fell attractively to one side, blunt cut midway on her long, graceful neck.

"Charlie has spoken of you as well. 'The manager he'd been looking for' were the exact words, I believe."

"I've been here a little less than three years, but it seems so much longer, and I mean that in the best possible way.

Charlie's made me feel, and Fentry and Victor, too, like part of the family."

Hudson looked out to his right across the 26-A's large, two-tiered main dining room, and up to the open staircase on the left to another mezzanine dining level and bar. A quiet hubbub filled the airy rooms, a discreetly shifting sea of summer sounds and colors, as the attractive and well-to-do from miles around arrived or departed through the beveled-glass front doors or the tall arch of the adjacent lower bar, or stood or sat in small groups along the paneled side banquettes as they waited for their tables.

"Must be a handful."

"Never a dull moment. In a former life I taught second grade for a few years. 26-A is *almost* that exciting." She had a rich, low voice, with humor in it. "You teach, don't you?"

"Freshman and AP English."

"Well, then you know what I mean."

"I've only been back at it for four years. They wear me out and I absolutely adore it."

"We'll have to trade war stories some time," she smiled.

Charlie, who had been waylaid by old acquaintances as soon as they'd walked in, now broke free and joined them.

"Greeting your public?" said Hudson.

Camilla whispered conspiratorially, "Just like a royal walk-about. Fentry and I amuse ourselves by watching who gets how much time."

Charlie laughed. "Now, now. You know," he said, leaning in, "I'm getting better. I am. Really curbing it a bit. For years I've felt I had to talk to everybody and his Aunt Sally who set foot in the place. Every local celebrity and VIP real or imagined. Now, if they're not old friends or acquaintances, forget it."

Camilla nodded with a hint of sarcasm. "Mr. Tough Guy." She rolled her eyes at Hudson, then looked back at Charlie. "The royal table awaits."

◇◇◇

Hudson sat back, enjoying the view from Charlie's table, fairly secluded at the far end of the mezzanine level but with a sweeping prospect, not only across the room and into a part of the upper bar (half of which was a clubby interior and half, through sets of French doors, a palm-embowered roof garden), but over a good bit of the large room below.

Charlie's visual signature was the elaborate system of pin spots, each one focused, without a millimeter of spillage onto a patron, on an arrangement of flowers at the center of each table. With only a pale golden ambient light lightly washing the walls as barely discernible background, the flowers looked like exotic, brilliant jewels, floating in the shadowy rooms.

"I had forgotten just how beautiful it is."

"Thanks." Charlie grinned.

◇◇◇

For their second drink, they had detoured downstairs to the main bar. Without having turned from a conversation at the end of the long mahogany and cane bar, Fentry seemed to have sensed their presence, as he seemed to sense every seismic shift in his domain whether physical or psychological. He had quickly wrapped up his regalement of the little group, turned dramatically, and said in his most musical Barbadian tones: "Good evening, Mr. Brompton. And *you*, Mr. H! How good a sight to see."

*"Oh, Lord,"* Charlie had said. *"He's in top form tonight."*

They drank their cocktails standing there, chatting, Fentry managing his seemingly effortless trick of giving them his undivided attention when in actuality his attention was dividing simultaneously in a dozen different directions. Not particularly tall but with posture approaching that of a dancer, Fentry did indeed seem in fine fettle, the voice running agile scales, the smile ready and brilliant, his starchy white shirt and black bow tie gleaming against his cinnamon skin.

At one point Charlie had been drawn away, and Fentry had suddenly fallen silent; he leveled his enormous eyes, even more glistening than usual, at Hudson, reached across the bar, and patted his hand in a kind, all-encompassing gesture.

Dinner was a succession of triumphs from Victor's large and capable hands. The big man himself dropped by the table early on to say hello and inquire after the salad (which looked like a Matisse floral still-life on the plate and memorably involved julienned beet, walnuts, arugula and cream). He couldn't linger; he was dealing tonight with what he called in his softly gruff Australian baritone "a careful sauce, calls for a bit of attention." Hudson didn't know Victor terribly well, one or two conversations, usually with Charlie; but Kate had twice spent long afternoons, at his invitation (rare, according to Charlie), in the 26-A kitchen, learning about soup stocks and some of the finer points of shellfish.

*"He looks like a great bear, but in that kitchen, in his element, he moves like Baryshnikov,"* she had said.

Now, Victor hesitated for a moment before leaving and then, with the same gentility that Fentry had shown, though in a more awkward and reticent style, he had nodded to Hudson, looked at a spot on the table for five seconds and then back up at him, and said quietly, "I'm very sorry for your loss."

◇◇◇

"What's on your calendar for tomorrow? I guess schoolteachers try to stay away from schedules in the summer, though, right?"

Charlie sipped his brandy. They had driven back to his house for a nightcap and were seated in comfortable chairs up on the gallery. He had dimmed the lights inside, the only light on the long verandah a small shaded lamp on a table nearby. They looked out into the great trees, silhouetted in the moon. There was a smell of magnolia and the darkness quaked with the cascading rhythms of cicadas and tree toads and, further out, nearer the beach, the occasional jagged cry of a gull.

"Exactly. I'm trying to avoid even the semblance. But I do have work to do. Lots of reading. And there's the collection. I suspect when I get back into some of these reviews I haven't seen or thought about in so long, I'm going to want to revise or, at least, re-edit some of them. I think I'm going to let the weather set my pattern. You know, beach or other activities before eleven or after five, and hole up for the heat of the day."

"Very civilized."

"And you?"

"Well, I have to get in gear. My cousin's son and his new wife are due from Atlanta on Monday, for about two weeks, and I have to 'do around' as my daddy used to say."

"You've talked about Peter, of course, but we were never here at the same time."

"I appreciated your letter, Hudson." He paused. "This is his only child, my namesake actually, but he goes by Chaz. He had some pretty rough patches growing up and into his twenties, but I'm proud of him. He's thirty-five now and he really seems to have gotten it together these last four or five years."

"You must miss Peter."

Charlie's jaw tightened and he looked at Hudson with unchar-acteristic sadness in his eyes. "Well, we didn't get together that often. Every few years I'd go up or they'd come down. But yes, yes I do. Sweet man. You may remember, we were really close growing up together in Louisville. My mother's sister's son. We went through UK together and then he went to law school at Emory. Joined a firm there and married. His wife Nancy had a lot of family in the Carolinas, and never was much of a beach person. Sometimes she and Chaz would go there for visits and Peter would come down for a few days by himself. Occasion-ally Chaz would come with him. Always behaved himself. He likes the Gulf, and I think the fact that I'm gay sort of appealed to his rebel instinct or something. Oh, he may have smoked a little dope while he was here, but most of the time he was on the beach or sitting around the house reading, happy and good-humored. And through all his troubles and all the disappoint-ment he caused them, he never went out of his way to actively antagonize his parents. He had a grudging respect for his father and adored his mother."

He smiled. "We're a family of only children. Peter was the closest thing I had to a brother. Real family. I do miss him, and I suspect a good deal of it may be that thing you apparently start saying when you reach a certain point, the one about losing part of yourself when you lose the people who remember."

"You have friends. Many, who love you."

"Yes, I do, and for whom I am eternally grateful. But you know, Hud, over the past, oh, twelve or fifteen years, I lost three really dear friends to AIDS. And though I've certainly made my peace with it, I always, always, wanted Andrew and me to work out a life together. Not meant to be, and I finally had to draw a line under it, but...still...."

Hudson realized for the first time, and felt incredibly self-involved and stupid at the discovery, that Charlie, at least at times, was lonely. That though he was still attractive, apparently fit, and as charming as ever, he was looking old age in the face.

He said: "Alex the shrinking priest has asked me a couple of times, 'Wouldn't you rather have discovered, rather know, that you have the capacity for love, than not?'"

Charlie searched Hudson's face in the near-darkness: "What did you say?"

"I said 'yes,' but I also...."

"What?"

"I also worry like hell that love is not just a matter of developing a capacity, but that it's a call and response. That an unused capacity begins to atrophy."

"And what does Alex say to that?"

"He says, 'So use it. Any way, no matter how small, no matter what or where.'"

Charlie reached over and gripped Hudson's shoulder, and smiled at him. "Sounds like Alex doesn't cut any slack."

"He looks like an intellectual linebacker and made me do homework. I had sessions for which I had to bring in discussion points based on everything from Plato to Emily Dickinson to Psalms. Kierkegaard. Winnie the Pooh. Sondheim lyrics."

They laughed, leaned back in their chairs, stretching, and talked on until almost one. Chaz, it seemed, was now Charlie's only living relative. A smart kid but an indifferent student, and perhaps a bit too good-looking for his own good, he had slouched through high school with a leering attitude and a guidance counselor's rap sheet of disciplinary problems, not so much at the flamboyant end of the scale but more to do with the sins of omission: skipping classes, some drugs and alcohol, the concertedly averted gaze and monosyllabic contempt for his teachers. He managed to slide into the University of Georgia where, away from Peter and Helen Cullen's salutary concern, he really cut loose. He majored in art and dabbled around with the notion of being a painter, but his last two years of college and his mid-twenties apparently were a fast white flash of coke, Ecstasy, and booze. Nearly a decade passed without Charlie seeing him. It was his beautiful mother's impending death from cancer that seemed, finally, to wrest a change from him. It was an untimely death; she was only sixty. During her final illness, Chaz promised to clean up his act, after serial failed attempts, once and for all.

"He's been down to visit a couple of times since Peter died. He seems to have found his stride," Charlie said. "He and a partner opened a little art and antiques gallery in Buckhead. When his mother died he came into a little money and used it to buy out his partner. I've only been up there once, but I think he's doing well. Good eye, nice sense of style. I think he's settling down and making a good life for himself.

"After so many years of not seeing him, I'm glad we're building our relationship again. He was down a couple of years ago, and was here in early March—that's when Peter was to have come."

"And he's just married?" Hudson asked. "Do you like her?"

"They came down a few weekends ago. Very attractive. Intelligent. Seems very nice—Peter had said he thought she was good for him. Chaz had told me a lot about her during his first visit, said he was really eager for me to meet her. He's always had somebody, but I knew this was serious. I told them I'd love to have the wedding here if they wanted, but they eloped to the mountains in April." He laughed. "They called, actually, to apologize. Apparently, between her work schedule—she's a creative consultant or something for a film and video group—and the logistics of her family, elopement seemed in order."

"So, this visit is your opportunity to fete the happy couple?"

"Well, I want it to be relaxed. An intimate dinner or two, maybe one larger party. And there's something I want to ask you." He paused. "Will you help?"

"You want me to make my world-renowned macaroni and cheese casserole?"

"Well, maybe one night I'll take you up on that, but, no, I mean…just in general. I want you and I to have time together and I need time with them, so may I count on you to, well…to be part of it? I mean, they'll be off on their own a lot, and she mentioned some business in Tallahassee, so it's not like this will be all-consuming. And they only have a couple of weeks. You'll be here for another three weeks after they're gone." He stopped suddenly. "I don't want to presume. You know other people in Laurel, and I know you have to work a few hours every day. And need some time to yourself. It's just that I want you to know them. I know they'll enjoy having some time with you and I hope you will them."

"Of course. I appreciate being included." They had gone back through the upstairs sitting room and down the large curving central staircase. They walked out through the heavy sub-tropical night and Hudson climbed into the Highlander.

Charlie leaned a forearm on the doorframe. "I think, after fifteen years, even though we don't see each other as often as I'd like, that we probably come close to qualifying as family by now, don't you? And now, with that fine cottage, I *expect* to be seeing you more."

He leaned his head back for a moment, looking up into the dark, massed shapes of the trees scattered with moonlight. "I have some things to put in order, and that's another reason for

Chaz's visit. We talked a little about it in the spring, but I want to go over some things with him."

"Are you all right?"

"Oh, I'm fine. Really. I've made a decision I've been weighing for a long time, and that feels terrific." He paused and smiled. "It's still private, nothing for publication for awhile yet. But it's something I want to make official with Chaz and Sydney. Why don't we plan on dinner here, say, a week from Saturday? A little celebration."

# Chapter 17

Hudson surveyed the early evening scene on the deck of the Blue Bar and sipped a gin and tonic. He had walked over just before six and the timing was well judged. A few afternoon lingerers who had come in from the rain were dispersing, some with the glow of a couple of extra, unanticipated beers, and the dining crowd, which would include everything from middle-aged couples to college students, young singles, and every sort of family grouping, had not yet arrived.

The cocktail hour had materialized slowly but surely throughout the long, ruby and mauve sunset, and was now in full swing in the cool, rain-clean gloaming. The last light was radiant behind a bank of clouds in the west. The temperature had dropped with the storms and hovered in the seventies, and a fresh breeze curled in from the backside of the departing low pressure system, now a charcoal smudge far out to the southeast over the Gulf. Just to the left, due east along the edge of the surf, the moon, pale as a wafer and nearly full, ascended.

Ensconced on the bench in one corner of the deck, Hudson leaned back, one arm stretched along the railing. The bar ran half the length of the deck, in the center, and then L-shaped into a back corner of the restaurant, where a short passageway led into the kitchen. There were stools all around it and, on the side looking out across the beach, a scattering of small tables. The windows of the restaurant looked onto the deck all along the back wall of the large back dining room, and he could see a few early diners taking their seats.

He listened to the pleasant clink of glass for awhile longer, idly observing, and then decided on a walk. He wandered back into the pleasant maze of the Blue Bar. He went along the wide hallway that skirted one end of the back room, the largest of the three, and then, three steps down, into the other bar, a cozy nook. That, in turn, opened through an archway and down another two steps to the front dining room where, in a bay off to one side with an old stone fireplace, the occasional live music group or singer would hold forth. There wasn't a level floor, step, or wall in the entire place, and that was, of course, exactly the way Charlie had kept it. Unevenly paneled with various eras and grains of dark old wood, lighted at night by shadow-casting sconces and candlelight, the Blue Bar was romantically rough, the sort of fabled old Gulf retreat that no longer existed.

As he made his way across the end of the bar toward the front room, he decided to visit the gents and turned into the little passage to the right. The tight space barely had room for a tall young man encumbered with a backpack, waiting outside the restroom door, and another man talking quietly, but rather excitedly on the pay phone. When the doors to both restrooms opened simultaneously and the occupants excused themselves toward the bar, Hudson stepped back, and the backpacker went in.

"Not *now.*" In one move, the man, of medium height and stocky in a wiry sort of way, hung the phone up and swung around quickly, almost stepping on Hudson's feet. His eyes rounded in the shape of his wire-rimmed glasses, startled with some surprised, vague recognition.

"Terry? Hudson DeForest. Friend of Charlie's." Hudson made room for á handshake.

The man, whose complexion was unmistakably fair and freckled despite the burnish of a light tan, blushed deeply and instantaneously, from his throat up to the receding sandy hair close-cropped around his bald crown.

"Sure, sure! Good to see you! Wow, long time." He had been breathing heavily and now exhaled slowly and lowered his voice. "I was sure sorry to hear about your wife." He shook his head slightly, looking earnestly at Hudson.

"Thanks. How've you been? The place looks exactly the same. Thank God."

"That's for damn sure." He smiled briefly and laughed, resuming a hearty tone. "Oh, I'm toolin' along just the same. Same old Laurel same old. I love it." He paused and looked sternly over his glasses at the phone on the wall. "If I could just get my distributors to *do their jobs.* Oh, well, it's always something."

"Terry! Julie needs you out back," said a young man hurrying past the hall with a tray of beers.

"Duty calls," said Hudson. "I'll see you around. I'm here for a few weeks."

Terry Main seemed distracted. He smiled at Hudson and nodded as he stepped sideways toward the bar, saying, "You bet. I guess Charlie mentioned that awhile back. I forgot—you bought a house, didn't you?" He seemed to sense that his stab at gregariousness wasn't quite compensating for a certain anxious preoccupation. He touched Hudson's elbow. "See you later. Take care." He turned into the bar and disappeared.

Minutes later, Hudson went down the steps of the small porch outside, making way for two interesting parties. First, a handsome pair of women, in their eighties at least, one with a cane and both of them chatting hell-for-leather, snow white hair and tasteful cotton shirtwaists. Patiently behind them, talking quietly with a pretty blonde in a sleek white halter dress, came a tall young man wearing a University of Virginia ball cap, two large gold hoops in one ear, a chartreuse tie-dyed tee shirt, and, knotted around his waist, some sort of brilliantly colored Polynesian skirt.

Radical chic comes to Old Laurel, thought Hudson, smiling to himself.

Moseying up the road, he breathed the spectacular air, moist and cool. He headed west, toward the darkening twilight of the beach and the rough whisper of the waves, wrestling with his own preoccupation.

◇◇◇

Behind the houses that fronted the beach and across the end of Yaupon Lane, he trudged through the sugary sand. He passed a few people here and there in the near dark, walking or sitting, but within a half-mile he was alone.

He pulled his shirt over his head and wrapped his keys and money in it, kicked off his Birkenstocks, and ran into the surf before he could talk himself out of it. The water was slightly warmer than the cool air, a summer rarity, and the stiff breeze made his blood race.

Just beyond the breakers, he swam laps for several minutes, until the choppiness wore him out. He then sat at the water's edge, looking out until the horizon vanished and the infinitely rippling moonlight on the waves became, after quite a long time, less agonizing, and more an indifferent, beautiful monotony.

# Chapter 18

On the brief flight from Atlanta, Sydney reread the letter. Twice.

February 16th

Dear Charlie,

   It's always a joy to hear your voice. And it's been far too long. What, almost a year? Alas, I have no excuse. I really have retired, except for a couple of dear friends who are convinced through sheer habit that I am the only decent estate lawyer in Atlanta. Other than golf and racquetball, some church work, and my ill-informed but constant commitment to Helen's roses, I truly don't know where the time goes. Remember how time seemed so limitless when we were young? When Helen died, time sort of yawned open again for me, and I thought I'd never fill it. Now that I've found ways of filling it, it seems once again to have accelerated. But I have no complaint with that. (I don't want to be too old.)

   Thanks for the invite! I can't think of any place I'd rather be than with you in that incomparable early March sunshine on the coast. I'll drive down on the fourth, probably arrive around four or five, and will plan on staying until probably the tenth.

We'll talk more when I'm down, but I just want to say again that I think you are making absolutely the right decision about the land. I know exactly what it means to you. When you made your will fifteen years ago, you were insistent that should you die before me you wanted me to have it because you knew I would honor your wishes and see that it wasn't badly developed. You gave me the choice of keeping it intact or of ensuring some sort of appropriate, low development. I was deeply honored at your entrusting me both with the inheritance and with the decision about its stewardship.

But, Charlie, I am now nearly sixty-eight years old, and you are a *much* younger man of sixty-six. And while we never know how our days are numbered, I firmly believe that the two-year gap in our ages will continue to "widen" as I have seen it do ever since we both hit middle age and you somehow just seemed to stop while I kept going. No one on the planet can be more pleased than I that you have decided to go on and make a great dream come true in your lifetime (and in mine, too). My only regret is that I suspect you maundered too long over letting me know your decision. That eighty-five acres of paradise east of Seagrove is a part of the enormous love for the Gulf that has defined you. I'm proud of you for seizing the opportunity to help define it, and doing it now!

Although if you were to go first when we'd both made it to ninety, I would have carried out your wishes as planned, I don't need to point out to you that you are actually saving me some measure of headache. Whether I'd decided to go the route you've now settled on, and which is clearly the very best possible—a land preserve or trust in perpetuity—or had decided to oversee some respectfully indigenous, low-density development, I'm afraid my window of opportunity for being a young turk has decidedly closed. My vision has narrowed; my energies are sufficiently absorbed by my duties as treasurer of the board of Peachtree Battle Presbyterian Church and in trying to break seventy on the back nine at the club before I move on. Why in this world would I want suddenly to have to deal with sixty or eighty million dollars or more? I am a comfortably retired attorney and, as you know, Helen had a nice trust from her family as well.

Which brings me, finally, to your question about Chaz. As you saw yourself when you were up a couple of years ago, he really seems to have overcome his problems and found a direction that suits him. It took Helen's final illness to bring him to, but I truly believe he will cleave to the promise he made her. We had determined long before her death that to set him up as a "trust fund baby" would not only be doing him no favor but could actually undermine his resolution to settle down. He used the money she left him to get started and he has worked hard to make a go of it. As far as I can know, he is a disciplined social drinker and is off the other stuff entirely, he's in that shop five or six days a week, and, best of all, he seems really to enjoy it. You know how art has always been the one thing that held his focus, even in the rough stretches, and his most important inheritance from Helen was actually her marvelous taste. I think his fiancée, Sydney, is good for him, too. She's smart and confident and very good-looking. Strong. Purposeful. She's attentive to Chaz, without hovering, and I like that. I think you'll like her, too, when you meet her, and I know they're eager to come down when their busy schedules allow. They've been seeing each other for almost two years, she moved into the house a year ago, and he gave her his grand-mother's ring at Thanksgiving.

It is specifically this incremental growth, this integra-tion, that Chaz has needed in order to build a life. And frankly, Charlie, I don't want anything to cause him to fly off in different directions again. The best thing that has ever happened to him was realizing, in that year before she left us, how much his mother loved him, how he had hurt her, and how desperately he needed to let her know he was serious about changing. He got some help, but primarily he did it by himself, for her. By the time she died, he was a new man. It was miraculous, but it has proven real. He is working for everything he gets, he's responsible, he has goals and even, I think, ambition.

I am proud of him. For so many years he was a troubled young man in seemingly needless but nonetheless unrelenting escape. Now he seems to be a man who is living fully in the moment and who plans for tomorrow. He's quite obviously in love and, I pray to God, he's happy. When I am gone, he (and my *grandchildren*???) will inherit not a great deal but enough to help make their lives a bit more secure and afford them some pleasure in their maturity. If I presume in believing that that is enough for my son, it is the experienced presumption of a loving father.

As I have told you several times over the years, I have never mentioned to him anything at all about your will or its directives for me, and now, I think it just as well, that I need never do so. Neither you nor I have been very much at ease with the implicit fact that on my death that responsibility would pass by default to Chaz, but you, of course, have been too good to bring it up. In many ways, that land is your child just as Chaz is mine. You want to go ahead and see for yourself that it will be safe and be the best that it can be. I want the same for Chaz. He has traveled far these past few years. But my pride and my love would be less than genuine if I were to be less than honest with myself. Chaz is a young man who needs parameters, who needs work even more than most of us, who needs discipline and focus, and only lately has he found the truth of this and begun to benefit from that truth.

I don't want that sense of purpose to become confused, and I simply cannot believe Chaz's progress would be best served by overwhelming temptation and limitless norms. For some it might be a kind of freedom; for him I think it would be, if not an invitation to disaster, at least the loss of ground that has been very hard won. This is not, ultimately, my decision, of course. It is yours. But I just wanted to say again how much I support it, and why.

I thought about e-mailing you, but it wouldn't be appropriate for this communication and, besides, I never have really gotten the hang of it. The last note I sent someone I discovered two weeks later was *unsent*; apparently I'd hit the wrong icon. Even though I'll see you in a few weeks and we can talk more at length, I wanted to say these things to you now. I am sending this letter by certified mail and no doubt you will want to burn it when you have read it.

In closing just let me say that I think your idea of leaving Chaz your beautiful home seems ideal to me. And sharing your intention with him soon, yourself, rather than letting him hear it read from a sheaf of documents years from now, is characteristic of you. Very warm and very thoughtful. Some of Chaz's happiest memories are of our times in Laurel.

I am delighted as well that you feel you have the right team now to take on the 26-A and the Blue Bar. I know that for you they are far more than businesses and that you want to place them, too, into caring hands.

Feel wonderful about your decisions! You deserve to. They are not only wise, they are right and good. I know that you'll work out the details with your attorney there; Dan is a great guy. But, of course, as you suggested, we can go over some options when I'm down if you want. Thank you again for having entrusted me all these years with what you, so characteristically, consider a profound trust of your own. I join you with every fiber of my being in preserving it. If anyone can be nearly as happy as you to see, in his lifetime, that tract of land saved, you know who it is.

And let me say how honored I am to have a man like you as my only brother in this world. What brother could have honored me more, not just for the past fifteen years but for over six decades, with such true intimacy, generosity, and confidence? My life is immeasurably enriched by your integrity and your love.

Always,

Peter

Although Peter Cullen did not get his wish about seeing in his lifetime the eighty-five acres of land just east of Seagrove become a wilderness preserve, he did get his wish about not growing too old. He had been discovered by a friend who had dropped by early on the morning of February seventeenth for coffee and to return a book. Not rousing Peter, the friend had walked around to the back to see him, one hand still clutching a hose, his robe drenched with the spewing water, sprawled close to the long bed of roses to which his wife had been so devoted. His face was free of pain and his physician later said that the coronary had, in all probability, killed him instantaneously.

◇◇◇

As the plane began its descent, Chaz looked over from his Bloody Mary and crossword at the letter in Sydney's lap. "Should you have that with you?"

"I don't think Uncle Charlie's going to go through my purse or bag. Besides," she smiled, "it holds a sort of talismanic effect for me."

She nestled into his chest, and kissed him.

# Chapter 19

Hudson slept well, was up by seven, and went for a run on the beach with Moon.

Over breakfast he decided that the work of the day would be reading, that he'd get back to the reviews tomorrow.

He tackled the project that interested him least, in order to get it out of the way: *Heart of Darkness*, a rough spot in the senior curriculum about which he continued to have questions. But for now, he had to work it up and there was no way around it but through it. He appreciated Joseph Conrad, he just didn't particularly like reading him.

At least that was the flippant assessment he currently held. More truthfully, it wasn't the author's alternating ham-handedness and opacity that rankled him, it was the novella's very effective delving into questionable motive and moral ambivalence that disconcerted him now more than ever. By one-thirty the weight of the story had pinned him to the sofa; he was slowly inching his way through the African interior, with Olive riding on his chest and a notepad at his side, when the phone rang.

"Hudson?"

"This is he."

"Well, I just wanna know this, is this the goodlookin' Hudson DeForest who makes me laugh?" The voice—pure old Memphis, rich, mature, deliberate and deep, almost a man's except for its distinctly feminine grace—poured into his ear like a commingled breath of cigarettes and bourbon. "The one whom I simply cannot *wait* to see?"

"Libby!"

"Well, I have to *call* to see how you're doing, because of course I know you've been here for a week and I guess we just haven't made it onto your social calendar and I really don't intend to wait much longer." Libby punctuated only rarely with full stops; implied commas and sinuously sustained run-on sentences, imbedded with dramatic emphases, sly one-liners, and droll parenthetical asides, were her forte.

"Five days. I was going to call you two tonight. I swear it."

"How are you, sweetie?"

"I'm okay."

"Really?"

"Yeah, I think so. What kind of trouble are you into this summer?"

"Not a damn thing that I know of and I wish I did! That old fool husband of mine has gone fishing up at that lodge in Montana with his card-playing geezer buddies and none of my girlfriends are here right now and I'm right lonely. Charlie says you all had a marvelous visit Saturday evening."

"It was, indeed. So good to be with him again."

"Bradford won't be back for two weeks. I know I'll see you for dinner next week with the young cousin and his bride. But I don't wanna wait to see you and I'm just sitting here reading...."

"So am I. Joseph Conrad's *Heart of Darkness.*"

"Well, aren't we fun? I mean I know you must have your schoolwork and all—oh, and I wanna hear about your book—but I was just wondering if you might like to get together for a drink and just talk some trash, I have to see for myself if what Charlie says is true."

"And that would be…?"

"That you just look *great.*" She said it in that Southern sense that translates as "You seem to be getting by okay."

◇◇◇

At seven o'clock Hudson mounted the wide steps of the big shingled house that Brad and Libby Lee called home seven or eight months of the year. They had owned the large saltbox at the end of Alexandria Lane, a cul-de-sac on the north edge of town shaded by large live oaks and myrtles, for more than thirty years. At first they came only a few weeks a year, renting the house out otherwise, but eventually they found themselves spending more and more time in Laurel. A few years back, on the occasion of Brad's third and final retirement from the brokerage, they had sold their home in Memphis, returning now only in late spring or at Christmas for visits with friends, Libby's brother, or Brad's sister.

The big Laurel house was now made available only to closest family and friends, and even then, at times, only with short notice. "I like to come and go when I want to," as Libby put it. In the past few years, Libby had come and gone—with Brad, alone, or with friends—to New York, New Orleans, San Francisco, British Columbia, Toronto, Nantucket, Tuscany, Lake Como, Austria, London, a ten-day hike along Kau'ai's Na Pali and a two-week biking tour of southern Scotland.

"Come in this house," she growled, swinging wide the door and throwing out her free arm for a hug. Libby's physical qualities uncannily matched her voice; she was an elegant voluptuary clearing a path to seventy with slyly vigorous humor, good breeding not heir to pretension, exceptional cheekbones, thick honey and gray hair, and watery blue eyes so penetrating that they would be almost disconcerting were they not also so ineffably inviting and sympathetic.

Hudson embraced her, producing from behind his back a rough bouquet of mustard yellow lantana he had snatched as he left the cottage. "Poor things, but mine own."

"No, they're beautiful, but let's go get 'em some water, they wilt so fast you know—you know I *had* a pretty good bush myself around back, it had grown up nice and tall, and then of course the workmen just *decimated* it when they extended that screened porch awhile back. It's just sort of pitiful now, hardly blooms."

She led the way down the wide dog-trot hall to the large, glassy kitchen, to search for a vase and situate the flowers, sustaining all the while a deceptively languid commentary that ranged from flowers ("You *will* be forced to look at my flower photos from the hike in Kau'ai") and local workmen ("They call the shots and you can just take it or leave it") to the big and fairly tacky house that had recently risen at the other end of her street ("The best thing I can say about it is that, thank God, they had the common decency to leave that stand of oaks and that big magnolia along the road so that I don't have to see most of it"); the afternoon's reading, a novel, from which she had sought relief ("So many people have told me 'You *must* read this book,' but I don't know—am I missing something?—I can't keep my eyes open, just duller than dishwater and *so* predictable, by the time something finally happens you feel like you've already read that it already happened"); an upcoming trip ("Brad has finally realized I guess that I'm not going to shut up about that Norwegian cruise, we're going in September"); and her volunteer gig at the child abuse center in Panama City ("I have to *make* myself go but then of course I'm always glad I did…").

Over drinks, she subsided: "I'm just *babbling* I'm so glad to see you." She leveled her dancing crystal eyes at him with unswerving focus, and said: "I mean *really* see you. In Memphis Christmas before last you *seemed* all right but I couldn't help but feel you were just acting like we're *supposed* to."

"Maybe that's why I very rudely kept our visit to a minimum. I knew I wouldn't be able to fool you. I was so grateful you came to see me, but also I couldn't wait for you to go back to Laurel or leave for Europe or wherever you were headed."

"Oh, honey, I understand, and that's why I've steered a wide berth and not bothered you. But we were worried about you. And you know you can talk to me any time of the day or night now or next year or any time at all or not talk to me one bit, I just want you to know we love you and we're pullin' for you."

She paused. "And I *do* just have to say, because it's true, that you really do look marvelous. You know, every time I see you after a long time you're even better looking than I remembered. That auburn hair with just a touch of distinguishing gray, and those green, green eyes. Those little girls at Elliott must absolutely swoon."

"And you, as always, are a woman of impeccable taste."

They laughed, and Libby reached over and gripped his hand for a moment. "I sure as hell am, and I'll tell you what. Now, this may be *importunate*, but I promise you it'll be my last unsolicited observation, all right?"

"Of course."

"That superb woman, Kate, wants you to *live*, you know that, don't you?"

"Oh, yes, I know that and I feel that. And I'm trying. And I'm trying not to try too hard." Hudson exhaled mightily. "It's hard. I'm doing it."

"Good for you. Are you still seeing Alex?"

"Just cut from once a week to twice a month a few weeks before I came down. He is a very wise, very compassionate taskmaster. I will probably be playing tapes of his voice in my brain for the rest of my life—I think of him as my voice of sanity. Kate, of course, is my voice of strength. She cuts me no slack. When I'm up against it, I think what he might say, what she would say. I trade on his rationalism, his emotional truth, and I trade on her strength. And when I've considered their perspectives, I force myself to make my own decision and get on with it."

Libby patted his hand and winked at him. "Bring your drink and let's go back on the porch—with the overhead, it's cool enough—and while you look at my Kau'ai flowers, you really won't believe them, I'm going to have just one little cigarette."

"How are you doing with that?"

"This will be my first of the day—never more than three a day, sometimes only two, and I think that's pretty good." They went through the French doors out onto the long screened porch, its wicker Adirondacks and ottomans lighted only by a couple of low table lamps. All around, the thick darkness beyond undulated with the interwoven rhythms of cicadas and tree toads and the evensong of birds.

◇◇◇

In the summer months, even Monday nights were fairly busy at the Blue Bar. Hudson and Libby sat in a corner booth in the back room, watching through the windows the ebb and flow of the deck bar crowd.

As she cased the joint, Libby filled him in on all the local gossip. "I have my role in Laurel society down to a fine science. I'm here just enough to know what I *want* to know about what's goin' on and I'm gone just enough not to have to deal with whatever I don't want to deal with."

Their talk soon turned to Charlie.

"What do you suppose this celebration, this announcement, is a week from Saturday?" Hudson asked.

"Intriguing, isn't it? But then one reason we've been friends all these years is that we share a high regard for privacy. I mean, we're as close as we can be, and we're not *secretive,* but we keep our own counsel, you know—Brad always says 'Charlie'll tell us when he's ready to'—and God knows I sort of go *my* own way. All I can think of is that maybe he's doing something wonderful as a wedding gift. You know, that boy's the only blood family he's got, and Charlie loved his father just like a brother." She paused. "Peter was a good man."

"Do you know Chaz?"

"Not really, haven't seen him in years—he was probably just graduating from high school and I believe Charlie said he's thirty-five, so, what? Seventeen, eighteen years? You know he's been down a couple of times since his father died, but we were away—in April, wasn't it?—I remember because we were still in Memphis the first time and then Hawaii."

"Charlie says he was a handful but that he's gotten his act together."

"He seems to be very proud of him. Apparently has a thriving little art and antiques business in Buckhead and apparently madly in love with this Sydney. I think she does something with some video production group or something like that—Charlie offered to do a big wedding party here, but their work schedules wouldn't allow it...."

"Sounds like her family would've been a lot to contend with, too."

"Smart girl, and besides I just *love* the idea of elopement. Brad wanted to, you know—wanted to come down here—but I wouldn't hear of it." She shook her head. "One of the best ideas he ever had."

"Charlie seems pretty happy about the marriage."

"Oh, yeah, I think it's all part of his being pleased that Chaz finally settled down and straightened himself out. He told me he knew how much Chaz loved her from the way he talked about her."

"I had the feeling the other night that Charlie may be putting his house in order. He's the same as ever. Energetic. Happy enough, I think. Glad to have divested himself of most of his holdings, and having a good time with 26-A and this—" he gestured. "But—I don't know—I sensed that somehow he may feel in need of some investment, some stake, in the future."

"Just a little bit lonely?"

Hudson nodded.

"That's why if he's finding pleasure in Chaz and Sydney, I'm all for it. If something makes Charlie happy, I'm happy for him." She reached over and squeezed Hudson's hand. "And, need I add, you gorgeous man, that goes for you, too." She straightened her neck and lifted her head imperiously, fixing him with a wry stare. "It goes for all of us. We're all a little bit lonely and we all need to help one another. God knows *I'm* not getting any younger."

Neither of them had noticed the figure suddenly approaching from around the high back of the booth. "*Who's* not getting any younger?"

"Charlie!"

"Libby, you know you're one of the youngest people any of us knows."

"You're a liar but you're cute," Libby said, looking around. "Have you all been here long? We just demolished two of those divine shrimp salads. And where *are* the newlyweds?"

"Out there," Charlie said, nodding at the window. "We just had a drink and I had to go up front to talk with Terry. They're waiting for me—we're about to walk on back to the house for a sandwich."

Hudson laughed. "I've just been watching them, thinking what an attractive couple they are!"

Libby twisted around and followed their gaze. "Tall, chestnut hair with the broad white headband? Nice-looking gal, and look at Chaz...." She trailed off in the memory of a gawky, sullen adolescent, shaking her head. "Mnh, mnh, mnh. I *cannot* believe it. Aren't they a handsome pair?"

Charlie beamed. "They are, aren't they? Come on out!"

◇◇◇

They seemed to Hudson the sort of couple whose complementary strengths and exchange of mutual support were immediately apparent, beginning with their physical appearances.

Chaz was about Charlie's height, just under six feet, and rakishly thin, not unhealthily, but in a rather aesthetic way. His bearing might almost be described as languid or willowy, except for the restless energy that seemed to bring his frame to alert, erect attention now and then, and to pulse behind the large, dark, watchful eyes, wide-set in a very fair face. His mouth's expression, seemed, too, to have a life of its own, now upturning the entire face with a sudden, brilliant smile, now falling into a line of distracted repose. His hair, dark, shiny, almost black, was not long, but it curled cherubically around his face. His brow was high. Something almost Byronic about the guy, Hudson thought. Something at once easy and potentially volatile.

Her voice was arresting, measured, low but lilting. In fact, everything about Sydney was artfully modulated, yet seemingly genuine and spontaneous. Hudson thought her blue-grey eyes

teemed with intelligence and was bemused at how the fine care-
fulness of her demeanor occasionally erupted into high-spirited
humor. Of medium height, she seemed taller: slim, long legs,
full breasts, a long oval face with the chin carried at a proud
angle. She wore only light makeup, and her rich brown hair
was pulled back from her face with the white headband; she
was dressed simply but strikingly in a short lilac sundress. Sexy
in a cool way, Hudson thought, and a conscious, but not self-
conscious, sense of style.

The anchor of Chaz's focus was clearly his wife. He was
cordial and attentive to them all, but he watched Sydney like a
movie. Hudson could understand why, and he didn't imagine
it to be merely a honeymoon mooniness that would wear away
with the ongoing intimacies of married life. Hudson knew a
powerful woman when he saw one, and he was seeing one now.
And he could see that, whatever else they might or might not
have going for them, Chaz Cullen willingly gave his wife his
undivided attention, and, in return, she gave his life direction
and interest.

After a few minutes of pleasantries, Charlie said, "Well, I
have to get these two back home. I have dinner waiting and
they didn't have lunch."

Libby laughed. "That's not the strongest endorsement I've
ever heard for the Blue Bar's kitchen."

"Oh, we'll be sampling the fare from time to time!" said
Sydney. "Chaz tells me the fried shrimp and hushpuppies are
unsurpassed."

As they began to move away, Charlie placed one arm around
her waist and the other around Chaz's. "Hudson and Libby will
be joining us for dinner on Saturday."

"Great," said Chaz.

Sydney added, "We'll see you then," looking back over her
shoulder at them.

Hudson imagined that the brilliant smile, for the first time
and only for a moment, faltered.

◇◇◇

Once back at the cottage, Hudson could not settle. He sat with Moon for awhile on the porch. Finally, he decided to check another review. Perhaps meeting Sydney guided his hand to one that in some odd way seemed *apropos* to the evening.

## Quality Star
### In *Afterglow*, the incomparable Julie Christie shows the kids how "It" is done

More than thirty years after initially falling in love with Julie Christie, I realized as I viewed her new film *Afterglow* that I was falling in love all over again with Julie Christie. Then, she was the wide-eyed, bekerchiefed Lara of *Dr. Zhivago* and the wistful, desperately glamorous model in *Darling*, for which she won the Academy Award for best actress, and I was in braces.

Since that time, both Julie and I have been around the block a few times. Her face is artfully, and ever so slightly, touched up; my hair is beginning to gray. But the strong feeling that her riveting performance in *Afterglow* evokes is not mere nostalgia nor some middle-aged desire to *recherche le temps perdu*. It is how her longtime fans are likely to appreciate Christie now that is of the essence. Thirty-five years ago, American teens found her sultry New Wave English looks either the stuff of exotic fantasies or the ultimate role-model for hair-frosting and *sang froid* stylishness. It is we who have matured. Even though the Christie of *Afterglow* is more interestingly attractive, intelligently sexy, and husky-voiced than ever before, we are better able at this perspective to see that she is a fine, fine actor, and one of the most satisfyingly watchable film stars of the past three decades.

At one point in Alan Rudolph's absorbing and entertaining new film, someone asks Christie's character, Phyllis Mann, "Oh, are you an actress?"

With a flash of that fabulous grin, unconsciously sharp timing, and painfully self-conscious irony, she rasps: "All the time."

Phyllis knows, in a mid-life best described as manageably bitter, that the modest talent that led to her only claim to fame, years ago, as a minor movie queen in B-minus (mostly horror) movies, has also been the primary bane of her existence. Rudolph explores, through an odd sequence of coincidental events, what it takes to break her out of her latest, long-running gig as a frustrated wife and failed mother, a beautiful woman in her early fifties whose tragedy is that she actually no longer has a role to play, and who drifts, watching videos of her old movies and dodging the threat of any real emotion with self-deprecating wit and too much qin.

With *Afterglow*, writer-director Rudolph continues to hack out his own distinctive path through the sulfurous urban angst, the postmodern moral and cultural detritus of our times. He has, on occasion, lost his way, as those who managed to sit through his *Love at Large* a few years back will remember. *Afterglow*, produced by his mentor Robert Altman, is Rudolph's most compelling film to date, marking a subtle but substantial advance over his previous best, 1984's *Choose Me*. As in that film, here we are treated to the same lush visual vocabulary, the same cool affect that somehow manages to quicken rather than alienate. *Afterglow* is a wonderful mood piece; but it is more than that. Integrating coherently Rudolph's dreamy, bracingly eccentric style, his sense of societal anomie, and his writing's oblique narrative investigations into human relationships, *Afterglow* takes great cinematic risks. What gives the film its own afterglow is the grace with which Rudolph manages to keep his three-ring circus balanced. We leave the theatre not only not particularly bothered but actually invigorated by his unique capacity for juggling icy surrealism with an almost giddy lyricism, and clinical dissections of the human heart with plot elements straight out of Restoration farce.

The ruefully smoldering heart of *Afterglow* is Christie's performance, which, short of a possible "Brit-split vote" benefiting Helen Hunt, should win her another best actress Oscar. Also helping Rudolph hold this odd, fascinating, and ultimately moving entertainment together are the three other lead actors: Nick Nolte as Phyllis' cheerfully philandering handyman husband, Lucky, and Lara Flynn Boyle (of television's *Twin Peaks*) and Jonny Lee Miller (*Trainspotting*) as a young couple facing their own marital challenges. More accurately, it is the fact that the couples are not facing what ails them that leads them astray, albeit eventually, to a sort of enlightenment. Miller's character, Jeffrey, a prissy young financier whose emotional circuits are clogged by his pretensions to a cold perfection of hi-tech, hard-edged style, seeks to revive himself through an affair with Phyllis. Her maturity and romantic air of loss have the effect of turning the jaded young man into a positively medieval, chivalric knight. Concurrently, with each pairing unbeknownst to the other, Nolte's Lucky has struck up a liaison with Jeffrey's lonely young wife, Marianne.

What begins as a cold examination of estrangement, set against the gray stone buildings and wintry sunsets of Montreal and musically edged by that master of film score chill, Mark Isham, ends, after all is said and done, as something quite different. The characters have come to a new place, and so have we. From a film of high artifice, with a vivifying sense of something rather magical, some real-life lessons have been learned about breaking free, and about the even harder business of breaking through, of expressing need, and of granting forgiveness whether to others or ourselves. As one character in *Afterglow* (speaking, one suspects, for the filmmaker himself) repeatedly exhorts: "Take a flying leap into the future."

# Chapter 20

A few nights later, after a run of evenings out, Charlie, Sydney and Chaz dined in the bosom of the family, on the lower screened veranda. Charlie grilled red snapper and yellow corn, Sydney concocted the salad, and Chaz churned fresh lemon and pineapple ice cream. More than once Sydney saw Charlie beaming at Chaz, and at one point when Chaz and she were looking out to the sunset-russet lagoon, the older man came up and stood behind them, wrapping his arms around their shoulders.

"I'm so very happy for you two."

Around ten, Sydney said, "Let's go to the Blue Bar for a nightcap."

Charlie looked tired and had already stifled a yawn or two, but he said he was good for a few minutes.

The three of them ambled over around eleven. Earlier in the day Chaz had called from the bedroom and ascertained that the Bar closed at twelve on weeknights. And that Terry Main would be there.

They had spoken briefly to Terry when they arrived. He had been behind the bar in the small middle room. "Sure, I remember Chaz. You were here a few weeks back. This must be your bride, Charlie mentioned you were coming down." He nodded appreciatively. "Congratulations."

They stood on the back deck with their drinks for nearly half an hour. It was a crystalline night on the coast. Even the lights of the bar could not obliterate the shimmering stars, and what was left of the thinning late crowd had wound down to quiet laughter and intermittent conversation.

Finally, Charlie drained the last of his scotch and said, "I'm leaving you kids to it." He kissed Sydney on the cheek and patted Chaz's shoulder.

Sydney returned the kiss. "Oh, I feel I could stay out all night, just walking the beach. It's *so* glorious."

"Do it! Come in whenever. You know the alarm code, and we have no plan for the morning except to do whatever you please whenever you please…." As he walked away, Chaz said, "We won't be too late."

Blue Bar patrons apparently knew the drill. There was no hue and cry about last call and by twelve the place was deserted.

◇◇◇

"Would it be an imposition to ask for some of that?" Sydney approached the bar where Terry was sipping a cup of coffee while he closed out the register. Chaz followed her in.

Terry swung two mugs from the rack. "Not at all. But I need to warn you, it's high octane."

"We don't drink it any other way," Chaz smiled. "Mind if we join you here for a minute?"

If Terry found the attempt at after-hours socializing odd, he didn't let on. *When they had discussed strategy earlier, Sydney had said, "You're the boss' family. What's he going to say… 'No, get out'?"* Dinner service had stopped at ten, so the night kitchen staff was already gone, along with most of the waiters. Terry called out a couple of orders to his two remaining staff as they came and went from the front room and the back deck, cleaning up. Then he looked noncommittally over his steaming coffee, first at Sydney and then at Chaz. "Having a good time?"

Chaz said, "Yeah. Great weather—not too hot yet."

Terry smiled and sipped his coffee. "Yeah, this is as good as it gets for summer."

Then silence.

Chaz looked down hard at the bar for a moment, and when he looked up at Terry his eyes had become searching, vulnerable, even humiliated. "Charlie…"

Sydney casually reached over and rested her hand on his, and said softly, "It's not *quite* the trip we'd hoped for." She noticed a slight flash somewhere deep in Terry's otherwise impassive brown eyes, and he seemed to forget for an instant the bar towel he'd picked up.

"Nothing wrong with Charlie I hope…,"

"No," said Chaz, "…and, yes." He looked up earnestly at Terry. "Does he seem different in any way to you lately? Has he done anything…well, *to* you?"

Terry looked like a man drifting into uncharted waters, but his eyes became more interested, alert.

Chaz exhaled deeply, and smiled with a little shake of his head. "Hey, man, I'm sorry. You don't even know me. We're just kinda worn out with a bad situation and have been trying to figure out what to do about it. But we shouldn't bother you. It's just old family stuff, and Charlie's your employer and you're probably crazy about the guy like everybody else seems to be down here." He stood and put his arm around Sydney's waist.

Terry hesitated only a second before laying the towel aside and taking two steps down the bar. He lifted over a bottle of good brandy and three glasses. "Let me send Jake and Marcie home. If you'll take these out, I'll be right behind you with the coffee." He winked at them as they picked up the bottle and glasses.

"Thank you," they both stammered in the tones of lost children.

◇◇◇

Over the first brandy, slowly at first, in a very credible agony of fits and starts, with occasional sympathetic urgings and amendments from Sydney, and finally in almost uninterrupted transports of passion, Chaz confided to Terry that his family had known the dark side of Mr. Magnanimous, Lord Bountiful, a.k.a. Charlie Brompton. That his father who had been like a brother to Charlie had been repeatedly ill-used by him in business ventures. That Charlie's success over the years had been built as much on bilked relatives and friends in Louisville as on his own entrepreneurial skills. That the easily summoned graciousness and flaunted acts of generosity masked, and, in Charlie's own sense of self-esteem probably atoned for, an essentially ruthless, cold, self-absorbed nature.

"We never knew what to expect. He could be the nicest guy in the world. I think he's always really wanted to stay on an even keel. But it's almost a sort of Jekyll and Hyde thing, you know? We've seen it take on some pretty frightening aspects over the years. Black depressions. Have you ever noticed? But usually he keeps to himself then. Irrational fears and anger...." Looking and sounding spent, Chaz tapered off. "My father died, unexpectedly, four months ago. He was supposed to have been Charlie's heir."

Sydney tenderly picked up the thread. "And Chaz would then inherit. We've discovered through some letters between them just before Chaz's dad died, and which Charlie doesn't know we've seen, that Charlie is planning to cut Chaz out of most of his inheritance."

"He doesn't know we know. He's just acting like it's old times and everything's fine."

Terry had lighted a cigarette and exhaled into the cool, light breeze. "Why don't you confront him?"

"He'd deny it like he's always denied his schemes in the past," said Chaz. "And, unfortunately, we have no proof. My father was a fine man, a good man, but he was a little eccentric. And very old school and very proud. He could never bring himself really to admit just how badly Charlie had always behaved in their business dealings. They had grown up together more like brothers than cousins. Dad was kind and generous toward him to the end. He knew he was leaving me a decent little trust and probably thought he was doing me a favor by not contesting Charlie's usurpation of the land agreement. Thought he was saving me a lot of heartache."

"And saving you from any more disappointments in your only 'uncle' beyond those you'd already seen," added Sydney, her hand on his. "They're a small family."

"I did have some good memories of this place when I was a kid. I didn't catch a lot of what was going on." Chaz paused. "Terry, we know, too, that he's cutting you out of the group that's getting this place and 26-A."

Terry didn't bat an eye, merely tapped his cigarette, drew a last drag, and ground it out. He looked out to sea. They sat in silence for awhile. The moon tilted, a ghostly half ring in the west, and other than a low bar light inside, a candle on their table, and the pale suffusion of a distant streetlight around near the front, the world was awash with stars.

Terry looked back at the two of them, his head just perceptibly nodding.

◇◇◇

Over the second brandy, Terry told them everything they needed to know.

Even more important, as Sydney, in a rapturous whisper, pointed out as they walked back to the house later, was how he told them. They had broken the ice sufficiently and, as if someone had suddenly thawed him, he began to gush his own account of betrayed understandings, two-faced dealings, arrogant presumptions, unfair and capricious decisions. As he warmed to his subject, Terry easily segued from the demeanor of laid-back, laconic beach guy to that of a former corporate attorney as if reverting to a more natural state.

"I've been in or around Laurel for six years, since I decided to leave law and come out here on the coast to slow down. Worked for a contractor for the first couple of years. I've been with Charlie for four years. He's said, and I think not just to me, that I'm the best manager he's had since he bought the place twenty years ago. I really like it, I treat it like it's mine. I like the area and I like the people, and I treat them like they're mine as well. It's become home.

"Charlie knows this. We've always had a good professional relationship. I know he relies on me when it's convenient for him to do so. I thought he trusted me. And, occasionally, he allows himself just a touch of that warmth with me that he seems to spread around pretty easily with everyone else. But there's always been a slight reserve, something held back. No matter how I prove myself, it never seems enough to get close to him.

"I make no bones about the fact that in these four years I've grown increasingly interested in the question of Charlie's retirement. Lately I've been fairly up front about my desire to take over when he decides to go from this sort of 'semi-state' he's in now into the real thing. I was never able to pin him down and talk details. I guessed it was at least partly that emotional thing people go through when they're at this point, you know, that he probably felt some denial or at least some conflict about laying down the reins. So, I never pushed hard. I've been a gentleman. Just let him know from time to time that whenever he was ready, I'd appreciate the opportunity of sitting down and talking turkey, that, for me, it would really be a dream come true. I could tell that he believed I meant what I said: that I wasn't interested in turning around and selling the place as a ten-floor pre-fab condo or miniature golf course, but all he'd say was 'Okay, okay' and go on about whatever he was doing.

"I trusted him to do the right thing. I really believed he'd give me first option whenever the time came, and I just kept my nose to the grindstone and tried in any way I could to let him know I was there for him. The best option. I'm his right arm. Anticipate things without being told. Keep the tone of the place the way he likes it. The kitchen is superb. Someone who knows and loves the place, who understands what it means as a tradition in this burg. I actually thought I'd earned enough confidence and respect that he might give me the best possible price. Maybe even help me secure the business loan." Terry paused and gave one of his quick generic grins. He leaned back in his chair and briefly considered his fingernails. "Silly me.

"He called me into the office over at 26-A about three months ago. Very businesslike yet very fatherly. To let me know about his decision regarding the new management and investment group for both the restaurant and the bar. His embarrassment was obvious and excruciating. I can't truthfully say that I cared.

I was furious. He reassured me three times that everyone was pleased with my management skills and liked having me at the bar and that no one wanted me to leave.

"'You've become part of the Blue Bar,' he said, as if that should be a suitable consolation prize for missing out on something I'd hoped for and had pretty good reason to plan for almost four years...."

Silence again, for two or three minutes. Seventy or eighty yards across the dark, wide beach, the surf tossed and slithered restlessly.

Chaz said, "We have something in common."

"A sense of fairness abused?" Terry asked, his brows raised.

"How about anger?"

Terry smiled and did not protest.

Chaz continued. "How about doing something about it? How about fighting for what should rightfully be ours? Has that crossed your mind?"

"It seems to have crossed yours."

"Yes," Sydney spoke up, "it certainly has." She smiled, wide-eyed, purposeful.

"And?"

"We have to get back to the house now. When and where can we meet again briefly? And privately?"

"We don't open for lunch Mondays, so I'm not due back here until about three-thirty. How about you taking a walk toward Seaside around one o'clock and my happening to drive past on my way to the post office and giving you a lift? How much time do you have in mind?"

Sydney answered, "Twenty minutes. No more than thirty. We want you to see the letter we mentioned...."

"And we're working on a plan. We hope—we think—you'll be interested."

# Chapter 21

Hudson realized he had been staring at his last sentence for probably eight or ten minutes. He was working on a few minor revisions in one of the reviews that was to go in the book, and, of course, it was becoming apparent, as it always did, that there was no such thing as a minor revision. He remembered, however, that it was this fierce concentration that he loved about the act (or perhaps it was more the *state*) of writing. Sustaining for moments at a time, word by word by word, the closest thing he knew to pure, unadulterated, obliterating focus.

He had been writing about film since he'd moved back to Memphis almost ten years before and had not tired of it yet. Someday, he imagined, he might try some other form. Some critical overview of a period or genre, perhaps, or even a novel or short stories. But for now, his lifelong love of movies still provided what seemed to him a fortuitous excuse for putting words on paper.

His relationship to writing, like everything else, had undergone changes since Kate's departure. For more than a year, he had considered telling the paper that he needed a sabbatical. Films with probing thought and genuine emotion were hell to sit through, much less re-examine to the nub for hours at the computer. And the frequent fare of banal action flicks and mindless comedies was no better: worlds without meaning were no escape from a world without meaning. Putting each word behind the last was as painstaking as it had ever been, but the concomitant reward had paled. Instead of spending his usual three or four hours to write about two movies on his Saturday mornings, he would often find himself still staring at the screen late in the day, having had nothing to eat. Sometimes he would even have to finish on Sundays, thereby crowding the day with whatever preparation he needed to do for his classes.

And, of course, there was the gnawing empty place in his schedule where an irreplaceable routine had developed. On Friday afternoons, he had usually gone directly from school to whatever new openings he was covering, and Kate would meet him for whichever of the two she most wanted to see. Afterward, they would stop somewhere for a bite to eat or, after the long day, head home for an easy dinner.

Whether whatever was left of his common sense prevailed, or perhaps because he was afraid of opening even wider the void that gaped beneath him, he kept doing it. "Putting each word behind the last is as painstaking as ever, but without the accompanying reward," he had told Alex. To which Alex had replied, *The process may not be for awhile what it was for you before, but now is most certainly not the time to give it up.* He had looked sternly at Hudson. *I don't think I need to tell you what a metaphor is, do I?* Hudson thought that beyond process, the work itself was off. It read to him like what it was: ideas dredged from an opaque consciousness and expressed as tediously as nails pounded through concrete.

It was instructive now, as he sorted through his years' worth of disks, deciding what to include in the collection, to see that several of the reviews from that darkest era were among his best. He could see now that, just as was true of his teaching, the focus required for his writing had not only gotten him through, but now helped him to reconstruct himself on the other side of the abyss, to know at least some semblance of who he was.

It had seemed to him at the time that that first year in the classroom after Kate was gone must have been a complete loss for his students. He scarcely knew where he was, or why, much less what page they were on, what he had assigned for homework, or how even to begin explaining what Tennyson was getting at with "In Memoriam." Only recently, looking over those notes and files as he made his way through the past year, did he begin to think that perhaps it had not been a total wash after all.

He was surprised to find lesson plans far more meticulously ordered than the rough sketches he usually relied on, like exhaustively detailed roadmaps he had instinctively created to keep himself moving from one point to another without stalling by the wayside or taking one of the myriad side roads into despair. And it seemed evident that he had toiled at compensating for the loss of humor and flights of imaginative give-and-take, with which he liked to think he had previously engaged his students, with a clear sequence of practical how-to's, challenges and positive reinforcements tailored individually, precisely, and a certain calm atmosphere in which the girls seemed to thrive.

So it seemed with the writing as well. In most of the articles the arc of thinking was carefully built and, if not stylistically superior, had at least integrity of shape and tone and what must have been a very well hidden, subconscious delight in language.

◇◇◇

He put his final touch on the sentence, getting his thought down exactly and in exactly the way he wanted to, and stood up and stretched. Cocooned from the midday heat, he'd been at it for nearly two hours. He took a carton of yogurt from the fridge, grabbed a spoon, and opened the front door. Immediately, an oven-like wave shoved in oppressively and, although the sun was behind the house now, the largely shaded front yard wiggled like an incongruous mirage. Flecks and shards of the blistering sun seethed like scattered bits of fire trapped beneath the canopy of trees. Moon, who had roused himself from a long nap on the cool tiles of the kitchen floor and was almost always ready for an adventure outdoors, paused at Hudson's feet, feeling the blast on his face, and looked up. "Al fresco is not an option, Mr. Moon," and the retriever smiled in agreement. Olive, who had never moved from the arm of the sofa where she reposed with one leg draped off the end like a rather relaxed sphinx, looked at both of them and then looked away again, as if they were pitiably insane.

Hudson closed the door and paced around the cottage for a few minutes, eating a piece of fruit, straightening some books and papers, walking back to put laundry into the dryer, and pausing on his return to look through the tall windows of the hall into the side yard, where only two young wax myrtle trees stood against the blazing afternoon of the Gulf midsummer. He thought again about what might do there. He had decided just the day before that he would definitely come back during his October break, and he wanted to plant something else there on the south side. Today he inclined toward a magnolia and some other evergreen, perhaps a red cedar.

As he sat down again at the computer, Hudson became aware that the oddly pleasurable feeling he had sensed these last few days was a luxurious sense of time. Time unhurried, unscheduled. And unfearful. Last night, he had wandered through early 20th-Century English choral music, the companionable blues of B.B. King, and some humorously elegant Cleo Laine jazz, until at last he realized that, on this particular evening, he really didn't particularly want to hear music.

Suddenly, he was remembering that time and space were precious necessities, not merely the nightmare projections of his loss. Precious for someone whose life for nine or ten months of the year churned around impossible amounts of work, relentless schedules, and being on every single minute of the day, day in and day out.

"This," he said aloud as he put in a new disk, tilting his head back and drawing deeply on a bottle of water, "is, perhaps, a bit of heaven."

He began to read:

# Home Before Dark
## Director and actors make *One True Thing* one truly fine film

Some of the early buzz about *One True Thing*, which is based on the 1995 novel by former New York Times columnist Anna Quindlen, is further proof, as if we needed it, of the barbarian dumbing-down of the media. Filmgoers should not be deterred by reviewers resorting to "weepie," "melodramatic," "heavy," and other lame-brained labels that do not begin to describe *One True Thing* but that certainly swell the sad commentary on the state of critical thought in our society today. If Quindlen's storyline has a few too many broad strokes and neat tucks, it is on the whole an intelligent, thoughtful, and moving study of a complex family dynamic.

Directed by rising star Carl Franklin, working from a screenplay by Karen Croner, and featuring a remarkable ensemble of actors, *One True Thing* is that rare project in which the creative elements, each strong in itself, combine in a memorable incandescence of filmmaking. In an era when many films assault the audience with cacophonous appeals to our lowest possible common denominators—negligible attention spans and desensitized appetites—*One True Thing* insists that the viewer lean in. It has a largeness of scale that has nothing to do with special effects; it has some violence but it's of a psychic sort and discreetly deployed; its humor is credible rather than banal; and it has naked emotionality rather than maudlin sentiment. It is a real human journey that moves with the thrilling suspense of a dream and holds us fast. And though viewers may leave the experience with differing perspectives, when we reach the end we know we've been somewhere.

Franklin's directorial artistry first caught the eye of a small but enthusiastic following seven years ago with the little sleeper *One False Move*, starring then relative unknowns Bill Paxton and

Billy Bob Thornton. (The movie played at theatres for about a minute; word-of-mouth subse-
quently generated video interest among film buffs.)
Next came *Devil in a Blue Dress*. Even in these
modest neo-noir projects, the insight and technical finesse were unmistakable. Franklin's work
has a muscular elegance of narrative, tone, and
pace, and a canny capacity for exacting rich and
subtle characterization. His films are seductively
compelling: they move well and move us; they're
good-looking, smart, humane, as unafraid of stylistic adventure as they are of the small telling
gesture and psychological and emotional complex-
ity. With *One True Thing*, Franklin gets the sort
of material and high-powered cast he deserves, and
the result is an artistic whole even greater than
the sum of its superlative parts, a poignant and
passionate examination of one family in all its
human seasons, sorts, and conditions.

The film is set in the late 1980s. George Gulden
(William Hurt), a professor of literature and literary critic of some note at a college up East,
asks (rather, insists) that his daughter Ellen
(Renee Zellweger) come home from Manhattan to the
small college town to care for her ailing mother,
Kate (Meryl Streep). On a journalistic fast track
at *New York* magazine, Ellen's first impulse is that
a nurse should be hired; she agrees to leave the
city primarily to please her adored father. Ellen
is not heartless, only ambitious. A word child,
she has always emulated her father, not her mother,
who is, by her own cheerfully tacit admission, one
of the last of that breed of 1950s women who went
to college (a) to find a husband and (b) perhaps
to have a teaching certificate "to fall back on."
Ellen wants more than anything not to be like her
mother, whose homemaking skills and interests seem
to lack seriousness beside the intellectual glamour of her father. Even her mother's pleasantness
rankles Ellen; she has always associated it with
insubstantiality. Her father's irony has always
suggested sophisticated depths of sensibility,
her mother's earnestness and uncomplicated smile,

triviality.

In the hands of lesser actors and a director less imaginatively cinematic, the film might well have turned out to be arid and pretentious, an *Ordinary People* redux. Franklin illuminates, with a dramatic arc not unlike a suspense thriller, the unexpected and profound alterations in Ellen's world as she comes to realize that neither her father not her mother is the person she has grown up perceiving them to be. The film is essentially a delicate character study; there is no overt action, only the course of an illness and a series of small epiphanies that accrue until they ultimately transform the characters' understanding of one another. And of life. Franklin's eloquent psychological realism, his embrace of emotion, and the brilliant deployment of detail in his *mise en scene* bring us into the story, face to face with the actors' vivid performances; *One True Thing* is never less than absorbing; it is frequently, for long passages in which time seems suspended, riveting.

Zellweger, who proved her ingénue mettle opposite Tom Cruise in *Jerry Maguire*, stakes out a new level of her actor's craft as Ellen. It's the sort of big role in which the sheer volume of screen-time itself can become a performance's worst enemy, constantly threatening credibility pinpricks. Zellweger manages to navigate cleanly the subtle shadings in Ellen's transformation. She never shows her hand by overdoing her initially unsympathetic chilliness or her subsequent warming and enlightenment; it's an intelligent, evenhanded performance that draws the viewer into Renee's shifting viewpoint.

Hurt, a skittishly self-conscious actor and one who, perhaps for that reason, has been known to grandstand occasionally, allows a notable degree of self-effacement here. Perhaps his recent turns in the classics on stage are proving instructive for his film work: there's a fine Chekhovian obliquity in his George Gulden; perhaps it is Franklin's tutelage. For whatever reason, this performance is Hurt's best in years. It submerges itself thoroughly in the character and serves, shoulder to shoulder with his fellow actors, the exceptional sense of ensemble. His George is affable, attractive, self-absorbed, weak, and ultimately heartbreaking.

When Meryl Streep first appears early in the film, readying a surprise birthday party for George to which the guests come as their favorite literary character, the viewer fears that something may be terribly wrong, that the movie, along with Streep's performance, is irremediably off on the wrong foot. We share for an uncomfortable moment the sullen Ellen's view of her mother as a bit ridiculous. Even for a costume party, the sight of tall Kate Gulden bustling around the kitchen in short gingham pinafore and pigtails with bows seems ill considered. In retrospect, we see that there is nothing about the scene, or about Streep's choices, that is ill-considered; they say a lot about Kate and about Streep's genius. The wife of an academic star, Kate has chosen Dorothy of *The Wizard of Oz* as her favorite character in literature, Dorothy, whose defining truism is "There's no place like home." And, as always, Kate is busy spreading good cheer and enjoying the moment; the last thing she would consider is that she might look faintly ridiculous. The scene prefigures Ellen's, and the viewer's understanding of this woman and is testament to Streep's risk-taking commitment to her character. She is almost over the top in this scene, but as she then goes about layering Kate's character, we realize how absolutely right she was to begin here.

Even ardent fans of Streep may often be heard to say that their favorite performances are the more "Streepless" roles, those in which the famous cerebration and technique, and even the distinctive swan-like visage, become transparent in the interest of a character whose persona we assume to be quite different from Streep's own. (*Silkwood* is a good example; others might include *Death Becomes Her, A Cry in the Dark,* or even, to some degree, *Out of Africa*.) *One True Thing* allows Streep another opportunity to become, very fully, Streepless. Her Kate is galvanizing in her simplicity. This is not to say that Streep doesn't bring her formidable battery of skills to bear; as a matter of fact, she is able in *One True Thing* to combine nearly her entire range of styles into one keenly felt, beautifully detailed, luminous performance. Streep's unpatronizing respect and affection for Kate provide the key, not only for Kate's family's deepening perspective of her, but for the viewer as well. Kate is a capacious role, an essentially generous role, and one of the most moving aspects of the film comes in having one of our great actors give her to us with such generosity. Kate's illness demands a re-framing of the Gulden family's shared truths, and the raw, sweet, power of Streep's performance caringly ensures that Kate's modest but nonetheless transformational spirit transcends the theatrical frame. The triumph of the film, and particularly of Streep's performance, is the universality of its intimacy. This is a common touch of uncommon brilliance.

There are a couple of scenes, one a climactic Christmas moment in the town square, that do, indeed, seem stagy and dramatically overripe. It may also be noted that Streep gets a few standard diva shots meticulously calculated for garnering Academy Award votes; they never, however, seem appended, they arise naturally within the film's emotional rhythm. If the film is occasionally manipulative, it's a thoughtful manipulation, one with dramatic integrity, which it earns as it goes along. Franklin's missteps account for perhaps a total of four or five minutes in an otherwise masterfully conceived and articulated two-hours-plus film. In these actors, he had rich natural resources with which to work; it is clear not only that he fully appreciated and was inspired by the potential, but that his cast wisely allowed his brilliant eye and rich sensibility to guide and inform their work.

One of Anna Quindlen's professional precursors, journalist Adela Rogers St. John, was asked in her early seventies, during a television interview, if she was afraid of dying. She answered quickly, "Oh, no, not at all. It's just that I want to see how it all turns out." Quindlen, Franklin, Streep, Hurt, and Zellweger argue an unsentimental, and therefore all the more deeply moving, case for the importance of making "*it* turn out."

On a daily basis.

A keeper, he judged, and with little or no revision.

He went to bed early and read for nearly two hours, putting the book aside from time to time, simply lying there, listening. An owl somewhere in the trees over the lagoon occasionally struck a contrapuntal rhythm with a couple of frogs. Otherwise there was silence; he felt the space of the cottage around him, and he felt time, and he didn't, for the first time in a long time, feel threatened by either.

# Chapter 22

The next evening, he had Charlie and the newlyweds, Libby, Susie, and Camilla over for dinner. Rusty at entertaining, he planned a simple menu: ceviche to start, which he'd prepared before they arrived, to be followed by a simple pasta with vegetables and parmesan.

Sending out a few showers ahead of it, a feeble but nonetheless very welcome cool front had glided through around six, and now, an hour later, Hudson was able to sit on the porch waiting for his guests without ruining his freshly laundered polo shirt. He had, almost with a feeling of inconvenience, eschewed what was becoming a basic uniform of old khaki shorts and a tee shirt for a decent pair of baggy cream-colored pants. The thermometer outside the kitchen window showed the temperature had dropped from eighty-eight to an invigorating seventy-two.

"Auspicious," he said to Moon.

Even Olive, who usually took her fresh air only in the early morning, had sensed that it might be reasonable to leave her air-conditioned domain, and lounged at the top of the steps, nudging her nose delicately into the gentle breeze that stirred the oaks. A fat drop of water from the eave of the cottage striking the top of her head startled her momentarily but she recovered quickly, shifting almost imperceptibly to one side and grooming behind her ears as if she'd ordered up the unexpected shampoo from room service.

As he waited, Hudson finished reading a story by Alice Munro he had not known and, as he breathed deeply of the cool wetness, he saw the evening world in a slightly altered state, with that quickened sense of discovery that can occur along the border between art and life. He lay the book aside on the small table and watched the light change in the rain-clean gloaming.

Back behind the house and the woods beyond, far down the beach and out over the water, a fairly magnificent sunset must be transpiring. The air, cleansed of the sluggish heat, took on a limpid radiance. At the end of the walk, the white crushed shell and sand shoulders of the road beyond were glowing a pale shade of rose, and the tall live oaks that had seemed exhausted earlier in the day now looked strong and vital and stirred with an easy majesty. Louie and Martine looked new, as if perhaps they had just sprung up from magic seeds in the past half-hour, laden with bright mustard-yellow blooms. And everywhere in the yard a vibrant chorus of greens emanated, from the flat ruffles of the scrub oak, the soft pine needles weeping their scent, the yuccas' fleshy spikes, the magnolia's leaves no longer brittle and dusty but brilliantly polished, relaxed with moisture.

It occurred to Hudson that it was a fine thing to be sitting on a village porch at the outset of an evening with old and new friends, anticipating a glass of cold white wine and some good conversation, here, in this dream of a cottage, in this out-of-the-way corner of paradise, tucked among its trees, beside the glittering turquoise expanse of the Gulf.

How could it, then, be so hopelessly far from perfect?

But he also felt, for the first time in as long as he could remember, extraordinarily grateful. The evening touched him, a cool hand lingering on his face.

◇◇◇

"You must be livin' right, Hudson." Libby was the first to arrive—she had walked—bearing a handful of hawthorn and hydrangeas swaddled in damp paper towels. "Where do you want these? What a *gorgeous* evening." They kissed one another on their cheeks and Hudson took the heavy-headed flowers. He found a large square vase that seemed substantial enough and they put them on the table.

"I want you to know that the last time I had people over for dinner and had planned to have little tables on the screened porch and the yard was a mass of dogwood and azaleas and I had chairs all around the garden and had made all these fancy-ass canapés and just every little thing—and it was the end of April thank you very much—I'll be damned if we didn't have a completely unforecasted drop to about forty-five degrees at six o'clock with almost a gale blowing."

Hudson poured himself a sauvignon blanc and a gin-and-tonic for Libby and they went back onto the porch. Libby gave "a woman of a certain age" every possible happy connotation. She wore a long gauzy dress in pale lilac, just the right amount of makeup, good silver jewelry; her soft honey-and-gray hair was caught back on one side with a silver comb. As always, her eyes were kindled with sensuous energy and interest, and her voice was full of shrewd humor.

"I'm sure you adjusted with aplomb," said Hudson.

"Well, I tried but I'm afraid the effort showed. I had Brad and the bartender we'd hired wrestling all that stuff inside and everything got wet and it was just a big oogey mess. I was having it as a welcoming party for our new young rector and his wife at St. John's—I got nabbed again for the vestry last year. And I had thought I was just gonna be so calm and collected and show them what a grand gracious lady I truly was."

She reached over and patted Hudson's knee and laughed at herself uproariously. "I had an old aunt in Birmingham who was right—she used to say 'Party pride cometh before destruction....'"

She paused and fixed her sights on Hudson. "I *knew* it! This place *is* good for you—you look so marvelous. Great color. Rested. Exercised. That *gorgeous* auburn hair." She paused, sipping her drink. "Brad sends his best. He called last night. Said to tell you he looked forward to seeing you after the Fourth. I told him not to worry about it, that I was gonna run off with you."

She asked Hudson about his work on the book and what he was reading and which was "homework" and which for pure pleasure. Warming to her voice as most creatures did, Moon had come to sit beside her and she stroked his head and shoulders.

"Where's Miss Priss?" she asked, looking around the porch.

"She was with us earlier but has retired either to my bed or perhaps to the desk chair in the hall where she sometimes takes light therapy under her favorite lamp. She doesn't do crowds. And on any given day that might include either Moon or me."

"I won't take it personally," said Libby.

◇◇◇

Camilla came next, having driven from her house in Seagrove. "It's good to see you again," she said to Hudson, handing him a bottle of merlot. "And what a treat, much as I love my work, to have dinner in someone's lovely home. Hello, there," she smiled, taking Libby's outstretched hand.

While Hudson got her a drink, he could hear the two women chatting familiarly. Libby had been thrilled that Hudson was inviting Camilla. *"She's a woman of substance—a godsend to Charlie. Smart and funny. We get together every now and then. And just as nice as she can be. I like her a lot."*

When he emerged from the house with her glass of wine, he thought again, as he had when he'd met her at the restaurant, what a serenely attractive woman she was.

The others suddenly convened at the cottage, Susie, from the north, having walked around the long block from Yaupon Lane, and from the other direction, Charlie and his young relatives. Charlie and Chaz each carried a bottle of something Hudson knew would be very fine.

"We're being inundated with good wine," he said to the two women.

"What a horrible fate," said Libby.

◇◇◇

They arranged and rearranged themselves, at times all together, at times in twos or threes, in an extended cocktail hour that seemed to take its pace, Hudson thought, from the fact that they were only a few days past the longest day of the year. The long twilight, both on the porch and throughout the cottage where only a few lamps were lighted, was, as Sydney Cullen observed, "magical."

While Charlie and Libby better acquainted themselves with Susie on the porch, Hudson took Camilla and the Cullens on a tour. Sydney asked all the right questions, with Chaz occasionally joining in. They thought the renovation was "perfect" and said they'd be "tempted never to leave" and wondered where this chair or that fabric had been found. Each had an affinity, in the way of newlyweds, for calling the other "honey." Camilla didn't say much. She smiled often, however, reflectively, attentive to what Hudson said and, it seemed to him, how he said it, taking her own measure of the place.

Later, with everyone sitting around the porch—Hudson had brought three extra chairs from inside—the conversation veered to Memphis. Chaz had said to Hudson that, oddly enough, neither he nor Sydney had ever been there, and Sydney pursued this as an open-ended conversational gambit: "What's it like?"

"Who goes first?" laughed Hudson. "You have three Memphians, two former, one current, here."

"You're kidding!" said Sydney, her eyes widening.

"Well," said Chaz, "I guess Charlie has mentioned that Destin and the area in general do draw a lot of folks from Memphis."

"Always has," said Libby. "They were among the first to discover its charms, even before the tourist boom after the War." She paused. "What Hudson was too polite to say is that you have three *generations* of Memphians before you." She looked at Susie. "I've just barely met this delightful young woman, myself. I'm the old lady, so I'll go first. And each of us can say one thing about our hometown, and we'll just go around a few times and see what we come up with. How's that?"

"It sounds very interesting to me," said Camilla. "I'm a North Carolina girl myself and I've only been to Memphis once, years ago, for a wedding."

Susie added, "The good, the bad, the Elvis."

Hudson laughed, "The dirty laundry…"

"There's not time enough in this world for *that*," said Libby.

"Anyway…" and as Charlie poured more wine, Libby began.

◇◇◇

"Let's see. In the springtime Memphis is without a doubt one of the most beautiful cities in the world. I've seen a few. Your city, of course, is lovely then, too. And Atlanta has hills. Memphis is so flat. But there's just something about the feel of March and April and May there. The Delta. The earth is so rich and the air is so soft and the world is so alive and green. Everything grows. My mother used to say that there must be something *not quite right* with anyone who didn't have a green thumb in Memphis."

"And there are wonderful old residential neighborhoods with marvelous houses and huge trees arching overhead, and deep wide lawns where white dogwood and crabapples seem to float in the shade like fireflies, with great fountains of forsythia and japonica and Carolina jasmine, and the redbud trees and saucer magnolias and spyrea and viburnum, snowballs and cherry laurels, enormous beds of azaleas and camellias, iris and dahlias. It really is breathtaking."

Sydney looked at Libby as though transfixed. Chaz, looking first at Hudson and then at Susie, said, "Tough act to follow."

"*Really*," breathed Susie. "You're up, Hudson."

"I moved back ten years ago after living for several years in Nashville, and I had lived in New York for awhile, and had work assignments from time to time in Atlanta and New Orleans and Denver. I knew when I returned to Memphis that there were plenty of aspects to living there that I didn't like. We hear that most people, in some degree or other, have love-hate relationships with their hometowns, and I think that's particularly true of Memphians. The place evokes subtle passions that can be confused and contradictory. There are days when I know exactly why I moved back and that seems enough. So long," he made a gesture around the room, "as I can get away from time to time. And there are days when I become extremely impatient, disgusted even, with how narrow and provincial and backward and mean it can be.

"It doesn't have the brash cosmopolitan air and healthy sense of humor about it of a Nashville or the energy and money and, pardon me, I mean this well, the sort of heady pretensions of Atlanta. Memphis is not without its sophistications, but they seem diminished, a bit faded, largely of a former era. And in that sense it's a very nostalgic city, an urban metaphor for everything that's *gone* from civilized living. Its newness, like a lot of American cities, is generic and fairly tawdry.

"It's a city that doesn't seem to learn from its mistakes. A lot of the great trees that Libby just mentioned—the oaks and poplars, maples and hackberrys—are old, and very few people even think to replace them. Hideous planning decisions, driven solely by development greed, are made that ruin the look of the city and no one raises a hue and cry. There's a pervasive sense of learned powerlessness. The only thing thicker in Memphis than its humidity is its chronic inferiority complex. It accepts metastasizing strip mall development, billboards, and every other sort of urban blight without much of a whimper.

"Most older guard Memphians talk with a sort of mildly irritated indulgence about their city, as if she were an inconvenient relative whom it has fallen their lot to put up with."

He paused. "There are also some of the kindest people there you'll ever hope to meet. Good-hearted, generous. Genuinely thoughtful and friendly."

If Hudson had had any concern about Susie being comfortable enough with these more mature people she'd just met, her eager face now dispelled it.

She took a sip of wine and then took up the thread immediately.

"Memphis is a small town, not a city at all really. Everyone seems to know everyone, or at least know of everyone, else. Or at least think they do. Libby and I just now in—what?—a five-minute conversation, discovered that her father is my father's second cousin once removed and that we have at least two sets of fairly close family friends in common." She threw up her hands and giggled. "This is *not* atypical. Memphis developed as the only sizeable city in the middle of the Delta cotton fields and hardwood forests. I suppose farmers and rural folk for hundreds of miles around thought it was the big city, but those of us who live there know it's really just a great big small town. Whether rural poor or former landowners, most families are just a few generations out of the country. And I think this common agrarian background blurs some of the lines of economic and racial differences and causes others to loom extremely large. There are a lot of old Memphis families, and some new industry barons, who are incredibly wealthy, and there are also tens of thousands of people living in poverty. High rates of adolescent pregnancy. A functional illiteracy rate of about thirty-three percent."

She paused and smiled. "But then there's the music, you know? The great meeting ground for Memphians and our gift to the world. It's almost always what people ask me about first when they learn it's my hometown. The blues. W.C. Handy. Alberta Hunter. Elvis. B.B. King. Tina Turner. Jerry Lee Lewis. Stax Records. Gospel. Memphis really has been the melting pot for a lot of American music: hillbilly ballads from the Scottish and Irish settlers in the Appalachians melting into Creole songs from the islands, and African rhythms mixing with European sacred music to produce spirituals. Blues out of slaves' work songs eventually fusing with Mississippi River jazz and then country with rock. It's *fabulous*."

Susie was wearing her horn-rimmed glasses this evening and looked quite studious. She pushed a stray lock behind her ear, and continued.

"And, of course, there's the inexplicable fact of our literature. We always resort to the best guess—that we are 'word people,' anecdotalists, storytellers by nature. Whatever. But there's just no getting around that in our general vicinity we grow great American writers at an amazing per capita rate. Faulkner, Tennessee Williams, Eudora Welty, Robert Penn Warren, Peter

Taylor, Maya Angelou, Willie Morris, Elizabeth Spencer, Jesse Hill Ford, Shelby Foote, on and on and on...."

She paused, and lifted her glass. "I suppose that's what means the most to me."

"And to me," said Hudson, joining the toast.

"Let's not forget the river!" said Libby. "Now admittedly it's not a pretty little blue-green sort of thing. It's huge, sprawling, muddy, a force of nature. But its beauty is in its power, its majesty. In the last ten or fifteen years, Memphis finally seems to have realized it's its greatest natural resource. I'm delighted to see all those nice houses going up on the island and people converting old storefronts and cotton warehouses into restaurants and clubs and galleries and co-ops and all that. Downtown is at least sitting up and taking notice of itself again. High time."

"It was wonderful when Brad and I were first dating in the early '50s. We'd often go sit on the bluffs under the trees and feel the evening breeze come up off the river and watch the sun go down, and then we'd go for a drink and dinner at the Peabody and then on up to the roof garden to dance the night away. Oh, it was *so* romantic."

Susie: "Heinous winter weather. Not enough snow and way too many ice storms."

Hudson: "If you meet the right person—like Libby, for example—one of the most attractive of all Southern accents. If you meet the wrong person, one of the most gratingly god-awful of all Southern accents."

Libby: "The worst drivers in the country."

Hudson: "The best barbecue in the country. The only real barbecue, despite what a lot of deluded Texans may think."

The three of them looked at each other, and then Libby looked at Sydney and Chaz. "Enough! Did that just wear you out?"

◇◇◇

During the ceviche, it was the Cullens' turn. They were asked about their childhoods, about their work, how they'd met, life in Atlanta. Sitting beside one another and occasionally holding hands, they more or less held forth together, trading off the various parts of their story to the appropriate partner, balancing the juicy bits of their repertoire with delighted aplomb. Sydney seemed to Hudson especially adroit at pacing their narrative, of throwing in a spontaneous, humorous aside just when it was needed, of deferring to Chaz at just the right moment, of graciously turning questions back to the others, eager to incorporate their opinions. Tremendous poise, he thought; she wasn't an actress for nothing.

He noticed that she had two strikingly developed capacities. The first was for making her listener feel as if he had her absolutely unwavering attention, as if he or she were the only person in the world who mattered. The second was the imperceptible speed and finesse with which she could adapt herself to a completely different rapport with a completely different person. She seemed almost to become each person with whom she conversed, picking up on their personal style, the tone and rhythms of their speech, their concerns, their humor, temperament and emotions. Hudson realized that this was only natural, in a way, that different people and situations evoke different responses, and he had, of course, known people who seemed more inclined this way than others. Southerners could be famously gracious and sympathetic. It was one of their greatest claims to real charm and, even more important, to true civility; but the quality in Sydney seemed quite remarkable to him, almost extraordinary.

◇◇◇

With the pasta, and then following through the ice cream and blueberries with coffee, the table conversation carried on in two- and threesomes: Hudson talked mostly with Sydney, on his right; Libby, Chaz, and Camilla were engrossed; and Susie and Charlie got to know one another and occasionally served as free agents, with topics they felt deserving, of general table conversation. Hudson thought Charlie looked relaxed and happy, if somehow a bit wistful, and noticed how often his gaze rested on Chaz and Sydney.

"Charlie tells me you'll be bringing out a collection of your film reviews," said Sydney.

"Well, yes," Hudson smiled, "but it's just a small press sort of thing. I don't think Pauline Kael's place in history, or even Gene Shalit's for that matter, is in jeopardy."

"You must enjoy it, though, film, and writing about it."

"Yes."

"Is there any one aspect of film that's the particular draw for you?"

"Oh, the writing and direction of course. But actually I think it's probably the art of acting that most fascinates me. That's why I was interested in hearing about your tenure with the Alliance. What was it exactly that made you decide to give up the boards?"

"I couldn't see myself doing it for the rest of my life. I loved it. But it began to feel like a season in my life rather than a career. I wanted to do other things."

"It sounds as though you're a busy woman, working with Chaz in his business *and* making videos?"

"You ought to know. I can't imagine how you do your film reviewing and teach a college class one night a week *and* do all that class preparation for your real job!"

"I've pieced together a life that I enjoy, and I suppose I'm afraid to let any of it go—just now."

Sydney spoke in a lower, very gentle voice. "Let me just say that I'm very sorry for your loss. Charlie has told us about your wonderful wife."

"Thank you. And, yes. She was. What sort of videos do you do?"

"Mostly corporate work. Training, human resources, et cetera. Some educational ones. I don't really do the technical production. I produce and script and recruit talent." She laughed. "And put on my thespian mask when needed. Actually, however, I see this as a phase, too.

" I have liked learning more about art and antiques than I ever would have guessed, and Chaz and I really love working together. We're a good team." She paused. "And…we want children. Before too much longer."

◇◇◇

Before the evening was out, Libby had developed such a fondness for Susie that, on their way out the door, she paused and rifled through her purse for a photo of her grandson.

"He just graduated from Washington and Lee and he's brilliant. He's coming down to Tallahassee for graduate school—to be close to Laurel, which he has always loved—in theatre. Wants to direct and teach. And just *look* at him—and he's good and he's kind and he's fun—and I just bet he'd *adore* you." Susie had looked at the photo and smiled, not without interest. "Cute."

"Very," said Libby. "He may be a year or two younger than you. But that's fashionable nowadays, isn't it?"

Hudson followed everyone down the walk. Charlie, Sydney and Chaz made their way down the road, turning to wave under the streetlight, and Susie walked north. Libby was getting a lift from Camilla, and as she got into the passenger side amid the general goodbyes, Camilla stood near her door and thanked Hudson for the evening.

"It was fun, wasn't it?" he answered. "But I'm afraid you and I hardly had a chance to talk," he said. "Isn't tomorrow your other day off?"

"Mondays and Tuesdays are my weekend."

"I'm driving into Destin late tomorrow afternoon to see a re-release of a film I really liked. *Afterglow?* Julie Christie? I'd like to give my review one more check."

"I never saw it."

"We might stop somewhere for dinner afterward?"

"I'd like that."

# Chapter 23

On Tuesday evening at five minutes to eight, Terry Main reached into the pocket of his old khakis and began to draw out a pack of cigarettes. Four or five years ago he had begun paring down his pack-a-day habit, and for the past several months he had been down to three or four smokes a day. He'd only had two today, but he hesitated as he looked again at the man who sat beside him on the bench of the pier. He withdrew his hand, without the cigarettes.

The other man sat motionless, looking toward the west. Although the sun must have slipped just moments ago into the Gulf, there was no evidence of it. A bank of darkening gray and purple clouds that had been building since late afternoon had overtaken the entire sky, now moving fast and low. The man nevertheless kept his eyes fixed intently on the horizon, as though he expected to see something or could somehow see through the approaching storm to the last molten light of the day. His head leaned slightly forward from his shoulders, and the rising breeze lifted his lank dark hair in ribbons and made his bushy beard vibrate. His hands lay on his blue-jeaned thighs, one turned slightly upward as if in supplication.

The two men sat about halfway down the hundred-yard-long Laguna Beach pier, between the beach and the big old wooden pavilion at the end. Twenty-five miles east of Seaside, Laguna Beach is one of the old beach towns that have been amalgamated over the past thirty years into the westward sprawl from

Panama City. Overdeveloped, badly developed, loud and tacky, this stretch of Highway 98 along the beaches has earned the possibly ungenerous, but nonetheless accurate sobriquet of "The Redneck Riviera." Young men with already soft bellies and young women with crudely bleached hair and crude mouths to match overpopulate the area on an endless daytrip basis, from south Alabama and the small interior towns of the Florida panhandle. They cruise the strip, eating fast food, swilling beer, and yelling to one another from their trucks and their SUVs with oversized wheels. They litter the beaches, fry their skins, trash the cheap motel rooms they inhabit now and again, get ritualistically drunk out of their minds, and generally make themselves obnoxious. With the abbreviated afternoon, however, and the promise of a downpour, they seemed temporarily to have disappeared into the low-rent sports bars with widescreen TVs, or the discount malls, or whatever other noisy cheap dives they hovered in until the weather cleared and they could begin, like a gaudy fever, to rage forth again.

Small in the distance, a few young teenagers gamboled at the shoreline, their intermittent shouts and laughter scrabbling indistinctly over the white-capping waves. Terry watched as from the other direction a few couples strolled past, heading in from the pavilion. A few lone figures sat here and there, looking as if they couldn't decide whether to come or go, and most of the remaining diehard anglers pulled in their lines and began to pack up their gear. He then looked toward shore again, toward the main set of wooden steps that led up and over the dunes to a boardwalk on top and the car park out of sight on the other side.

As if to assure himself as much as his companion, Terry said, "They'll be here soon. I think the rain's still an hour or more away, but we can sit in the pavilion if we need to."

The other man turned and looked at Terry. "It don't matter."

Terry pursed his lips and nodded his head slightly. "Yeah, I guess you're right. A little rain's not going to stop us now, is it?"

The comment seemed to jog the man from his silence, and he began talking rapidly, with a low, uninflected intensity.

"When I met Miss Rachel she said that God had led me to her and that you were God's agent. That you brought us together. Just like He brought me to Pensacola. To hear the Word and be sanctified."

Terry eyed him carefully and, after a minute, said, "Ever miss your home in South Carolina? Your sister?"

The man looked up, a pained expression quickly replaced with something like scorn. "I didn't really have no home. I tried to. People oughta have a home. We lived in one of those big complexes, you know? It wudn't too bad. Two bedrooms and all. I planted some flowers and stuff in some pots on the porch like my mama'd done before she got sick and I kept things clean as I could, workin' all hours and all. But my whorin' sister kept bringin' those lowlife men around all the time."

He paused, looking again toward the hidden sunset. "One of 'em shoved four cigarette butts and a empty half-pint of whisky in one of those pots and killed that plant. It was just ready to come out. Called a moss rose? I loved my sister but she's dead to me now. She's a whore. She mocks the Lord." He paused again, and looked down at his paint-spattered work boots, and said softly, "She mocked me for going to the Lord." Turning suddenly to Terry, he said, "I looked in the mirror last night, at how God has made my outside new like he did my inside, you know, the beard and all, and I said to myself 'If God had meant for me to have a home, he wouldn't have set my feet on the path they're on now, he wouldn't have led me out of South Carolina, to here.' When God leads us into exile it's not for us to question and it's never just for…for nothing. After *this* I don't know what he has in store for me, but that's not for me to worry about. Just like if I saved only one sweet baby, then even if I smite the devil just once it'll be for the greater glory of God's war against evil. I'm only a poor example, but if God sees fit to use me as an example then why should I fear anything?"

Terry reached over and grasped the man's shoulder, and the man turned to look at him.

"Michael, you are not a poor example. And, as Miss Rachel says, God most certainly has not led you here for nothing. Just as He most certainly also led you to that painting job at the Blue Bar back in the spring. He wanted me to find you, you know? To recognize you, my man, as the only person brave and worthy enough of confronting the devil here. Of helping Miss Rachel alleviate her pain and being the Lord's own helping hand in carrying out his divine judgment."

Suddenly, nearly over them, a woman's voice, strong but gentle: "You are God's precious angel, Michael. You are part of the great ongoing mission in Pensacola and you are part of God's larger plan for this sick and troubled land from which we wait to be translated into glory. He has already set your feet on that path and chosen you for his work."

❦❦❦

Neither man had noticed the two figures, a man and a woman, slowly approaching in the gloom, and both looked up, startled. At which point the woman quickly knelt beside the bearded man and, looking up into his face, said, "He has chosen you for greatness."

The man called Michael uttered a choked cry, rising, and awkwardly lifting the woman with him to her feet. "No, no, Miss Rachel...you mustn't do..."

"What?" she said. "Look into your face and see God's salvation there reflected in your eyes?" She reached out her hand and lightly touched the man near his right temple. Her eyes matched his in intensity, but she smiled warmly. "Come, Michael, and walk with me."

The three men and the woman moved slowly toward the pavilion. Only a few older people passed them coming and going, getting in their power walk laps undeterred by the encroaching weather, and one small group of teens lingered nearby, calling to a couple of their friends still surfing off one side of the pier. The atmosphere was heavy with that dull, quickening current of latent force, of waiting, just before a storm. But there was still just enough human activity that the foursome was not particularly noticeable as they walked, the woman in front with her arm linked through the arm of the man called Michael, Terry and the other man behind. And their low, earnest voices would not carry far in the rising wind.

◇◇◇

The woman walked slowly, very erect, like someone in a ceremonial procession, her head held high. Her gaze seemed fixed somewhere beyond the looming pavilion as though on a point far out to sea, but occasionally, as if awakening from a trance, she would turn to Michael with rapt attention, searching his face with wide eyes, her serious expression warmed slightly by a knowing smile. She leaned in toward him when she spoke in her cadenced but somehow softly thrilling voice. When she did, he would steal sidelong glances at her and answer, quietly, like a child, enthralled.

When they reached the pavilion, she led them toward the side farthest from the few remaining people and sat down, her legs straight to the wooden boards, her feet together. She indicated that Michael sit to one side and Terry the other. The other man sat, still silent, behind Terry. She folded her hands in her lap and looked intently at Michael until he overcame his apparent shyness and stared expectantly back at her. Her eyes were an almost surreal robin's egg blue.

She was dressed very plainly, in a longish dark gray jumper with a simple white blouse underneath. What little could be seen of her lower legs and ankles revealed dull whitish-gray hose, and her feet were encased in flat, round-toed black shoes. Though far from unattractive, there was an ascetic air about her. She wore little if any makeup. Her hair, a dark honey blonde, was long, parted in the middle and pulled back just over the tops of her ears, hanging straight down from a large barrette at the nape of her neck. The severity of her appearance seemed to set off, by contrast, the controlled but unmistakable passion in her face. Her expression was one of gravity and peace, yet at the same time shadows of emotion coursed somewhere behind her patient, almost stoical gaze—flickers of beatific joy alternated with the pained look of inconsolable longing. For a long time she did not speak.

Finally, turning her body slightly and peering even more deeply into Michael's eyes, she said, "I have spoken with my brother, Reverend Oakley, Michael. He has prayed about this mission for many weeks, and now he has received God's answer. The revival in Pensacola will continue in some form, but his role, after these three glorious years, is ending, and he must take his call to other people in need. He told me last night that God has revealed to him that you are his chosen servant for this task, and that this glorious sacrifice will bring a fitting end to this phase of the Lord's ministry here." She paused as tears sprang up in her eyes. "That you have been chosen to honor our brother Timothy's death through this vengeance against the Devil."

Michael's body went rigid, but after a moment he breathed deeply and seemed to settle slightly, resigned, within his work clothes.

He said, "I've heard your brother every night that he has preached since I got down here. He's been just like my pastor back in South Carolina and the ones I listen to on the radio while I paint every day. I've learned how we *are* in a war and that we cannot turn our back on what's right."

"Praise God. He has a plan for each of us if we are to have victory over Evil. That is why God directed you to Terry. And let Terry know that it was you who did His work in South Carolina. Someone else would have had you put into prison, Michael, but Terry knew that you had been sent to continue helping God make an example of the wicked. And now we are one in God's purpose. My brother says that when the news of this sacrifice is made known, it will help others come to the truth and join in God's war against the Devil. Fewer babies will be killed by the abortionists and fewer young men, like my brother Tim, will be converted to evil and even killed by the sodomites and the plague that God has visited on them. Because of your example, more money will be raised to support the effort. With this brave act you become a part of my brother's great work, and that of

God's other specially chosen servants, part of the great Pensacola revival and—who knows?—perhaps part of the ongoing work when he moves on. He thinks God is calling him to Galveston next or, possibly, Merida, in Mexico. The Great Gulf Revival! Remember. Once we are done with this work here, Michael, we want you to join us in some role in God's new mission."

"I don't know what I could…"

"We will see. Leave it to me, Michael. And remember what we discussed at our first meeting. Do not seek out Reverend Oakley. In these next few days, when you go to the meetings, as I know you will, to hear God's word urging you on, don't seek out my brother, don't try to find him and say anything about our plan. I am his agent, as you are mine, and we are all one. Each has his own job to do, Michael, and we must leave my brother to his. Just as Terry must continue to pretend that he is a bar manager so that he can serve as the eyes and the ears of the Lord." She smiled. "Within our family of Christ he is sometimes called 'the undercover disciple.' He has done so much good, gathering information about the enemy and helping us to know how we can best target our efforts. And, of course, God directed Terry to know that you were the one He had sent for this mission. You understand this, don't you?"

Just then, the thin man who had not spoken, dressed in black pants and a white shirt and seated behind Terry, rose, shaking slightly, looking as if he might begin to cry. Instead, he hesitated, and then went down on one knee in front of Michael. He looked up at him through thick black-rimmed glasses, and took his hands in one of his own and patted them slowly with his other.

"This is the Reverend's and my cousin, Michael. This is Joseph. Joseph cannot talk. Like all of us, in his own way, he is one of God's 'peculiar people.' He is a soldier, too, in God's war. He's done some work like yours and he manages our website outreach program. Do you know, he had hoped very much to do this mission, but God has told us that it is only you, Michael, whom He wants." She touched the kneeling man lightly on his shoulder. "You want to pray with Michael, don't you, Joseph? May I speak for you?"

The man called Joseph nodded. "We are one in God's work," she continued, extending one hand to Terry and sustaining with the other her hold on the kneeling man's shoulder.

The three or four other people remaining nearby had left the pavilion by now, heading down the long pier in the gathering darkness. As the heat lightning on the western horizon began to erupt into writhing horizontal bolts, the foursome held hands, and the woman prayed.

◇◇◇

Without further words, the woman then led the way back up the pier toward shore, one arm linked as before in Michael's, Terry and Joseph behind. They climbed the wooden steps and then descended into the car park. Just as the first fat, round blobs of tropical rain began to pummel them, the woman turned to Michael, took both his hands in hers. Her face glistened with rivulets of rainwater and her eyes welled with tears, but she did not blink and held him fast with her piercing gaze and a slight smile that suggested patient determination and a deeply shared intimacy.

"My cousin and I must return to our work now in Pensacola, Michael. Terry will go over the final details of the mission. We are honored that God has brought you to take such an important role in this glorious revival, this crusade for His truth. And Reverend Oakley and I thank you, too…" she hesitated, closing her eyes for a moment, "…personally. For our little brother Tim. We are with you and we love you, Michael. And until we meet again, you know that God is guiding your every step."

With that, she got into the car with Joseph, who started the engine and turned on the lights and wipers, smiling diffidently and lifting his hand in farewell. They drove away into the early darkness of the downpour as Terry and Michael, drenched, climbed into Terry's pickup.

# Chapter 24

The film, as it turned out, was even smarter and more surprising than Hudson had remembered.

"I hate to resort to a cliché, especially with a movie critic, but that last scene really put my stomach in knots," said Camilla as they dashed back to the car in the downpour.

"Mine, too," Hudson said. "Do you think a drink might unknot us?"

They stopped at a funky seafood place renowned for its oysters and clams, on Highway 98 near the turnoff to Santa Rosa. The place was crowded with an amalgam of locals, tourist families, and tables of local laborers stalled by the storm from going on home at the end of a hard day. It was loud and clattery and, quite uncharacteristically for him, that suited Hudson just fine. Is this a date? he had asked himself throughout the day. What's going on here? He had interrupted the short stories he planned to use with the freshmen and the David Hare play he was considering for AP, interrupted himself, over and over, questioning himself, no matter how absurd he knew he was being.

"You're a good host. Last night was great fun."

"Thank you. A little out of practice."

Her hazel eyes were frank and warm, and when she tilted her head very slightly her blunt-cut brown hair, finely streaked with gray, fell softly along one side of her face, not quite touching her shoulder.

"You've been on your own now for—two years did Charlie tell me? I'm very sorry. It must be hell."

She was taking it head-on. Probably, he thought, very wise.

"Almost two and a half. It has been hell. Just recently I've come to think that I'm not in hell anymore. Just rather awkwardly in life. It's not a lot easier. But I think it may be progress of a sort."

She smiled gently, and Hudson suddenly knew what had caught his attention the first night he'd met her at 26-A and several times in the course of the previous evening. Her gaze was discreet but steady. Her smile was not brilliant or dazzling, it was slow and sure. She seemed to know something about life. They were the eyes and smile of someone who is not easily fooled, who is judicious and yet who—and this, he realized, was the great thing—manages to be kind.

He relaxed. They behaved shamelessly with the baskets of shellfish and slaw and hushpuppies, and laughed, and talked easily. About Laurel, teaching, the weather, movies, books, food. They lingered over a last cold beer.

◇◇◇

"I'm on my own, too.

"As of four years ago. Divorced. I was married for sixteen years. My former husband is a cotton merchant and shipper. We divided our time between a wonderful, quaint old house in Mobile, where his offices are, and a place in Seaside; we were among the 'early settlers.' We have one wonderful son who is studying in France this summer and will be a sophomore at Sewanee in the fall.

"As I said last night, Charlotte is my home. I went to college in Charleston, then lived in Boston with a friend for a couple of years. Came back south to teach, in Atlanta, and met my husband there. He commuted from Mobile every weekend for nearly a year. I finally gave in. He made me laugh, he was very nice looking, and he had a generous nature and…he meant well.

"Unfortunately, not many years passed before I realized that there simply wasn't much *there* there. No core, really. I stayed busy teaching and I didn't want my son not to have a family. And there was actually very little unpleasantness. We just grew apart. There were a series of women. He was discreet. I blame no one, not even myself now, though I did do that for awhile. I was disappointed, and I've come to think that living too long with disappointment can eventually make people feel like something less than whoever or whatever disappointed them in the first place." She smiled.

"My husband has kept the house in Seaside, though he and his new wife who, according to my bemused nineteen-year-old, just celebrated her *thirty-third* birthday, spend less time here than before. They do come into 26-A, of course, from time to time…."

"Hmm."

She laughed. "Oh, no. That's nothing. We're all very amiable and everyone knows I'm happier than I've been in years. I know I do. The divorce and his almost immediate remarriage are far beyond their shelf life as local gossip. I'm old news now. I can't tell you what bliss that is.

"I love my work. Teaching the little ones was great. I did it for eleven years. But I came to a point where I needed a change, and I opened a small retail business with a friend. I learned a lot but it just wasn't the right fit, so I sold my interest to my partner. I ran into Charlie—we'd known him socially for years—at a party several months after the divorce. He got this funny look on his face when he saw me across the room, and we ended up on this patio discussing all the reasons why I should think seriously about taking over at 26-A. His manager was about to move on to open a place in Key West and he hadn't found anyone he felt he could really entrust his 'baby' with. He was ready to start pulling back. I said yes." Camilla's smile grew broader.

"And every minute since I've been so happy I did. Charlie's a good man and he's created an exceptionally fine place. Victor and Fentry are treasures. I feel at home there, and the work offers me just the right context in which to bring together my interests and skills. I like the routine and I like the unexpectedness: it's like teaching in that the form remains largely consistent and yet every evening, every moment, really, is in some way new. Plus I get to do things that I just plain like and enjoy and am good at. It suits me."

◇◇◇

As they drove through the pitch-black Gulf night, even more seamless than usual in its enveloping rain, Camilla said, "It was good being with Libby last night. I hadn't seen her in too long a time."

"As we say back home, isn't she *something?*"

"Indeed," she laughed. "I'm crazy about her."

"Me, too."

They rode for awhile in silence, staring ahead as the headlights followed the broken center line of the road through the storm.

Then Hudson asked, "Had you met Chaz before?"

"Only briefly in March. Charlie and he were in for dinner. Twice, I think."

"You and Libby seemed to be keeping him entertained at your end of the table."

"Mostly Libby—which was just dandy with me. I enjoyed your wonderful pasta and pretty much sat back and watched the show." Hudson looked over just in time to see her eyes shift to the dark masses of trees hurrying past the windows. "We certainly talked, though."

"They're a handsome couple aren't they?"

"Yes."

"Charlie's very happy for them."

"Of course."

After another silence, Camilla said, "I enjoyed meeting Susie. She's so attractive and bright."

"A passionate reader and an inquiring mind. Gives me hope that all of America's youth aren't turning into passive video heads." He paused, looking over again for a moment. "Will I retain whatever status I may have as a gentleman if I say I think I just sensed a change of subject?"

"Oh? Chaz, you mean? Well, I don't know."

"I'm wondering if Charlie has shared some of the same things with us."

"About Chaz's background? Yes. It's not that exactly."

"I'm sorry. I'm not interested in prying."

"No, I know that. And I'm not trying to be mysterious. It's just that until you brought him up I hadn't really sorted through some impressions I had last night." She turned to him, and smiled. "And I've enjoyed our evening and don't want you to think I'm some sort of madwoman."

"Hadn't really *occurred* to me."

"Okay." She pursed her lips, then said, "I don't want to be unfair. It's just that something about him, oddly enough, reminds me of my former husband."

"Attractive and charming, I think you said."

"Yes, and that may be part of it. But that's not what struck me. There was something more intangible yet somehow more specific than that." She paused. "It was the way he talked about his business, I think. He seemed knowledgeable, had lots of humorous anecdotes. A natural marketer. I remember thinking at some point in the evening that if he really wanted to, he could do very well indeed in Atlanta."

"And?"

"Well, what I'm remembering now is the precise phrasing of that observation as it formed in my mind. 'If he really wanted to.' That seems odd."

"Is that it, do you think? Did your husband not really care about his business?"

"Well, he cared very much about the idea of it, about the idea of being chairman of the board, about all the trappings that go with it. But I think he cared even more that his father had built it and that his brother, for all intents and purposes, ran it. He talked a good game, he looked involved, and occasionally I think he even wanted to believe himself that he had it in his blood. But I'm relatively certain that for all those years, even the early ones, his office was just a brief stop on the way to the next golf or tennis game, or long lunch. Or, later on, girlfriends."

She paused and looked levelly at him. "And now you're going to think that I have some sort of sick obsession about my former husband, which I assure you I do not. My passing impression may be utterly wrong, anyway, and it's incredibly rude of me to be discussing someone I don't even know like this. I can't imagine what, as my mother used to say, got into me."

"I *asked* you. You feel as though something is missing."

"But that's incredibly presumptuous. There's nothing wrong with not loving your work. That's the natural state of most human beings, isn't it? I think *we're* in a very tiny, very fortunate minority."

"But your husband not loving his work was not, alone, I take it, the only problem. You spoke earlier of 'no core.'"

"Yes. I suppose less than passionate involvement in the firm might even have been desirable, if there had ever been any real engagement with anything else. An avocation of some kind. Public service. Charities. Faith. Our son. Anything." She paused. "I was young but I should have known better. I mistook his rather vain expansiveness and animal energy for character and spirit."

"And you think it's something like that you may have glimpsed in Chaz?"

"*May have* being the key words. You know, though, this impression may have much more to do with my feelings for Charlie than anything else. I have such high regard for him and am so fond of him, and I know how much his cousin Peter meant to him, that I may be holding this man up to some unrealistic and completely unjustified standard. Chaz is not Charlie. And apparently he's come through a lot, and that's admirable. And this is really none of my business. I'm behaving like one of those people I loathe. All that I need to do is wish them the best and be glad that Charlie's happy."

Hudson pulled over in front of the cottage, behind Camilla's car. He turned and looked at her.

"That's exactly what I told *myself* this morning over coffee. When I found myself wondering what had gone on last night at *my* end of the table. Why, instead of feeling some sort of personal response to Sydney, I went to bed with my film reviewer's hat apparently sitting squarely on my head. 'Great performance,' I thought. And, in order to get to sleep, I finally wrote it off to the fact that she had been an actor and that even when some actors leave the profession they never really retire. But this morning I thought, no, it wasn't anything that simple. Or that obvious. Oh, she may have been a bit eager, but I'm sure she just wanted to please Charlie's friends. She's attractive, charming, intelligent, good-humored, extremely poised but evidently capable of spontaneity...."

"And?"

"I have no idea. But perhaps almost the opposite of 'something missing.' Something more like, like something *extra*. Like a great actor trying not to grandstand, trying to make the harder choices, the most subtle ones. Trying to disappear as an actor and cross that line where they really become the human being, really live it. It's rare."

The windows were coated with condensed moisture, and he turned off the engine. They looked at one another in the tree-and-rain-dappled light from the old wooden streetlight down the road. "You were *impressed* with her? Would that be accurate?" asked Camilla.

He looked out into the darkness and they listened for a moment to the sounds of rain and wind. "Exactly." He turned back to look at her. "I could find no fault with her. But this morning I felt somehow, *disappointed*, may be the word, that that was the best I could do as a response. As you say, perhaps we just have unjustified expectations for Charlie's sake."

"And," said Camilla, "you know he'd be the first to say that Chaz and Sydney are their own people, living their own lives, they obviously are bright and attractive, and they're not bothering anyone. So who are we to judge?"

"Right. He's happy enough that Chaz isn't dead from an overdose or living in a halfway house somewhere. And that he's found a capable, good-looking woman whom he loves and who loves him."

Smiling, she asked, "So what's our problem, do you suppose?"

"We're idealists?"

"Okay, let's go with that. It's so much nicer than busybodies. Frankly, I'm just pleased that you shared your, whatever it is, with me. I certainly never intended to spend the last part of a very pleasant evening doing this rather bizarre post mortem, but at least now I don't have to go home knowing you must think I'm some sort of, I don't know, *misanthrope*."

Hudson laughed. "Misanthropes don't have smiles like yours."

◇◇◇

He couldn't sleep. He managed to finish off a *New York Times* Saturday crossword puzzle that had frustrated him for three days. From the porch he watched the last of the rain dripping from the eaves and heard it in the silhouettes of the trees. He wandered the cottage. Finally, he decided he might as well work. There was no need to revisit his appraisal of the Julie Christie performance, but the conversation with Camilla brought another film to mind. He took up his station at the desk in the hall, scanned a few files, and began to read.

## L.A. Confidential
### From Noir to Neo-Puritanism – Catching the American Conscience at a very specific moment

There has been much comment about *L.A. Confidential*'s style, particularly the palpable authenticity of its sense of time—it is set in the early 1950s—and deservedly so. From the upholstery on a diner's banquettes to the bands on men's hats, from the snout-nosed Ford coupes on the streets to Kay Starr crooning on the airwaves, the production design by Jeannine Oppwall and costumes by Ruth Myers are seamlessly accurate. The idiom of the dialogue, refashioned from James Ellroy's thriller by Curtis Hanson and Brian Helgeland, snaps with the breezy be-bop slang of the '50s, punctuated here and there by monosyllabic tough-guyisms still in post-War favor. Hanson, who also directs, and cinematographer Dante Spinotti unfurl the movie with a perfect texture and pace, equal parts seedy *film noir* and brassy "Show of Shows," that catch that very instant when America, and most emblematically, Hollywood, were poised between the school of hard knocks (the Depression and the War) and a jarring array of social revolutions (the '60s and beyond). If the 1950s may be described as a period for self-satisfaction, a time simply to keep up with the Joneses and contemplate our blessings, then certainly no one aided and abetted our strictly enforced sentimentality more avidly than did Hollywood. The conformist morality of its product was never more sanctioning, or hypocritical. The world of *Written on the Wind* and *Magnificent Obsession* did not invite an introspective splitting of the fine hairs of conscience; it was a broad-brush canvas, a midnight or noon world of fraught but tight-lipped consensus.

In the 1952 of *L.A. Confidential,* the facade of the American Dream is getting a good buff everywhere, but nowhere as energetically as in the city that has become the western outpost of that dream, where people get off the bus to do, well, they may not even know, but something better than from whence they came. You can eat oranges right off the trees and stars are born every day. And if the American Dream, like any great dream of mankind's, needs a face in order to move the masses, then Hollywood is the place that gave it to us. L.A. is the Face Capital of the World. Through the depths of the Depression, the movies reflected an American public that had grit and sentiment, laughter, and even glamour, whether the mirror was accurate or not. And during the War years, they showed us all together on the home front, waiting for victory, in one homey back lot hometown, as often as not, singing and dancing. After the boys came home, Hollywood (almost despite itself) gave us some faces more troubled, less certain, less composed, faces that had seen some trust, whether with the American Dream or a buddy or a dame, broken. Hollywood, however, doesn't ever flirt too long with the dark side. So now it's 1952, and Ike's been elected and McCarthy's going to get rid of the Communists, and we're all learning How To Win Friends and Influence People. We're putting on a happy face and a busily moral face, and if you can't be happy and be moral, you sure as hell better *look* that way.

*L.A. Confidential* is not merely appropriately named, it is, like many a fine film or novel, so steeped in its sense of place that it is impossible to imagine the story coming to life anywhere else. Its themes—appearance vs. reality, corruption, heroism, and love's redemption—are universal. And the fact that these forces are at war for the soul of an urban police department seems broadly applicable: after decades of serial television and investigative news stories, the institution has become one of our most visible moral battle-grounds, a microcosm of society's fault lines. Not only is *L.A. Confidential* not just an easily trans-plantable *NYPD* episode or *Serpico* gone south, its title city transcends its function of background to become one of the primary characters. Not one of the film's intricately woven plot lines could breathe anywhere but in the hothouse atmosphere of La La Land; none of the story's central characters would confront their demons or their dreams as they do here, interacting with the schizophrenic entity that has become the church and state of illusory values. *L.A. Confidential* brings us face to face with Los Angeles, home to human expatri-ates in exile from themselves, city of angels rising and descending, improbable earth mother, waterless, glamorous, putrefied. This unique city is as uniquely inescapable in a consideration of this film's impact as it was in such memorably L.A.-centric works as *In a Lonely Place, Sunset Boulevard, The Bad and the Beautiful, Day of the Locust, Chinatown, Tequila Sunrise,* and *The Player.* Not to mention that Jacobean soap opera, the O.J. Simpson case.

At the heart of *L.A. Confidential* is the relationship between Bud White (Russell Crowe), a tough, sad-eyed, loyal young cop, who wants to do the right thing but is painfully suspended in a state of suppressed fury by department superiors who use his brawn for their back-room intimidation sessions, and Ed Exley (Guy Pearce), a rule-book model officer whose ambition and unyielding standards do not make him popular with the rank and file. There's plenty not to like about both. One of the beauties of the film is that it never rushes our sympathies; it gives us just enough about each man to *interest* us as the film's convoluted plot lines slowly come together for full gallop to the finish. Only in the final scenes of the film do we experience, all the more powerfully for it being something of a surprise, a depth of feeling and of respect for them both.

One of their colleagues is Jack Vincennes (Kevin Spacey), a guy who's gotten so smooth he can't stop himself from outrageous displays of verbal smarminess, even though we can see there's an acrid taste of self-loathing, or at least self-fatigue, when he does it. Vincennes is adviser to the TV cop show "Badge of Honor" and something of a minor celebrity. He takes small pay-offs and we sense that his inner barometer about what's too small to bother with or too vile to touch is less reliable that it used to be. He turns his head so often it's in a perpetual swivel. Spacey is extraordinarily adroit at making Vincennes, at once, faintly disgusting and touchingly sympathetic. When he tries to turn what we know could be a big corner in his life, we root for him; and it hurts when he answers Exley's question about why he became a cop. It's Spacey's most galvanizing moment: there's an attempt at the usual glibness, followed by a wide-eyed, wordless straining at truth; followed by the actual, crushing truth: "I don't remember." Vincennes is the perfect cop for a world founded on duplicity; he's acting, and he's been acting for so long that he's forgotten to remember where all the bodies are buried. Too late he realizes that among them is his own.

Danny DeVito is exuberantly trashy as Sid Hudgens, verminish reporter for *Hush-Hush* magazine. He and Vincennes occasionally trade favors: Jack'll set up the vice bust of a starlet and tip Sid to be there with his cameras. James Cromwell plays Lieutenant Dudley Smith as a benign Irish patriarch and, amazingly, does so without resorting to cliché. It's a cunningly crafted performance and should dispel the notion, held in some quarters, that his Oscar nomination three years ago for his role as the farmer in *Babe* was a fluke. As Pierce Patchett, an elegantly tailored Brentwood gentleman who runs a high-class string of hookers, whom he sends to hairdressers or even plastic surgeons to heighten their resemblance to stars of the day, David Straitharn continues a string of low-key but vividly eccentric performances that are mesmerizing in their variety.

It's hard to imagine any two actors being more suited, more innately *right*, than Crowe and Pearce for the two leads. Which is precisely the point. In one of the smarter moves made on any major film this year, Hanson wisely avoided using better-known stars (and managed to talk the producers into it). The pay-off for the audience is enormous; we are allowed to experience fully our seduction by the film's suspense, its sensuousness, its ideas, because we are not distracted with projecting star expectations onto the personas on the screen. There's nothing to get in the way of the good work here, and it's very good, indeed; the characterizations are finely drawn. Even the physical opposition of the actors' good looks have room to work: Crowe's heaviness of experience sits uneasily on his brow; Pearce's chiseled righteousness is matched by his cheekbones.

In another instance, it's hard to imagine how what the audience *does know* about an actor's historical baggage could add more to a performance. The face that is most familiar among the cast of *L.A. Confidential* belongs to Kim Basinger. Her performance as Lynn Bracken, a Veronica Lake look-alike from Patchett's agency, accrues its emotional heft precisely because moviegoers have watched her migration in recent years from blonde sexpot to would-be dramatic and comedic actor, to owner of a small town in Georgia, to bankruptcy and box office poison after being sued for conduct deemed unbecoming by a major studio, to marriage to Alec Baldwin, motherhood, and a measured, modest comeback. It's all there. And it makes her love for Officer White nearly unbearable in its wounded tough-cookie need.

Hanson and Helgeland have handled the neat convolutions of Ellroy's crime thriller with cinematic finesse, and even though Hanson's sense of pace and stylistic integrity are sinuous and sophisticated, the real fuel here, as in the *noir* classics of the '40s and early '50s, is emotion. Last week, speaking at the fifth Film Preservation Festival, director Martin Scorsese said of those films: "They were about descending into a labyrinth where anything can happen, including the death of the protagonist."

For 135 minutes, *L.A. Confidential* takes us with it on such a descent, and not one frame of this remarkable film tips its hand as to whether we'll go to hell or, if we do, whether we'll come back. We end up on the edge of our seat, yearning for two protagonists, both anti-heroes—one of whom, not long before, we'd taken to be a psychotic thug and the other a reptilian prig—to gun their way to a compromised moral victory, to make us believe again in at least the possibility of integrity.

Odd that for many who see this movie, in which the city of movies looms so large, its white hot light streaked with the shadows of palm trees and ghosted with celluloid shadows, it may be, in the end, not other movies about L.A. or the movies that are recalled first to mind. It might well be a film made in 1952, *High Noon*—another exploration of the American Dream, violent evil, and our constantly reforming need to find a face, however unlikely, we can trust.

# Chapter 25

Terry watched the highway intently. They were driving through the deluge in tarry blackness. Michael kept his eyes on the road, too, as though he were deciphering Terry's instructions on a watery grid in front of the headlights. Terry spoke slowly and distinctly as the torrents slashed noisily around them.

"The people who are staying at his house will be out of town a week from Sunday. He usually goes out for dinner and gets home between eleven and eleven-thirty. He's always up in the bedroom by midnight and asleep by twelve-thirty."

Occasionally he would make a point by turning for a moment toward Michael, inviting a quick return glance.

"You have the gun?"

"Yes. I hid it like you told me to when you gave it to me."

"You're sure you're comfortable with it?"

"Oh, yeah. I had it out in the woods just that once to fool around with a little bit. If you grow up in the hills of South Carolina, you gonna grow up with guns."

"Okay. Good." They drove along 98 in silence for a long time, the rain billowing in concentric waves against the truck as the storm rotated around them and moved off toward the east. About three miles east of the 26-A cutoff to Rosemary Beach, Terry pulled off into a gravel and shell lane that led into a small stand of pines, coming to a halt just behind another pickup off on the right side. He cut the engine and turned slightly toward Michael, reaching out and laying his hand on his shoulder.

"Michael. Like Miss Rachel said, the Lord is waiting for you now, and we are all with you. I will get a copy of the key to you next week and I will have tried it to make certain that it works smoothly. And I will have the alarm code. We have thought of everything. Taken care of everything. All will be well for you to carry out God's justice as he has called you to do. And to leave the letter exposing this evil to the world." Michael looked over his shoulder into the backseat, at the two videos he had brought back to Terry when they'd met to go to the pier. He shook his head, and he looked at Terry with barely suppressed disgust.

Terry said, "I know. It's sickening and it's the very face of evil. I could only watch part of one and it made me throw up. But Michael, I wanted you to watch them again for a reason. I wanted you to look one more time on the work of this monster and to think again about what he did—and what he will continue to do, unless you help God make an example of his evil. He recruited the Reverend's and Miss Rachel's little brother into that world of drugs and sodomy and sadomasochistic evil and that poor eighteen-year-old boy was innocent. That boy is dead of AIDS now, and dozens like him, and that monster goes on, making more of these films, this devil's work, and it is up to us to stop him. To let the sodomites know just as we are letting the abortionists know that God-fearing people are rising up in the army of the Lord and bringing our nation back to Him."

"It's hard to believe people doing that stuff." Michael shifted in his seat and scratched his shaggy beard.

"Recruiting young people and converting them to their ways and then using them like you wouldn't use a yard dog. Timothy is dead because of this man. But because God has sent you for this mission, he won't be seducing any more young people into sodomy and evil and death! While he makes his secret money off their innocent flesh and his despicable perversion. And lives in his big house and acts like some big-shot pillar of the community, while his hired devils churn out this satanic filth in some back alley studio in New Orleans." He paused. "Are you ready to serve the Lord and do his holy work, Michael? To send this Charlie Brompton to meet his Maker?"

"Yes." Michael stared at Terry in the dim light from the dashboard. Then he turned and opened the door into the hot, heavy rain. As he climbed down into the darkness, he looked back once more at Terry, his eyes glowing, wide open in the sluicing water. "Yes. I am."

Terry waited for the other truck to pull away, and then turned around and began the drive toward his cabin in Blue Mountain. He reached one arm back and grabbed the two videos—truly creepy things, one titled "Dungeon" and the other something like "Boot Camp II"—that he had found in Panama City. When he passed the next large condo complex, he pulled up to a large commercial dumpster wedged between a row of palmettos and a low wall, and, lifting the top, threw the videos in. As he drove away, he nuzzled into his damp pants pocket, pulled out the pack of cigarettes, and lit one. He exhaled deeply, cracking the two front windows about half an inch. He hated for the truck to smell like stale smoke.

◇◇◇

Terry navigated carefully through the slackening shafts of rain, but though his eyes were riveted on the two-lane highway and his hands clenched on the wheel for any sudden reaction, it was as though he drove unconsciously. His thoughts kept crawling around the events of the past few days....

He had picked them up as planned near the bridge across Western Lake that leads into the new resort.

He had then pulled over on the north side of the highway into a small turn-out fishermen sometimes used.

After Chaz apologized—"You understand, of course…"— insisting they step back into the trees to search Terry for any sort of recording device and Terry, in turn, did likewise with them, they emerged back onto the turnout and conferred very reasonably for nearly half an hour. Occasionally Terry gestured here and there as if indicating points of interest to them.

In the first five minutes, he had read the letter which Sydney handed him in a book of maps. He asked them how he could possibly know whether the letter were even genuine, and Chaz said that he couldn't except that they had absolutely no reason to make it up. Over the next ten minutes, they agreed that the only thing keeping all of them from getting what they deserved was Charlie Brompton.

Finally, Sydney heard Chaz say—as scripted and yet with an unexpected pleasure that she found terrifying and exhilarating and oddly erotic—quite coolly, his large eyes locked on Terry's: "I want that land." He added, "If you'll help us get it, you'll not only get the Blue Bar, you'll get five million dollars."

Sydney thought Terry looked a bit stunned, but he rolled his eyes and gave a little snort. "One, how? Two, why me?"

For the next fifteen minutes, Chaz and Sydney outlined the situation.

Charlie needed to die before making changes to his will at the end of July. Although it was no secret that Charlie owned the tract (he'd regularly been approached by potential buyers and developers over the years) he'd made a real point of never talking about it. His friends didn't ask (many assumed he'd use his retirement to plan some low-development project), and Charlie didn't tell (even his attorney didn't yet know he'd seriously decided on the wilderness trust idea). Having the inheritance pass from Charlie's unexpectedly predeceased heir to his son, as the will now stood, should come as no particular surprise to anyone.

Terry interrupted. "How can you know that? About not even his lawyer knowing yet? Or believe anything your father said they'd talked about?"

Without missing a beat Sydney answered, "Because in March, in his emotionally distraught state over his cousin's death, he told Chaz so. And other than this rather sad exception of secretly taking sixty million out from under our noses, for his newly beloved Chaz's own good, he is apparently congenitally honest. A man, though it chokes me to say it, of integrity. All that stuff Chaz told you was, we now confess, to get you to open up. We knew you'd been shafted, too. We just didn't know how irritated you were about it."

Terry could do nothing but lean his head slightly to one side, as if in court, nodding, a faint smile tensing on his lips.

"And number two," said Chaz, "why you? Because, Terry, we have much in common here. This well-meaning, generally kind and generous man seems not to be giving you a fair shake any more than he is me."

"You would think a gay man would have some special empathy for black sheep trying to go straight, wouldn't you?" asked Sydney, with a playful smile.

"You know about my past."

"Bingo," said Chaz.

"How?"

"Doesn't really matter," said Chaz. "Old Southern gossip, you know. From a friend of a friend of a second cousin who, I believe, was your former wife."

"I hope you aren't thinking of blackmail. No way it could work. That family will never say a word. They didn't want it public then and they wouldn't want it public now. You think you can blackmail them? Over less than two hundred fucking thousand dollars that they immediately covered eight years ago?"

"Yes," said Sydney. "Because, Terry, it's a public company with ties to the nursing home business, and your former father-in-law is running for a city council seat this fall. The media love gothic family squalor and are at least mildly interested in a political candidate's having cooked his books, especially if it had anything whatever to do with senior citizens on limited incomes. Even in New Orleans."

Sydney saw Terry stiffen, though all he said was, "You have no evidence, and believe me, whatever there was is history."

Chaz said, "Terry, they despise you. And you know how sensation-hungry the media is these days. If it comes to allegations in the press, which choice do you think your in-laws will make? Living through a whisper campaign that'll run right through the primary about him being a questionable manager of the public trust, or a story that focuses on you, a criminal and a moral sleazeball who stole from his wife's family and walked out on his seven-year-old daughter? The good people of New Orleans would forgive and forget his justifiable error. You, on the other hand, would get no less than four to six years, even with parole."

Sydney added, companionably, "But we don't have to be wasting time thinking about this stuff. We have plans to make and business to take care of, and we have very little time in which to be successful."

"This is ridiculous. You folks are crazy."

"Far, far from it, Terry," Chaz said. "I think you can already see that. And within, oh, let's say, no more than one calendar year, you'll be perfectly certain of it. When you have both your bar and a previously undreamed of five million dollars."

"You think you're going to coerce me into..."

"No. There's no way we could possibly do that and we have no particular interest in trying to. The bar that should rightfully be yours anyway and the five million we're giving you from the sale of land that should rightfully be mine are simple motivation, Terry. We simply see your shady past as some insurance for us that you'll hold up your end of any bargain we strike."

"But I'm not a..."

Chaz didn't blink an eye and said as calmly as if he were discussing some theory about the weather: "We don't know what you are or what you'll do for five million dollars, Terry. We just know what needs to happen and we know what role we're willing to take in it and what role we're not willing to take in it. And we just don't happen to count any mafia folk among our acquaintances."

"Look, I made one mistake. Once. A long time ago. That's history."

"We know that!" Chaz said with conviction. "Believe me, I know what you mean. That's why we're here. That's what this is about. Charlie may have been a nice guy to some people but he's screwed you out of something you've earned and he's about to screw us out of ours!"

"For your information," Terry almost sniffed, "I don't happen to have close and regular ties with the underworld either. I'm not a thug."

"We know that," said Sydney soothingly. "We just know that you were a lawyer and that even though you got caught once, you're pretty sharp. And, to use a word that popped up here and there in our research, 'tough.' We know that you really did come out to the coast to ease back and settle down, and we know that most folks think you're a pretty decent guy, so long as you're not crossed and though you do seem to keep to yourself pretty much. And we believe that your designs on the Blue Bar have been relatively modest and relatively honest."

"In other words," said Chaz, "we felt you probably weren't so very different from us. Differences in degrees, sure, but similar situations, similar feelings, similar motivations. And, now, I hope you're beginning to see, a similar belief that we can correct what's wrong and make it right for ourselves. We can do this."

Sydney looked at her watch. "We probably shouldn't be standing here much longer."

She aimed a cool but reassuring smile at Terry and said casually, "All you have to do now is think about it. Take two or three days. If not, somehow, you—then who? Give us a pay phone number and a time and we'll call. No details over the phone. Just yes, let's arrange a meeting and proceed with the next step, or no, you're out. Consider what's at stake, Terry. Consider possibilities. Options. "

As Terry adjusted his sunglasses and his short reddish beard rose into a sudden, rather strange smile, Sydney, for the first time in the interview, drew a blank. She couldn't read what was happening behind the black wire-rims, as Terry, almost familiarly, leaned close to her.

"The most bizarre thing of all, in this already bizarre little encounter, has just occurred. I actually may have an idea. It's a long shot, but…" He looked up into the dazzling sunshine and shook his head with a little bark of a laugh. "It's all I've got, but—just maybe." He added mysteriously, "Something I saw just this morning, in the post office, as a matter fact."

Chaz put his arm around Sydney. "Leave a time and a number for our call Wednesday on a pack of matches and leave it under the real estate newspaper stand outside the bar tomorrow morning by nine. When I jog, I'll come around and get it."

Terry had lifted a hand in brief salute and turned toward his Jeep. The smile had vanished but Sydney thought he still wore an expression of animated bemusement, like someone who has suddenly wakened, not yet fully alert but deeply refreshed, from sleep.

◇◇◇

The young man called Joseph waited, looking around the mini-market gas station, his finger pulsing on the radio's search button. A succession of country-and-western, bland oldies, and ranting demagogues filled the rental Jetta, competing with the diminishing slaps of rain on the windows. Although the storm was beginning to let up, only a few cars pulled in and out, and a couple of kids, their bikes leaning against the wall, hung around inside, eating junk and talking to the young man at the counter. Four big trucks dozed on either side of the small building, their drivers either sipping coffee or perhaps napping out the downpour.

Finally, the woman called Rachel appeared from the restroom around back, jagging around the largest puddles, her large shoulder bag clutched under one arm, a smaller plastic one dangling from her hand. The man swung open the door and she climbed in just as the tuner came to rest on an ingratiating voice denouncing the "liberals' conspiracy" to control certain kinds of assault weapons with a conveniently edited snippet of Luke chapter eleven: "It is by the finger of God that I drive out the devils...."

The woman cocked an ear toward the radio and made wide eyes at the man. "Hmm. Might be my brother, the good reverend. You take this in," she said, dropping the key into his hand. "I doubt it seriously, but those redneck cretins *might* notice something *different* about me." She turned off the radio, shook her hair, and ran her hands up and down her glistening bare arms. "God, it's good to get out of *that*. I was about to faint."

He darted into the building and then back to the car. He swung out onto 26-A, and as they drove through the diminishing rain toward Laurel Beach they resumed their conversation.

Her voice was reassuring. "If Terry thinks it's necessary the night before, Sister Rachel may make one more fortifying phone call. But I really think he'll be fine."

"I still worry about Terry," he said.

"Terry isn't going to let anything go wrong. Sometime in the next few days, he's going to help poor Michael compose his letter of divine judgment. The rough draft, which he will manage to keep, will be his protection if something *does* go wrong. If Michael chokes, then Terry happens to find it somewhere in the bar, dropped apparently when Michael was on the painting job in April. He takes it to Charlie and tells him he had had a bit of concern at the time over some odd allusions the young man had made to events in South Carolina. It'll be Terry's smooth former-lawyer's word against the ramblings of a crazed religious fanatic, one who will be found to have bombed a women's clinic and who has hand-written a letter of intent to murder."

"Goddamn it!" he suddenly spat, his head jerking nervously. "It's like shooting a sitting duck." He hit the steering wheel with the butt of his hand, "For Christ's sake…what are we doing? What have we got against Charlie? We're killing a decent man!"

She turned toward him and rubbed her hand lightly along the back of his neck. "First of all, *we're* not killing anyone. Terry Main has his own score to settle with Charlie and has been considering this or something like it for a long time. We may be the beneficiaries but we're only protecting our interests. What we're doing is keeping an old man, however generally decent he may be, from taking your inheritance away from you."

She paused, and continued gently to massage his neck. "Someone needs to be realistic, and it may as well be us. The days of people playing with you and your choices, your future, are over. We both know life doesn't just hand over opportunities. We have to decide. And which do you want, my love? A couple of million when we're too old to enjoy it—or between sixty and a hundred before we're thirty-six?"

He didn't turn his head, but he reached behind his head and pulled her hand around to his lips and kissed her fingers.

She lightened her tone into a playful tease. "By the way, cousin Joseph, you were pretty *wonderful* back there for a non-Equity kinda guy. I've always said you take direction well." With this, he finally smiled. The rain had stopped and they were slowing for the stretch through Seaside. The choking humidity had broken and the air was fresh and cool. People milled to and fro across the road between the houses and the restaurants and bars.

"Let's stop for a drink," she murmured. "I could use a nice cold martini, and I'm not ready to go to the house just yet." As he parked near the little post office, she got her rings and a broad gold bracelet from her bag. She fluffed her chestnut hair in the mirror and then picked up the plastic bag from the floorboard. From it strayed one long tress of dull blonde. Stuffing it back and tying a knot in the bag, she said, "I was going to get rid of this, but maybe I'll keep it just for tonight."

She laughed. "Would you like to have a very special religious experience a little later with Miss Rachel?" She leaned in close to his face and her eyes assumed a piercing, otherworldly quality. "And if you are a *bad* boy, then perhaps Miss Rachel will have to discipline you."

When Sydney and Chaz entered the small bar just north of the Seaside town green, his arm around her waist, they were both smiling brilliantly. Several people looked up and noted that they were a very handsome couple—"extraordinary," murmured one older woman to an unhearing husband—and, quite obviously, very much in love.

# Chapter 26

Terry Main called at the designated time.

His response was affirmative.

They rendezvoused at an anonymous interstate motel forty miles inland. Terry had a backlog of vacation and told Charlie and his assistant manager that he was taking a day off to take care of some business errands, and Chaz "wanted to show Sydney some of the swamp country over near Apalachicola."

For two hours, over bad take-out Mexican and beer, Sydney and Chaz had listened as Terry unfurled an already remarkably detailed plan, and then as the afternoon wore on in the gray airless room they had gone over and over it, taking it apart and putting it back together.

It seemed that on the very day before their roadside conference, Terry had dropped into the main post office after shopping for some supplies in Destin. As he stood in the seemingly interminable line, his boredom eventually led his gaze to a small bulletin board near the door. To one side of some confusingly worded bureaucratic announcements were two small "Wanted" posters. One was standard-issue FBI—photos of a vague-looking skinny guy who'd killed a federal officer in Mobile and two fairly attractive women wanted for mail fraud. The other poster, issued by the Bureau of Alcohol, Tobacco, and Firearms, was older and less distinct, a composite drawing of a youngish man with sad eyes and an inch-long burr haircut. It made Terry think. Though, of what, he couldn't guess.

On his way out, he stopped and looked at the drawing, the basic stats, and a ragged photocopy of a newspaper account that someone, probably an outraged local healthcare worker, had stapled to the bottom. Mark DeWayne Lukerson. Possible aliases John, David, Michael. Possibly sighted nine months ago in Montgomery, Alabama. A year ago he had bombed a South Carolina women's health and family planning clinic where abortions were also performed. The explosive went off after most of the staff had left for the day, but one nurse, a father of two small children, who had been waiting outside for his wife to pick him up, was severely injured by a flying hunk of cinder block. Attempted murder, violation of clinic access, felony arson. When he'd left the post office Terry couldn't shake the feeling that the face rendered in the police artist's sketch seemed distantly familiar, but he couldn't imagine why. He didn't recall the story, but perhaps he'd seen the drawing many months ago on the news.

It may have been the strange, almost surreal discussion by Western Lake the next day that jarred something loose. (Or it may have been the invigorating prospect of more than five million dollars, it seemed to Sydney.) For whatever reason, just before he dropped them at the intersection near the Hibiscus Bed & Breakfast, Terry suddenly knew where he'd seen the face. In an instant his mind had come up with its own little composite sketch, relocating those sad, lonely eyes above a bushy full beard and under much longer, greasy hair.

It was the painter he'd hired a month earlier to do some outside work on the bar.

The two women he'd used a couple of times before had moved out of the area. This guy had put up a sign in the market and had a recent reference from the pastor of some small church over near Holley.

It all fit. He'd only been around three or four days, did good work and didn't talk much. But it was what he said when he did open up and how he said it that Terry remembered. He was polite in an almost abject way, and looked so hang-dog and lost that, around noon on the third day, Terry had taken a sandwich and a Coke out to him and tried, briefly, to shoot the breeze with him for a few minutes.

It hadn't taken long for him to realize he had a fundamentalist weirdo, not an unknown commodity in west Florida, on his hands. Lived in an apartment in Pensacola where he'd moved last year to be near that big revival. Drove all over the panhandle on jobs but was back home every night to clean up and "go with like-minded people to love the Lord" at the big tent. Like-minded people, he allowed, were of course those who hated abortion, homosexuals, taxes, government in general and Democrats in particular, artists, educators, the "liberal" media, and independent women, and who knew that they were on God's side in a war to win back America's soul. Terry, who had grown up in the crosshairs between a evangelical mother and a lapsed but not unleashed Catholic father, had merely finished his iced tea, smiled and nodded a couple of times knowingly, said that he, too, was a believer, and gone back in to work. He had needed the job finished.

The next day, when he paid him, the guy pulled two crinkled pamphlets from his overalls' back pocket and said he hoped that Terry would come over for the revival one night. Terry thanked him, the guy drove off in his old truck, and the pamphlets, of a particularly garish and virulent variety he had seen before, left on doorsteps or propped on supermarket shelves or urinals in men's rooms, went into the trash.

Despite the lank long hair and the scraggy prophet's beard that framed them, the scared, sad, lonely eyes in the ATF Wanted poster were undoubtedly his.

◇◇◇

"So the entire enterprise is riding on a volatile, probably schizophrenic, religious fanatic moron. *That* sounds good."

Chaz had tried to remain calm, but by afternoon, after Terry's initial outline, he looked harried, aghast. He sat cross-legged on the bed, anxiously poking through the acrid remains of chips and salsa. Sydney paced the room, stopping for moments at a time here and there as if to assess Terry's strategy from all possible angles, occasionally lighting in one of the two armchairs. Terry sat in the other, near the desk, the lamplight flicking on his glasses.

"It can work. He *wants* to be used."

Sydney scrutinized Terry, reminding herself that, so far, Terry had proven quite shrewd. "Well, that could certainly be true," she said. She had had in her own childhood enough warped zealotry to last a lifetime. "I know these people and that *is* what they live for. They're hopeless and weak and have no lives and they hate people who do, so the only way they can know power is to give themselves over to power. Masochistically."

"But how can you be sure you can control him?" Chaz asked more than once.

Terry looked now, it seemed increasingly clear to Sydney, like a man who, in the new conviction that he could have even more than he'd ever wanted in life, could think circumspectly and even imaginatively, wait patiently when necessary, and act, at the right moment, decisively. He removed his wire-rims and rubbed his hands over his eyes. He looked like a cagey attorney, back in the saddle, as he began to go over the rationale and the strategy, step by step, again. Sydney admired his performance.

◇◇◇

The night after he had met them on the road, he had found Michael, the painter's, phone number. He'd left a message on what sounded like a relic of an answering machine, saying that he was pleased with his work and asking him to call about another job as soon as possible. Michael had called back early the next morning and driven out from a nearby job later in the week.

"Right off the bat I apologized for having him come on false pretenses. Admitted that I didn't really have another job. At least not a painting job. He looked extremely nervous. But I proceeded to assure him that there was, indeed, a job. One of the most important missions he would ever have the opportunity of carrying out, a job that I believed God had sent him to 'us' to learn about. I had him then. Looked like a deer in headlights.

"He asked what I knew, and I said very calmly that 'my superiors' in the cause knew and had told me about South Carolina. But that no one would be going to the police. That we considered that wanted poster a badge of honor and that we needed him to work with us. That God had led him here for greater things.

"By the time we finished our little conversation forty-five minutes later—and we had prayed aloud together—he knew he was in a corner, and I'd helped him come to believe that not only was that not something to be afraid of but that God and I and certain powerful 'like-minded' religious leaders would shelter him there. And that it was really just the first stop on the road to glory."

"But does he believe it enough to actually *do* it? He understands what you were talking about?" asked Sydney.

"Yes. And that's where you come in, our 'religious leaders.' He'll stay on task and follow through if we stage just enough pep sessions to keep the pure flame of his purpose burning. He's looking for some kind of atonement or, at least, vindication. Not for having crippled the guy in South Carolina—he was, in Michael's cosmology, a misguided agent of the devil—but for not having made a bigger splash for Jesus. He didn't want limited fire damage and one injury, he wanted to blow that clinic and all the baby-killers in it out of existence. I'm also positive he's a lot more afraid of going to prison than of going down in flames as an officer in God's personal militia."

"Sounds like one of Bin Laden's boys," said Chaz.

Sydney and Terry both spoke at once: "Same thing."

◇◇◇

By five o'clock, Terry's voice was wearing down, Chaz's questions had become less plaintive and more probing, and Sydney's spirits were on a slow but sure rise. Their role would put them closer to the actual event, but there seemed no other way. And she was as certain of Terry's determination as she was of the set of checks-and-balances that would keep him in line and keep her and Chaz clear of implication. The fact that what Terry had actually begun to do was to create the outline of a play, a script for them, not only impressed but exhilarated her. There was a fine symmetry to the fact that they would all be actors. It would be the ultimate proof that what she had come to believe a few years back was true: the only interesting, and valuable, theatrical art takes place in the conduct of real life.

They spent their last hour before heading back to the coast fleshing out the roles, the timing, the nuances.

Terry had left it with Michael that he would be back in touch immediately. That he should pray about what a great gift God was presenting him. And that he shouldn't even think about getting away not only because God would punish him but because it was impossible. (Terry's "superiors in the cause" had authorized him to put a team of private investigators on twenty-four-hour surveillance until the mission was accomplished. "It's for your own good, son. They don't want you to blow your chance to get this right, to serve God in such a vital, once-in-a-lifetime way.")

"I also built up his feeling that he was a member of a team, a chosen MVP, by swearing him to secrecy. He's really locked into that Pensacola Revival thing. It's been his big spiritual teat, I think, since he hightailed it out of the Appalachian woods where he apparently hid out for several weeks last summer. Going to that tent with a few thousand other lost souls five or six nights a week has been an integrating focus. That's why I alluded vaguely to one or two of 'the superiors' he would meet when we got together again—and that they had close connections to the Revival."

Sydney mused, "He needs to have no doubt that he is needed, that he belongs."

"Exactly. It's the critical variable. The idea about the private eyes put the fear of God in him."

"But now we need to put a loving face on the mission. Ensure his motivation. To welcome him and lift him up in the loving arms of fellow-believers." Sydney knew the territory. "That's easy. We can do that."

"I thought you could. Some sort of special emissary from the upper echelons of the movement."

The first come-to-Jesus summit would be at some out-of-the-way location further east, to be followed by a last-minute hand-holding if necessary.

◇◇◇

Before going their separate ways, they reviewed each element of the strategy. They assessed the risks, over and over, reassuring themselves, individually and as a unit, with the various self-protections that could be reliably built in. With the various fallback options at every stage right up to the very moment of the event.

There was a provision for every possible development. If Charlie broke form and unexpectedly talked with anyone about the land, or somehow moved faster with his attorney and the will change, they would cancel. If the final seduction of Michael for whatever reason didn't work and he somehow got away (perhaps even, they had had to consider, by suicide), they would cancel. If he talked to anyone, it would be their very credible amazement against the outrageous babblings of a deranged criminal fanatic. Nothing would be lost. Terry could console himself with a little upfront money and Chaz and Sydney would have a terrific beach house for their sunset years.

They also reviewed every element of their business plan. Their talk was extremely candid, everyone knowing that they had already journeyed light-years and there was no time to waste. Instead of resenting it, Sydney found herself quite reassured by Terry's elaborately detailed selfishness and the unblinking eye with which he watched his back. She trusted his hungriness and his utter inability to trust.

For engaging in a more active role in the actual event, Terry was to receive fifty thousand dollars. Ten now, twenty if they decided on the final "go," and twenty immediately after. And the involvement of Chaz and Sydney, if indeed at a certain remove, was nonetheless his added insurance of their all staying on the same page. Should they renege on his cut after the disposition of the will and the sale of the property, he would talk. Even with no hard evidence like video or sound, he could give the authorities too good a story to ignore. Getting them to believe it might be a challenge, since in the current will Chaz was heir, no one knew that was about to change, and therefore he'd have no apparent motive. But Terry reminded them of their own threats about the media. This would be exactly the sort of juicy soap opera investigative journalists thrived on, with the two of them as the stars, day in and day out until they cracked.

As for their part, Sydney and Chaz knew that Terry wasn't about to risk prison by coming back to them for more.

Discretion was the very best part of valor for everyone concerned.

As Sydney put it, just before they dispersed, "The prospect of mutual poverty can do much to keep everyone honest. None of us gets a thing if this doesn't work, and if anyone turns on the other after we succeed, we lose everything. All we have to do is concentrate on making it work. We can all have everything we want."

Charlie, a nice enough man who had fatally presumed on other people's capacities and dreams, would simply make his exit a few years before expected, dispatched by a madman. And the madman, in turn, would, happily, no doubt, be dispatched by Terry from this corrupted mortal wasteland for an early meeting with his Maker.

Terry mentioned that he would probably sell the Blue Bar. Getting, Sydney and Chaz reckoned, at least a couple more million. That, plus the five, would make for a promising new start. He'd always wondered, he said, about Santa Fe. Perhaps, Antigua. Or even farther afield—Geneva or Florence, maybe Marbella.

Buyers would be lining up for that land. It could all be over and done with by winter, spring at the latest.

It seemed a bit of a pity to Sydney that there was little to no likelihood they'd ever spend much time in Laurel. From what she'd seen of it, it seemed, after all, in a ramshackle sort of way, a pretty enough little place.

# Chapter 27

Hudson and Susie had biked the trail from Laurel to Seaside, stopping for a paperback Susie had ordered at the bookshop and to refill their water bottles, before heading east along 26-A through Seagrove. After the houses and beach traffic thinned out and the road veered away from the sea into the bridge at the inland neck of Eastern Lake, Hudson called out to pull over into the shade of some pines.

Susie creaked to a halt beside him on the old clunker she had liberated from use as a hose rack in the Sandifords' tool shed. "I can feel the pounds evaporating into the torrid ozone." Susie drew her arm across her brow and readjusted her cap and sunglasses.

Hudson momentarily considered her willowy twenty-four-year-old frame. "A real problem, I'm sure."

"I'm reading Edith Wharton and, you know, all that Gilded Age stuff—it just makes me feel *fat*."

Hudson laughed. "Ozone? That's where things evaporate?"

"Oh, what do I know? I'm an English major. It just sounded appropriate. Are we nearly there?"

"I think so." Hudson scrutinized the hand-drawn map Charlie had roughed out for them. It wasn't terribly detailed but Hudson remembered enough to think that the area lay not very far ahead.

◇◇◇

Charlie's commentary hadn't been terribly detailed either, though he had volunteered the destination eagerly enough when earlier in the week Hudson had mentioned wanting to break in his new bike. "Some of the trails are just footpaths, though. You've been over that way once. I sent you and Kate on a picnic. I own some land over there," he had added dismissively. "That whole stretch of beach and wilderness is really something, the highest dunes on the coast. You told me you saw herons on the back lagoon."

Of course Hudson had remembered.

Kate, standing like a statue in the violet and green twilight, a full golden moon staring at her through the oaks and cypress and he staring at them both; the herons, some seventy-five yards away, seeming at once the masters of the scene and gorgeously, almost unbearably vulnerable, like an etching from memory of some dream of perfection.

He remembered, too, that a day or two later when Libby and Brad had had them over for dinner they had smiled at one another over Charlie's modest characterization of his property. "'Owns some property' is right," said Libby. "There've always been rumors about the exact acreage and value but we try to protect his privacy and not add to the speculation."

Brad had added, "Real estate has been the most popular topic of conversation in these parts for over fifty years. But that's just not Charlie, and that's one of the things we've always respected about him. He's said, and of course he's absolutely right, that it could become the only conversation of his life and that more agents and developers than already do would be bothering him constantly. I mean, I suppose it's a matter of public record if someone wanted to go down and look through the county assessor's office."

"In a way," said Libby, "that huge St. Joe Corporation resort development site has gotten him off the hook somewhat. For the last six or eight years that's been the big question mark."

"He's told us that every once in awhile somebody in the media will approach him but he's always declined to be interviewed."

Libby had smiled. "And isn't *that* refreshing?"
And that had been all there was to that.

◇◇◇

It was after seven when Hudson wheeled his bike into the large storage closet at the back of the cottage. He had been drenched, dried, and re-drenched in sweat so many times that his shorts, tee shirt, socks, and especially his skin felt as if they had been varnished. He changed into his trunks and headed for the beach with Moon.

This time of day, anywhere, was Hudson's favorite but nowhere, he suddenly knew, more than here. It was still warm, but the grinding white heat of the day had ebbed away with the tide and a breeze from the northwest brought the slash pines and tall oaks along Pendennis Street to life. The sun would be just on the horizon, but an hour before it had nestled into a mass of towering cumulus clouds which, except for their fiery coronas, were darkening by the minute into grays and indigo. Overhead, small land birds and terns cruised the opalescent sky and along the shore gulls awakened from one-legged slumber and began to bathe and strut.

A man watering his small patch of lawn and a row of hibiscus waved and said hello to Hudson. A band of kids loaded down with every imaginable sort of paraphernalia staggered past on their way from the beach, and Hudson suddenly saw himself at that age, never happier than dead-tired after a day in the sand with his head already filled with plans for the next. But, now, he was just another invisible adult to them. They said hello only to Moon.

Occasionally they passed through a riff of music drifting out from a screened porch or the low chime of ice in glasses. From the end of the road, where it elbowed east and became the main drag, he could see several vehicles lounging around the Blue Bar, people coming and going.

◇◇◇

The Gulf was as calm as a lake. He swam some laps until he realized that he had had more than enough exercise for one day. Then he contented himself with bobbing in the shallows while Moon pranced in and out of the low surf and for awhile they played fetch with a piece of driftwood. The walkers and joggers were thinning out and the last of the die-hard children were being corralled by parents who were long past their feet-up-with-a-drink time.

After an hour or so Hudson dried off, Moon shook with brisk efficiency, and they began trudging across the wide beach.

Suddenly, for several minutes, he lost his connection to the glorious twilight and fell into a cavernous maw of grief and rage.

The dog looked up several times and finally sounded a wistful moan. Hudson, finding that they were halfway up Pendennis, reached down and ruffled his neck.

"Thought you'd lost me again, huh? It's okay, boy. I'm here."

◇◇◇

That evening he knocked off a healthy chunk of reading for school, and even wallowed for an hour in the tawdry suspense novel that he had begun purely for pleasure. Then he checked another review.

The only difficulty with some of the reviews, of course, was that in selecting and editing them, he inevitably relived the particular afternoon or evening he and Kate had seen the film. Her reaction. To the film or to his review, or both. She always either read them or had him read them aloud to her. He remembered their discussions, how certain lines that had passed into their lore repeated themselves over and over again at opportune moments. Her face, now pensive, now smiling, as they talked. He had never in his life seen a woman whose intelligence was so ineffably related to her sensual appeal. He had once told her, "You are never more beautiful than when we're discussing ideas. I feel as though we're making love. And when we do make love I often feel as though we're talking." That had evoked one of her great murmuring laughs. But she knew what he meant and seemed pleased.

He had decided to arrange the book by emphasis sections. Directors, writers, performances, best overall, and, for laughs, a few representatives of the bottom of the cinematic barrel. But, for now, what he most needed to do was to e-mail Alex, something he'd been intending for the last few days to do.

Dear Alex,

First of all, I want to thank you for helping me.

Of course, I've been aware that I don't know what I would've done without you from time to time, but it seems that being here these past two weeks has enabled me to realize the full scope of your effort. Trying to determine whether its source is in your being a priest or in your role as a counseling psychologist seems a futile exercise. I simply know that you have a rare capacity for seeing into a person's heart and mind, for understanding, for communicating the difficult and the complex, and for knowing just how to inspire someone to help himself even when he can find very little, if any, reason for doing so.

You asked me for a progress report.

You were, as you seem to have an eerie way of always being, *right* about what coming back to this place I love could do for me. I'm seeing old friends and, I think, making a couple of new ones. I run on the beach every morning and pass the day working with pleasure. I had lost sight of how extraordinary this place has always been for me. It's that place in the world—I hope everybody has one—where time means everything and nothing, where the past, present, and future are capable of converging with less painful consequences than I had begun to believe was possible.

Coming through the door of this cottage was, as we'd imagined, the hardest thing I've done since I walked back into the house in Memphis that first time…

Alex, I have just come back to this letter, after being on the porch, sitting and staring into the night and having two glasses of wine. Now I'll say what brought me to a crashing halt an hour ago.

I sense that you will be expecting this. From a couple of our more recent conversations, I would guess that it is a progression which you probably have antici-pated, or hoped for for me, but which, of course, in your astute kindness, you have waited for me to dis-cover. To say.

Kate is becoming more like a memory.

If I live another fifty years, and no matter how life may become new for me or I for it, I will in all prob-ability forget nothing of our life together. It was life as fully as I've ever known it.

But I have, as I believe you've foreseen, ceased to struggle and I don't mean by that that I've given up. You always said that giving up would never prove an option for me. *"You're just a little too driven, I think, for that. No, you'll either go on, or go* really *crazy."* Your inimitable bedside manner at its best, eh, Alex?

I'm going on. Where? I have no idea. How? Even less. Why? I'm not sure. Except that it has to do with God, and the relentless sorrows and joys of being human. And Kate. And good friends and teaching and writing. And people like you. And trees, and the air at dawn, and the light of the world in the evening.

Hud

P.S....and Moon, who sends his warmest regards, and Olive, who doesn't give a rat's ass.

It was nearly one when he padded down the hall to the bedroom. He looked as he almost always did at the framed photograph on the old teak dresser. It had been taken at their engagement party and like most great true portraits, it had been spontaneous. They were holding hands and had just turned in toward one another and back at the friend who'd said their names. They were framed in a pale wash of late-afternoon radiance from the French doors just beyond them. They looked so indescribably happy that it seemed they might just have, together, only moments before, been born.

Hudson picked up the picture and carried it to the other bedroom, where he left it on a small table. Then he came back into his bedroom, went into the closet and found, in a box padded with socks, another framed photo which he placed on the dresser. It was of Kate alone, standing in the middle distance. They had been hiking in Colorado and she had gone ahead on the trail while he fiddled with the camera. Just as he was getting her in focus she stopped at a point where the trail jagged around an outcropping of rock. She had raised her hand to beckon him on.

Moon looked a bit confused by the unaccustomed trip to the spare room.

Hudson was not.

"Goodnight, Kate," he said.

# Chapter 28

Terry Main sat on one of the benches that faced the large fountain in the middle of the small city park. Despite the still-throbbing, early evening heat, there were, as he knew there would be, plenty of people milling about and sitting on the benches, on the grass, and along the ledge of the fountain. Giant live oak trees, some draped with Spanish moss, cloaked nearly the entire square block of the park with long shards of deep shade. Parents watched as squealing children took turns on the three-seat swing set, the slide, and jungle gym. A historical marker flanked by tall flagpoles bearing the colors of the various nations that had ruled Pensacola was always a popular site for tourists. They still wrangled cameras in the last light and bumped their knees with huge shopping bags; downtown office workers crisscrossed the square on their way from businesses, or to cocktails; people lounged or strolled idly about, chatting, while others sat here and there still reading, or listening to headsets; a few stalwart runners loped with fixed stares through the humidity.

He unfurled a newspaper he had already read and hoped that no one would take the other end of the bench. Three or four minutes passed before Michael appeared, also carrying a newspaper.

"Hey," he said quietly, scarcely nodding to Terry as he sat down. He looked around the park for a full minute, fingering his beard. He crossed one leg up over the other knee and spread the newspaper. After a few minutes he refolded one section carefully and lay it down.

"Mind if I take a look?" Terry smiled.

Michael nodded.

Tucked within the pages of the paper, Terry found one sheet of plain white paper, covered with cramped but neat handwriting.

He read with a concentration so fierce that he forgot about the rivulets of sweat coursing down his back. It was perfect. They couldn't have done better themselves. The awkward phrasing, the misspellings, the ignorance and fear transmuted by a steady diet of demagoguery into hatred and weird, grotesque logic.

◇◇◇

To whom it may concern (Police, FBI, the Media, Government Officials, the Public)—

"They will conform to my statutes and keep my laws. They will become my people, and I will become their God. But as for those whose heart is set upon their vile and abominable practices, I will make them answer for all they have done. This is the very word of the Lord God." (Ezekiel 11:20-21)

I take no credit for this act. That would be putting myself above the holy justice that is our cause. I am nothing. God has seen fit to use me and that is all I know. "You are my battle-axe, my weapon of war" (Jeremiah 51:20)

We are Godless in this country and we will answer for it. The colored races are God's children but they have got dominyon over us and they take the family values down. Some have gone over to the Infedel Alah and dress in his rayments and they want to get down and pray on mats in the schools when you can't even pray to the true God or have the Ten Commanments by the pencil sharpner. While our so-called leaders (New World Order) sleep with harlots the Devil does not sleep. His handywork is seen thruout the land. The

children have no respect for the adults and women
do not obey their husbands or God's laws, dress like
whores of Babylon and killing their inocent babies in
their own womb. The homosexual agenda is taught in
the schools and they infilltrate the t.v. and shown to
be acepptable everywhere even by some radicle pas-
tors who are in the cult religions (Jews, Freemasons,
Unitarions, Methodists, Episcable, xct.) God's wrath is
upon them with the AIDS (Leviticus 14,15, 20:13) and
they do not turn from evil but take more with them to
perdision.

Satan has control of much of the Media and Inner-
net except for some Godly men who have begun to
fight back in the Name of the Lord. Pornography is
rampet but it is most the ones that coruppt the soul and
the flesh of inocent young ones who must be stopped.
There are godless laws that protect evildooers but not
those who are inocent. Godfearing people must act.
I have been called and I am an obedient and humble
servant of The Lord.

This man Charlie Brompton has made millions of
dollars in the trade of Evil. He has a restrant and a bar
and owns property and because he has this power of
Mammon no one will speak against him or take action.
But mostly it is pornography and no one knows this.
But now some Men of God do know and it and his evil
will be made known. The Lord has said "Do not blot
out their wrongdoing or annul their sin (Jeremiah 18:
23). So now the sword of truth and Vengefull Justice is
risen up to protect other inocents from being abused
beyond belief in pornography and killed by AIDS at
the hands of this man. I have seen what he sells to make
his fortune and I will never forget it. Twice in my life I
have seen manifest the very face of the Devil, once the
Abortion killing on video and the other is this man's
videos. I can never forget. God has seen fit to torment

even my sleep. But I know that is His way of leading me to redemtion as a soldier in his Holy War and I praise His Name.

Someday you may know who I am. But it does'nt matter. I have been told that God has a plan for me in another place now and so I will follow his chosen leaders. But we do not know the days of our coming or our going. God's will be done and to Him all the glory. If we must be persecuted as His peculier people then we are truly in the company of angels. The law of man is coruppt and I must answer to the law of God. His is the only true judgment.

You will find a sacrifice here acording to God's laws of purification and atonement. When this is on CNN and in the papers, Godefaring people will know this for a Holy Symbol and even the others will know that God's army is no longer fearfull on the sidelines of this sick culture but on the march. Evil will be driven out by The Sword and Our House will be made pure.

"In order to rid the house of impurity, he shall take two small birds, cedar-wood, scarlet thread, and marjoram. He shall kill one of the birds over an earthenware bowl containing fresh water. He shall then take the cedar-wood, marjoram, and scarlet thread, together with the living bird, dip them in the blood of the bird that has been killed and in the fresh water, and sprinkle the house seven times. Thus he shall purify the house, using the blood of the bird, the fresh water, the living bird, the cedar-wood, the marjoram, and the scarlet thread. He shall set the living bird free outside to fly away over the open country, and make expiation for the house; and then it shall be clean."

Leviticus 14:49-53

Terry folded the letter and eased it into the fold of his own newspaper. He took off his round wire-rimmed sunglasses and squinted up into a slant of orange sunlight that penetrated the canopy of oaks. He rubbed his hand over his eyes, appearing to be on the verge of tears, and then he turned and looked at Michael.

"Michael."

Michael shifted, uncrossing his legs and, for the first time, lifting his downcast face, questioningly. "Yeah?"

Terry lay down the borrowed section of newspaper beside Michael and smiled, tapping his finger vaguely as if to indicate something he had read there. "I will take your draft of the message to Miss Rachel and The Reverend, as we've talked about."

"Sure. I don't have all the words...."

"We just want it to be perfect because it's going to be such an important statement. But Michael..."

"Yeah?"

"I feel confident that they will change very little, if anything. It is very powerful and very beautiful. This proves again that you are God's instrument in this mission. Oh, our leaders may want to touch up a spelling or a phrase just here or there. But this is from the heart and I know what they'll say. They'll say 'Well done, good and faithful servant.' This letter is filled with God's inspiration. I'm very...." He hesitated and pointed to another area of the newspaper. "Michael, I'm just very, very moved."

He looked away. He was thinking that Michael might not have time for his little ritual with dead birds and marjoram or whatever, but, as he watched some children who had taken off their shoes and were splashing at the side of the fountain, what he said was: "Those children are going to grow up in a cleaner world because of you and because what you are doing will embolden more people to join our cause."

He then gathered up his newspaper with the letter inside, and stood. Looking down, he said, "You know, Michael, I look forward to working with you in the open, out front and shoulder to shoulder, when this mission is complete and we go to Houston, or Merida, or wherever the Lord sends us to work with the Reverend and Miss Rachel."

Michael said, "They sent me a letter the other day." He almost smiled. "It made me feel pretty good."

"That's fine. I'm not surprised. They have grown to respect you very much." He paused. "I have to get back, now." He looked up again into the sunlight. "My pretending to be a bar manager has helped us gather a lot of useful information for our efforts—but to tell you God's truth my soul is sick with feeling dirty. I do not see many spirit-filled persons in that place. And if I were to witness, it would draw too much attention to us." He put on his sunglasses. "But we're almost there, my friend."

Michael nodded.

Terry locked eyes with him. "Are you ready?"

"Yes."

"You know every step of the plans?"

"Yes."

"You have nothing with any of our names or anything like that on it in your room, or in your truck?"

"No."

"I'll get you whatever few changes they may need in the letter so that you can copy it over."

"Okay."

"And should there be any changes in the plan we'll go over them in our final checklist the day before. I'll be in touch, the usual way. Goodbye, Michael. Godspeed."

"'Bye, Terry." He looked up, his eyes wide with the only hint of joy Terry had ever noticed there. "Godspeed." Clearly unaccustomed to the word, he seemed to savor it for a moment before releasing it like a kiss blown hopefully to one's beloved.

◇◇◇

Terry sauntered out of the park and walked over two blocks to his vehicle. He would, indeed, get revisions back to Michael for his final copying of his letter. They would be few and they would be minor. The real McCoy couldn't be improved on and, except to help keep poor Michael on task and feeling that his spiritual leaders were in there pitching with him, they really wouldn't matter. Michael might feel especially conscientious to think he had a brand-new final edit to leave in Charlie Brompton's house after the holy act was done, but Terry now had in his possession what he needed as insurance.

Just in case something went wrong once Terry dispatched Michael himself on an unannounced flight to paradise. Just in case, despite his meticulous planning, the worst case scenario occurred, and he was somehow discovered before getting away from the house with not one, but two dead bodies inside.

He would produce this perfect specimen (somewhat dusty, wrinkled, and torn), in Michael's handwriting (perhaps a draft?) of a disturbing letter that he had found under some paintbrushes while putting away cases in the storage room after closing. He would have remembered his concern over some passing comments that the painter had made. Despite the late hour, he would have decided to stop by on his way home to check on Charlie.

He would seem dazed, distraught, grieving.

He would have been too late.

# Chapter 29

Charlie's first stop had been the farmers' market in Destin. He spent quite some time foraging among the vegetables and fruit, gently testing the whorls of the endive, examining the edges of mushrooms and the bending points of asparagus spears, searching for the barely discernible scent that distinguishes the better blueberry, adjusting his menu slightly depending on his finds.

At one point the owner, a tall black man with stooped shoulders and a soft but very deep voice, walked over and said conspiratorially, "Can't give those strawberries much, but look at these." In each plump hand he held a small basket of raspberries, brilliant and perfectly globed. "Sweetest we've had this year." The man's face was gentle but solemn and he scrutinized Charlie's face as Charlie took a couple and ate them.

"You're right, Frank." He grinned. "I'd better have some."

Frank allowed himself a brief, small smile. "Always a treat, good raspberries. Just for you or you havin' folks in? I haven't put these out yet, they're in back."

"A celebration. Six people. Just family really, for my young cousin from Atlanta and his new bride."

"You don't mean. Well, now that is a special supper. You get you some o' that endive?"

"I sure did." He paused. "How do you fix it?"

Frank managed another smile. "Covered skillet, but not too long. Like it tender but firm. A shot of bourbon and a touch of bacon grease."

"Bourbon?"

"Now, that's the *secret* part."

"Of course. Have you tried that clove and lemon zest pork loin?"

"Third time last Sunday."

Frank was called away for a phone call, and Charlie finished gathering what he needed. They met again at the checkout counter, and Charlie asked, "When are you and Grace going to get out to the restaurant again?"

"Our daughter's coming down from the University next month for her brother's birthday."

"Just let me know. *University?* That can't be. Just yesterday she wasn't as tall as that stack of tomatoes."

"Twenty-one."

Charlie shook his head and said, "I better get out of here before I get any older," which made Frank actually let out a little laugh.

"You fix those young folks up right, tonight, Charlie. I know you will. A happy time for all of you."

◇◇◇

He picked up extra bottles of merlot and sauvignon blanc at Ollie's, seafood for the bisque at the fresh market on Highway 98, and bread from Cesaria. She was an ancient Portuguese woman who, with her daughter, had for years supplied markets in Fort Walton and Destin, and the 26-A, but was now retired. Her widowed daughter had remarried and moved away and Cesaria lived on modest but sufficient investments her husband had made during his years in the Air Force. She resided in a scrupulously and lovingly tended little house set in a scrupulously and lovingly tended little yard in an oak and cypress grove beside Redfish Lake. She spent hours sitting on her deeply shaded porch reading books of poetry from the county library, and in the evenings she listened to an odd assortment of music—Tony Bennett, the Police, zydeco, the odd Broadway anthology—rejects that her daughter had left her along with an old CD player. Cesaria had learned where the bargain bins were in the local stores and enjoyed passing long minutes flipping through the CDs, comparing deals from store to store, narrowing her choices, and finally, once every month, treating herself to something new.

She now baked only to teach her young nieces and nephews and for events at her church. She had once confided sadly, "*These* Catholics are not bakers. Italians. Irish. If it's not pasta or that flat hard soda bread, they do not know."

And, on occasion, she baked for Charlie.

Today, when Charlie drove up, Cesaria was reading Octavio Paz and listening to *Cats*.

He always wanted to kiss the fine olive skin of her lovely high cheekbone, but it was not Cesaria's way. She was capable of wonderful, sly humor, but she was very formal and, Charlie guessed, considered a friendly kiss, even with true affection, somehow a trivialization of the vigilant passion she kept for her husband, who had died in a freakish deep-sea fishing accident at fifty.

He held both her hands in his for a moment. "You'll never guess what I have for you."

He reached in the pocket of his baggy khaki pants and drew forth a CD.

She looked at the cover and her delicate brows lifted. "*Cesaria?*"

"Cesaria Evora. I've just discovered her and, naturally, thought of you. She's Cape Verdan."

"This is *your* CD?"

"No, mine's out there in the car. I've just been listening to it. This one's yours."

# Chapter 30

Chaz watched from the window of the upstairs suite as a small truck appeared through the trees, approaching the house along the long winding drive. It pulled to one side of the turnaround that circled a small stand of sweetbay magnolias. In a moment, the housekeeper, Marianne, emerged from below carrying two grocery bags and awkwardly balancing a rectangular box. Her husband got out to help her arrange them in the back and they drove away.

"She's gone." Just out of the shower, he stood naked, drying his hair with a towel. "Loaded down as usual."

Sydney crossed the room, pulling on a long white robe. "Oh, yes. I got an earful this morning when she was doing the library about how fine and generous, etc. etc. etc.… Charlie is definitely in a giving mood. That Libby woman mentioned the other day how 'good' he's been to some abused children's shelter. On whose board she sits. Of course. They're all so *appropriate*."

She put her arms around him from behind and they looked out into the scattered pools of sunlight and the shadows stretching toward them from the west. "If we decide to use Atlanta as our primary residence, I intend to rotate through every important non-profit board in town. It shouldn't cost that much. And I'll know how to help them give money a lot more usefully than some of these people who've always had their own."

"Charlie didn't always have his own. He earned it."

She cupped his cheek in her hand and turned his face toward her. She kissed him.

"He didn't earn it without using enlightened self-interest. And he didn't earn the right to revoke your birthright and set himself up as your own personal judge." She paused. "Terry's due at noon?"

"Yeah. I told him Charlie said he'd be back around two. If he gets back early or if anybody else shows up, Terry has stopped by to bring my wallet which I 'accidentally left wrapped in a towel' at the Bar last night."

"So we have safely at least an hour to go through it again and for him to look things over." Sydney sounded confident, even nonchalant, for Chaz's sake, but she was eager for the reassurance of a complete run-through.

"He says he knows the house fairly well, but hasn't been in it for nearly two years. He has to be sure about the keys and alarm. And where he'll need to be."

"And we're sure Charlie doesn't have a gun? It's not something he might advertise."

"I worked the question into a conversation about being isolated out here with such a great house. He said crime really isn't a problem on this stretch of the coast and that if anybody wants to rob him badly enough he doesn't intend to stop them just for a few pieces of art."

"But he's the sort who would register a gun."

"Terry says not even good law-abiding folks always bother in west Florida."

"So no one would particularly question him having one that no one knew about?"

"Apparently not. Hey, if Terry's comfortable with this aspect of things, I have to be. He's the one who's gonna shoot that moron."

A shaft of sunlight found its way among the trees and flooded through the window. The cushion on the window seat suddenly glowed a rich chartreuse, the pale drapes took on a slight cast of silver blue, and the kilim rug beneath their feet bloomed with extravagant hues of lime, rose, and ochre. The light rippled across the house in three distinct waves and as they watched, below and off to one side, it caught some tubs of geraniums which pulsed a thrilling blood red.

Sydney's face lit up, too, like a child's. "We'll have brilliant gardens everywhere we live. One season to the next. And serious gardeners. 'Out there, John, along the end of the vineyard, put in a line of lombardy poplars.' She turned back to look into his eyes and moved one of her hands down along his side. "You can just putter and do some fine detail work. Just enough to break a light sweat. And smell of the earth."

"How the hell does he get geraniums to look like that in this humidity?" Chaz asked rhetorically.

She slowly glided down along his body, her robe open, her breasts brushing his stomach, his thighs. She knelt, and began, with her mouth and hands, almost idly at first and then with slowly mounting purpose, to knead his tensed buttocks and the exceptionally handsome penis that she had always counted among his chief assets.

"I like this house," he said, looking into the full length mirror across the room.

She paused and looked at him in the mirror, her hands still engaged. "I know—it is good. *Remember?* He's *gay*. But we'll have other houses, far superior."

"Mysterious murders don't usually do a lot for market value."

"Men with close to a hundred million dollars don't worry about losing a couple of hundred thousand on one little property."

She didn't talk for several minutes and Chaz continued to stand, slightly arching his back now and then, keeping his eyes on the mirror. He locked his arms behind his head.

◇◇◇

Chaz glanced again at the clock behind Charlie. Four o'clock. Sydney would be back soon. When Charlie had refused her repeated offers of help in the kitchen, she had decided to drive in to Seaside for a couple of magazines she wanted.

He gave Charlie his most ingenuous smile, and answered carefully as if uncertain of the correct or preferred answer. "I think so."

Charlie was finishing up his early prep work at the block table in the center of the large kitchen, and had suddenly asked, almost abruptly, if Chaz thought he had "found his niche" with his work.

Chaz turned from examining the wall that led into the long hall to the dining room. It was crowded with years of framed photographs, apparently of Charlie's friends. "Of course, it's hard to get any business to stand out from the pack. The Atlanta market's huge."

"No," said Charlie, "I mean for you. Does it—*feel* right?"

"Oh, yeah, it's fine."

Charlie wiped his hands. "That'll do for now. How about some iced tea? Lemonade, beer?"

"Tea sounds good," said Chaz.

Charlie poured tall glasses from the pitcher in the refrigerator and the two of them went out into the shady glassed verandah that ran along the east side of the house, under a canopy of tall oaks and pines that bordered the lagoon.

The air conditioning formed condensation here and there along the slightly tinted floor-to-ceiling window. The light that filtered in through the trees was cool, green, unthreatening. It gently teased the color from the flowering plants and the palms and ficuses that seemed to anchor the room's serenity. The two men sat in silence for some time.

"Of course, there's a lot I'd like to do with the business. Ways of expanding. I'm a pretty small fish."

"Well, there's not a thing wrong with that. As long as you like it well enough and actually have some fun with it."

"Right." Chaz finished his tea, rattled the ice, and stood up. "Think I'll have another. How 'bout you?"

Charlie shook his head. "I'm fine." When Chaz returned a few moments later, he smiled and said, "I don't mean to pry. I seem to be developing that unattractive old folks' desperation to see everyone and everything *settled.*"

"No problem," Chaz laughed. "Dad was the same way."

"Do you know how proud he was of you?"

"I think so."

"So am I. And I want you to be happy."

"I am. Very."

"Sydney, your health, good work, some money. You really have everything, Chaz."

Chaz looked over at Charlie with a tight smile of something that might have been modesty. Then he shifted his gaze out through the trees, stirring now in a light breeze, toward the dunes and the sea beyond.

"We *may* be able to have drinks out on the upper porch if this breeze keeps up and the temperature drops just a few degrees," said Charlie, putting his hand on Chaz's shoulder. "I've told everybody seven-thirty. But will you and Sydney join me at seven? I want us to have a few minutes before they come."

# Chapter 31

Sydney had decided that a touch of glamour was in order for the party. After all, it was her wedding party and it would be expected. In fact, she wondered if she had been overdoing just a bit the image of the self-effacing good wife. This was the perfect opportunity to let the gentlewoman restaurateur and the wacky *grande dame* see, without inducing any competitive ire, that, on the appropriate occasion, the girl from Coweta County could clean up with the best of them. She wore her hair up in a classic French twist, and was virginally draped in a gauzy ivory sheath with a go-to-hell emerald green sari lightly brocaded in gold. A long single strand of pearls.

"My, my, look at you!" Charlie kissed her on the cheek when she reached the bottom of the stairs, Chaz close behind. He guided them to one of the sofas in the living room and asked whether they'd prefer champagne or a cocktail. When he returned with flutes of Veuve Cliquot for them and a gin-and-tonic for himself, he didn't sit in the chair nearest them but stood near the mantle. He raised his glass, "To your love and happiness."

"Thank you."

"I want to tell you about one of your wedding gifts," he said. Sydney thought his anticipation made him look ten years younger, a perspective that did much to reinforce her resolve. She smiled at him as she sipped her wine.

"I think you both know how happy Chaz's father was that you two had found one another. We all wish he were here with us tonight and, in a very real sense, of course, he is." He paused. "In some ways, you know, I almost feel as though I'm standing in for him."

"He told me, Chaz, just before his death, about how he'd set up your inheritance trust. I want to add something to that. I'm going to put $300,000 in trust for the two of you. You'll be able to access the principal in ten years. In the meantime, you can decide whether or not to draw down the interest; it'll be just a bit shy of $4,000 per quarter. If you let it reinvest, then…" He grinned. "When we celebrate your tenth anniversary it'll be up to about half a million."

Sydney had reached out and taken Chaz's hand. She now squeezed it. They both said, wonderingly and at once, "*Charlie.*"

"How *kind!*" she exclaimed as, together, they stood.

"That's very generous, Charlie. Thank you," said Chaz.

In a tight circle, they hugged one another. With the detached perspective that always played in her mind like a split screen, Sydney could see the stage picture they made, murmuring the sort of happy endearments that families do when the tokens of love are given and received.

"Ya'll go up and see whether the porch is bearable," said Charlie. "I'll be in the kitchen for a few minutes."

As they climbed the stairs, Sydney giggled in a whisper to Chaz, "I wonder if we're having small potatoes for dinner."

◇◇◇

"It just came to me," mused Libby, standing with Hudson at the far end of the porch. They had been watching the luminescent aftermath of the sunset spill toward them, up the long curve of beach, and now looked back at the others. "The evening at your house, sitting at dinner with Chaz."

Hudson knew the shrewdly meditative look in her eyes. "What?"

"I had the feeling that something about him was reminding me of someone I knew but I couldn't quite *get it* — and now—I do. It's *me* he reminds me of...."

"How?"

"Well, not now, but once. Years ago—long time—you don't even know this—Brad and I went through a bad patch with our marriage and I, very stupidly, started drinking too much. We fixed ourselves up, but by the time we did I found I'd really fallen into a habit. I got some help."

"You think Chaz is drinking too much. Or doing drugs again?"

"No, no, it's not that. I just remember that part of getting myself straightened out included a period at the start—well, I didn't know it at the time but I could look back and see it later—when I was *trying* too hard. I mean, being more concerned with proving to everybody else that I had kicked it than I was with proving it to myself.

"That's what I see." She paused, looking at Hudson. "Maybe that's just a natural part of any process like that."

"Maybe."

◇ ◇ ◇

Hudson had rarely been in a house so evocative of its resident, and this evening he felt especially close to Charlie. He had come in before the others, carrying down an empty hors d'oeuvres tray, and now relished several minutes of walking alone from room to room as the long twilight finally seeped away and the lamps and picture lights came on, the rooms glowing in a whole new incarnation of form and color. A typically eclectic mix of music floated harmoniously in the air. Fats Waller, Andrea Marcovicci, Finzi, Glenn Miller, Gershwin, James Taylor.

Like Charlie, there wasn't a single false note in the character of the entire house, and, like his personality, it was large and rich, even somewhat grand, without being pretentious. It was a house of comfortable, lived-in integrity. The burnished floors and panelling, the handsome art and rugs and fabrics, the impeccable but unobtrusive elegance in every decision, the loving sense of place that bound it all together and to its owner's heart. It was a fine enough home to hold its own anywhere, but here—overlooking the lagoon to the east, the pines and oaks and sassafras and sweet gums to the north and west and, just beyond the high dunes, the long wide sweep of whitest sand beach angling west against the Gulf—Hudson realized, more than ever before, it was the living essence of Charlie Brompton and of old west Florida.

◇◇◇

From time to time, throughout Charlie's supper, Libby's comment crept back through Hudson's thoughts like a shadow, an interference. Charlie had put Sydney and Chaz at the heads of the table. The tone of the evening was celebratory, with toasts to the couple punctuating the succession of courses and the table talk that was, though not trivial, light and carefree.

Why should he, of all people, question the need of someone who had come through a dark night of the soul to "try too hard" simply to be *okay* around other people, to try perhaps even to ingratiate himself with them? With life? Reality? For more than two years, he had grown used to the frequent sensation that he was separated from any group, any conversation, in which he found himself. That unless he forced himself to concentrate very hard and to participate through a sort of automatic response technique he would completely lose even the fragile thread of connection he felt to the rest of the world.

But he realized that that particular invisible wall was not there tonight. He knew that he was as content as he probably had any right to be. He was among friends, Charlie looked very happy, Camilla sat directly across from him, and the food and wine and flowers were superb.

It was Libby's observation, and the conversation a few nights before with Camilla, that, now and again, for moments at a time, pulled him outside the frame. The conversation among the six of them was mostly general, but occasionally it broke into smaller groupings or pairs. Of course, from long practice, he was fairly adroit at putting himself back in what, after all, was a very attractive and congenial picture. Once, however, he snapped back just as Camilla looked up at him.

She asked something about his work, but they were both immediately aware that it was something they had already discussed earlier in the evening. Her lovely, calmly watchful eyes said something else. He couldn't tell if it was a sort of understanding about his lapse that she was passing or a scarcely perceptible signal of her own tenuous engagement with the celebration. Or both.

◇◇◇

A little after ten, they moved into the living room, where the gifts were bestowed along with dessert and a round of champagne followed by coffee.

There was a heavy cut crystal vase from Camilla and a Chippendale silver coffee pot from Libby. Hudson had found a WPA-era survey map of Laurel Beach and environs. He'd had no idea whether their interest in antiques extended to cartography but he knew he'd have been happy with it.

And, in a plain white envelope, there was a check from Charlie. He brought it to them where they sat, side by side, on the sofa. Sydney opened it and looked at a loss for words. Chaz took it and then put his arm around her. They looked at it together. Sydney looked at Charlie, her eyes glistening. She bit her lip quickly and then said, in a hoarse, just audible whisper, "But—this afternoon...."

Charlie grinned. "That was this afternoon. This is now." He paused, adding almost as an afterthought, "Oh, and there's one other thing."

He stood on the polished flagstone hearth, his back to the large fireplace. "I'm not planning on going anywhere soon. But when I do...."

Hudson watched as Charlie gestured gently beyond their circle to the beautiful, capacious, warm, much loved house that held them.

"I want you to have this home. You, and your children."

# Chapter 32

Sunday dawned indeterminately, the air heavy like warm milk.

Hudson and Moon loped through town and out onto the sand. No one was in sight. The lazy filtered sun, slanting along the beach, pulled barely discernible shadows beside them as they ran. The Gulf rose up as a solid mass, unrippled, a grayish celadon, too flat and seemingly transparent to be called silvery or metallic or blue, a filmy texture like waxed paper, rising up heavily and blending on some indistinguishable plane with the pallid midsummer sky. A single gull, low over the water, gave one desolate screech as it labored slowly through the stagnant heat, never landing on the water or sand, until it was absorbed at last, an ethereal nomad, by the rimless wash.

Hudson passed the morning reading, paid a visit to Susie and had a frozen yogurt at the Laurel Market in the early afternoon, and then tried to clear his mind of everything but work.

He didn't know what else to do with himself.

Or with anything else in the world.

He forced himself to edit two articles.

Every word now seemed cast in the light of his unease, freighted and fraught, tinged with forebodings.

Indecipherable moral imperatives, inscrutable directives.

# Evil Under the Sun
## *Breakdown* is an elegant, well-acted thriller

*Breakdown* comes just in time to give us all some *serious* second thoughts about summer road trips. Driving through the expansively lonely, other-worldly beauty of the high Southwestern desert, on their way cross-country from Boston to a new home and new jobs in San Diego, a married couple, Jeff and Amy Taylor (Kurt Russell and Kathleen Quinlan), end up in the middle of nowhere when their deluxe SUV grinds to a halt.

A mechanical malfunction that leaves you stranded alone in the desert under a broiling sun can be serious business. It is a measure of *Breakdown*'s powerful assurance as a thriller that we scarcely have time to register this reasonable daylight concern before it proves to be merely the dangling latch on a door that opens, as in a nightmare, to another door, and then, faster and faster, another and another, a yawning chasm of constantly escalating paranoia, terror, and unreasoning evil.

In his first theatrical release, director Jonathan Mostow, who co-wrote the script with Sam Montgomery, has melded several strong elements into an elegantly crafted film with a deceptively simple structure.

The through-line of the story is a tried and true formula: Jeff waits with the Jeep while the seemingly kind driver (J.T. Walsh) of an 18-wheeler gives Amy a lift to the nearest roadside diner. Amy does not return. A conspiracy of bad guys begins to emerge in the parched, desolate landscape, at first like a mirage, but eventually becoming an unrelenting, horrific reality. Jeff must figure out what's going on, save himself, and find Amy.

It is *how Breakdown* handles its ordinary man in extraordinary circumstances, a favorite premise in Hitchcock's thrillers, that sustains the film's unsettling psychological suspense. It's *why* the bad guys are bad, *how* the arid landscape is hostile, *why* the situation defies understanding, and *how* the protagonist (an average, peaceable guy who wears khakis and a polo shirt) becomes a quick-witted, death-defying hero, that give the film its edge. It has the rush of a ghost story expertly told late at night by a campfire, a breathless, headlong freefall through anxiety without a ledge to grip.

Basil Poledouris' music, eerie synthesized staccatos that seem to skitter and echo around the desert rock formations, reinforces the director's frequent use of deep focus and sweeping aerial shots which induce a sense of vertigo to match the hero's panic.

*Breakdown*'s atmospherics provide resonant context for the actors. Without divulging too much about the wonderful J.T. Walsh's role and his band of bad guys, let's just say that his dead-eyed malevolence has never been employed to more chilling effect. His character and his fellow brigands haunt the desert landscape like a miasma of inchoate evil, all the more disturbing because they tap into our escalating societal fear of the gulf between haves and have-nots that produces children who shoot one another over a pair of sneakers and increasing numbers of people who do harm for very little reason and without any shred of recognizable human compunction. (The Tates' only crime is that they have a new vehicle with leather seats and a CD player and, though only middle-income folk, are *perceived* as having money.) These bad guys also share some frightening identity factors with the tunnel-visioned paranoia that nurtures the proliferation of extreme right-wing organizations.

Kurt Russell gives what may be the most compelling performance of his career to date. It's a big role—Jeff is onscreen for most of the film's two-hour duration—and Russell carries it very well, giving real emotional urgency to the character's progression from bewilderment to panic and, eventually, fury.

He is in proud company here. Like Jimmy Stewart

(in *Rear Window, The Man Who Knew Too Much,* and *Vertigo*), Cary Grant (in *North by Northwest*), and Henry Fonda (in *The Wrong Man*), his Jeff Taylor is the sort of Everyman character Hitchcock utilized to ensure audience empathy with the hero's baffling predicament, and Russell has the goods. Separated from his wife, he has the abject lostness of a little boy; forced into survival tactics, he has a ferocity that surprises even himself. The role dually functions as the psychological catalyst for the film's mounting suspense and as the emotional catalyst for the audience's pity, terror, and rage. And the range of Russell's performance keeps it all on the boil.

At six-thirty, Charlie and Hudson met at the tennis club in Seaside to play a few sets.

Charlie had a fairly decent game and Hudson had warned him that not only was he out of practice but that he'd never been any good to begin with. "My idea of a tennis match is a Grand Slam event on television. It's really the only sport I like to watch." But they had a good time, Charlie serving and volleying at a pace that gave Hudson a good workout and very little embarrassment. They had the courts practically to themselves anyway. By late afternoon, the clouds had begun strafing in from the west and the wind was rising. They knocked off a few minutes before eight, just as the hot rain began to plaster their already soaked shirts.

They discussed whether to have a beer or something to eat but decided that after the late hour and abundant champagne of the night before, showers and an early evening at home were probably in order for both of them.

"At least we've gotten out here and mortified our flesh a little bit," laughed Charlie as he waved and drove away.

# Chapter 33

At 11:20 the phone rang. Charlie had just watched a rental movie, one of Hudson's recommendations, and gone into the kitchen to put away a few things.

"You said you never go to bed before midnight. I hope you meant that. The time got away from us. We went out to eat late." It was Chaz. They had left around noon to make the two-hour drive to Tallahassee. Sydney had some "research to do in the university library" for one of her video projects.

"I was just on my way upstairs."

"Hi, Charlie!" Sydney had taken the phone.

"Did you get what you needed at the library?"

"Some, not all. But it was worth the trip. I got enough to know what to look for when I get back to Atlanta."

"How's that bed-and-breakfast?"

"Oh. They were booked. We're at some—" she laughed, "no-tell motel."

Chaz got back on. "Well, we won't keep you up. We'll probably be in around four or five tomorrow." Sydney said something inaudible. "Sydney says to tell you that we're still pinching ourselves about our wedding gifts."

"Well, they're true. I love you both."

"We love you."

"Good night. See you tomorrow afternoon."

◇◇◇

He went out on the upper porch. Down at the seaward end, he closed and fastened the shutters that sometimes tended to slap in high winds. The storm had been advancing some pretty stiff waves of squall lines and he had seen on the Weather Channel that the worst was still to come.

Once he got into bed, fatigue took him. He managed only to flip through the week's *New Yorker*, untouched since its arrival three days before, to see what he might want to come back to.

He turned out the light and lay back to enjoy the sound of the wind in the trees, but he scarcely managed to look at the clock before his eyes closed.

11:40.

◇◇◇

Terry Main moved methodically, as though on a hike, as though his nerves were soothed by another round of slashing rain. He slogged along the overgrown and almost never used path. Even if the oversized shoes he wore were leaving traces of his passage through the swampy underbrush, they certainly wouldn't be anything but a soggy, nebulous hint. A dog perhaps, a raccoon.

Deep in his pocket, under the protection of his poncho, was the first draft of Michael's letter. In the pack on his back, two towels, dry shorts, tee shirt, socks, gloves, and another pair of running shoes two sizes larger than his own. The .380 Magnum. A couple of hundred or so yards behind him, through the dense woods and scrub that ringed the lagoon, his truck sat in a pull-in off 26-A overhung with oaks and nearly obscured by tall sawgrass. If the worst happened, he would say that in his haste to get over to Charlie's he had forgotten that he needed gas. Had run out. Did the best he could trying to find his way through the woods on the old path that only a few locals knew about and even fewer ever used.

If everything went according to plan, he'd come back and get the ancient gas can he'd left buried under the top layer of garbage in a dumpster fifty yards down a nearby dead-end dirt road.

◇◇◇

Small garden lanterns lined the long drive that circled at the front door and threaded west through the trees, but they provided only dull nubs of light every few yards in the thrashing wet darkness. Otherwise, there were, as usual, just the two lights on either side of the door and, around back on the lagoon side, two lights by the French doors into the solarium.

He looked in a side window that gave a view through the hall into the kitchen. Dark. He looked in another near the back corner. The dining room and, beyond, a long slice of the living room. Except for one small lamp near the foot of the stairs, dark. As usual, drapes not closed in the second floor bedrooms. No visible light anywhere on the second floor. No reading light from the master bedroom. He looked at his watch.

12:40.

Kneeling down behind a tall hibiscus, the downpour sheeting off the eaves of the house inches from his face, he waited another three or four minutes, listening. Only the choked sob of the wind in the pines and the wild eddies of tropical rain.

Then he took the key from his pocket and made his way to the French doors.

◇◇◇

They had arranged two minor flukes with the alarm system, several days apart. The second incident, just yesterday, had prompted a call for service, scheduled first thing Monday morning.

He gently opened the door. There was no zone-sensor beep. He found the control panel down along the wall, behind the areca palm. He double-checked everything. When Charlie, who knew little about the system's finer points, set it, it would have appeared to be in order. But his wiring job yesterday afternoon, which he had explained and they had re-checked before leaving for Tallahassee, would have rendered it useless.

He got out of his sodden shoes and clothing, stuffed them into the small backpack, and pulled on the dry ones. With the first towel he carefully mopped up the floor around himself and then the wet trail to the alarm panel. He used the other to dry his hair, face, and arms.

Then he stood, without moving, listening, for three or four minutes.

◇◇◇

The heavy padded socks made the large shoes manageable. He kept to the hardwood floors, off the rugs, hugging the walls, risking a potential squeak rather than a footprint. He wanted to keep it neat. He didn't want the police looking for an accomplice, size twelve shoe or otherwise. And the storm provided good sound cover. He took one step at a time, stopping after each step for a full half-minute to listen. The stairs were the biggest problem. The best option was to the right side of the runner, but the fourth and eleventh steps were dicey.

By the time he reached the long gallery that ran the length of the second floor, he was sweating profusely despite the cool air on his still damp hair.

1:00.

A large Palladian window at the end of the hall behind him allowed only the barest illumination from the porch lights below, evanescent wisps of radiance that managed to work their way up like wraiths around the portico, through the rain and tossing shrubbery.

He inched his way toward the open door of the master bedroom. A flash of lightning transformed the gallery into a black-and-white photograph that hung before his eyes even when, after a split second, the darkness returned. He froze. Then he backed into the guest room and waited for one minute, two minutes. He re-emerged. Listened. There was no sound, no light, from the master bedroom.

He made the last remaining feet to the door without breathing. He stood on the sill, lining up the bed with one eye. Half of his face, half of his body, one foot still outside the frame of the door.

The body in the bed did not move. Between the sighs of wind and rain, there came the sound of heavy, regular breathing.

He stepped back without a sound and glided diagonally across the wide hall to the walk-in linen closet and a slight, welcome scent of WD-40. The louvered door opened silently and he went in.

In the darkness, he regulated his breath, and waited. The pale glow of lightning seeped less and less frequently under the door and along its horizontal louvers, and the ragged rasps of thunder were more distant. There was just the sound of a silent sleeping house and the steady, calming murmur of the rain.

1:05.

Although it felt like two hours, he had been in the house for twenty minutes, In no more than another thirty, he wanted to be driving home.

With his gloved left index finger he counted the louvers in the top panel of the door. At the twenty-third, just at his eye level, he gently lifted. The slanted inch-wide wooden slat moved. No more than half an inch. Just enough for an uninterrupted view down the hall and into the master bedroom.

He removed the glove. With his right hand, he clicked the safety.

When the time came it would come instantaneously.

He flexed the muscles in his arms and hands.

He waited.

1:29.

A blunted sound, distant, perhaps downstairs, and, minutes later, the slow elastic creak of a yielding stair.

Then, nothing.

1:35.

A shadow, discernible only to eyes adjusted to the darkness, began to pulse, inch by inch along the floor from the right of the closet. Seconds later, Michael came abreast of the door, one foot testing each step of the way. His right hand lifted forward just above waist level, the gun poised.

There were two hushed exhalations of breath. Two words, repeated, that would have been inaudible beyond a few inches. "Oh, Jesus. Oh, Jesus."

He moved on, nearing the bedroom door, his back now to the closet. He hovered only a minute in the doorway and then stepped softly into the room. He took three quick steps toward the bed, leveled his arm, and went momentarily out of Terry's field of vision.

◇◇◇

Terry pushed outward with his left hand, gun raised in his right, and was already at the bedroom door as he heard the shot explode. He waited until Michael began to turn toward him and fired twice from less than ten feet. The first shot tore into his stomach and the second took the body on over, backward, from the impact to the chest.

Charlie lay, his left arm flung back, his lead lolling foolishly off the side of the bed, his mouth agape. The top of the sheet was a creeping dark stain. His eyes stared, unseeing, at a point just over Terry's shoulder.

Terry forced himself to move. The blood was already beginning to seethe up from Michael's body and flow onto the rug. He pulled on the gloves and took the letter from the pants pocket. He lay it over to one side, stained but legible. He lifted the shoulders, angling the torso and legs slightly toward the bed.

The quiet was enormous, almost overwhelming. Time itself seemed to fall into the gaping silence, as if ceasing to exist.

But it hadn't ceased to exist because just as he finished arranging the body, there was a next thing and the next thing was not what he'd planned. The next thing was the faraway but unmistakable sound of a car, beyond the lessening rain, perhaps as far as the little road at the end of the long winding drive.

Perhaps already somewhere along the drive.

◇◇◇

He rushed to the bed and looked down. The eyes gawked senselessly past him, enameled, opaque. There was no pulse.

He wiped the gun one more time and then folded it into the lifeless right hand.

He walked back to Michael, checked the angle of trajectory from the bed, adjusted the body slightly, looked again, and then flew down the stairs, avoiding the rugs and the traces of water and muck from Michael's shoes. By the back doors, he stood for a minute, fighting to control his ragged breathing enough to listen.

The sound of the car, almost certainly out on the little-traveled road a hundred and fifty yards from the house, was fading into the rain.

Close enough.

In the dim light from the porch lanterns he took a last look down the shadowy hall to the dining room. He could just make out one end of the long mahogany table where, a couple of times, two, three years ago, he had been a part of Charlie's parties.

As he put his hand on the door to let himself out, he saw at his feet the wet paper bag, its top rolled down, creased and wrinkled. Knowing what he would find, he opened it. A jagged hunk of red cedar. A new tin of Spice Islands marjoram. A spool of red thread. A bowl. The carcass of a dead sparrow. Just outside the door, on the broad top step under the overhang, sat an old rusted cage that looked as though it came from a salvage shop. A small sandpiper cheeped in confusion, jerking its head from one side to the other, apparently terrified from the rough trek and by the water rushing down inches from its prison.

He set it just inside the door.

◇◇◇

The big shoes took him down to the edge of the lagoon. He went back the way he had come, wading knee-deep in the shallows for more than a hundred yards along the shoreline. To a tall live oak pine with its roots gnarling into the water and a broken lower branch. Another fifty yards through bruising, clawing undergrowth and sinkholes, and he picked up the old path. For long stretches, hardly any better.

He made sure no other errant vehicles were plying the last of the storm, and crossed the highway. He pulled the gas can from the forgotten dump, fed a gallon into the truck, and began to drive.

He made a quick sidetrack from 26-A onto the road that meandered through the woods to Charlie's drive. Only because he knew where to look, he saw Michael's truck, obscured by a wall of scrub oak, fifty yards from the entry to the drive. He'd walked straight up the drive as planned, and was going to take the time afterward for his "ritual." Ignorance and hatred, ignited by even the slightest touch of madness, could make for an unwavering flame of devotion. And the devout do nothing better than follow instruction.

He was home at 2:25.

It hadn't been perfect. Too rushed at the end. Who could have expected anybody to drive along that road in the middle of the night in a storm?

But nothing had really gone wrong.

Nothing that would suggest two people had been involved. Nothing obvious. And certainly nothing to implicate *him*.

# Chapter 34

Hudson had fallen asleep early on the sofa. One hand still lay on the crossword puzzle book, the top of which had come to rest on his chin.

Startled, he reached out and grabbed the phone in the other hand and was saying hello before it had become clear to him where he was, or why or when.

The aspirated whispering voice sounded like a small child or perhaps a very old person.

"Huh…duh."

Silence.

"C…cuh…come."

Silence. Then a muffled rattle.

"Charlie?"

Silence.

"Charlie?"

◇◇◇

He had made it to the house in less than ten minutes, slaloming down the drive just behind a county police car. The two officers made him wait in the Highlander. Five minutes. Ten. Fifteen. An emergency medical vehicle arrived and the man and woman went in, carrying a stretcher and a crash kit.

One of the officers jogged back through the rain. Hudson slid the window down.

"What was that name again, sir?"

"Hudson DeForest."

"Friend of Mr. Brompton?"

"Yes."

"I'm afraid he's been shot. Looks maybe like a burglar, we don't know." He paused. "It's pretty bad."

"Is he *alive?*"

"Just barely. He must have regained consciousness for a moment and hit a couple of his speed dials. His hand was near the phone. They'll be taking him to the emergency room at St. Andrews in Panama City. Any family we should call?"

All Hudson could think of for the moment was how pleased he was that Charlie had added him to his speed dial list. He could guess the names his fingers had missed. Libby. Camilla.

Seconds passed before he remembered Chaz and Sydney. "Only the son of a cousin. He and his wife are staying here from Atlanta for a couple of weeks, but they're in Tallahassee tonight. They're due tomorrow…I mean, this afternoon."

"You know where they're staying?"

"No."

They were bringing the stretcher out. He couldn't see Charlie's face.

"May I go with him in the ambulance?"

The officer went over and spoke briefly to the EMS people as they got the stretcher into the ambulance. The woman looked over at Hudson. The officer came back. The rain was a drizzle now, but it still poured in rivulets from his cap.

"They don't know that he's gonna make it to the ER." He locked his eyes on Hudson's. "It's bad. You can ride in the back with him. Just don't get in their way."

◇◇◇

At noon, Camilla took the job of waiting for Chaz and Sydney. Naturally, she would rather have been at the hospital with Hudson and Libby, but they decided that one of them needed to be at the house when they arrived.

By daybreak, the county sheriff's office had already tentatively ID'd the shooter, matching the tone and content of the letter with the ATF composite sketch. Three local investigators, under the direction of a team of four ATF agents, combed the house and grounds.

A county policeman stood at the entry to the drive, lifting the yellow crime scene tape that stretched between two stanchions only when an official vehicle entered or left. Trying to read, occasionally turning on the radio, Camilla waited in her car for nearly four hours. Occasionally, the officer would come over and make polite conversation. At one point, she thought she would have to make a run to the restroom at the Blue Bar. She told him she didn't want to leave even for ten minutes. They might come. He got permission from one of the agents for her to use the john in the ATF mobile unit. The agent accompanied her and stood just outside the small compartment.

The plan was to take them first to the hospital. Hudson would put them up in his guestroom until the agents allowed them back in the house. It might be, they were told, as long as three or four days.

Later they would tell one another that they'd each had to fight a gut-level rage of resentment. They wanted to be near Charlie, even though there was nothing to do but go in one at a time, once an hour for only a moment, to look at him—and the ICU waiting room was a claustrophobic nightmare.

But, at the time, looking out for these two people with whom none of them had been able to grow comfortable seemed something they could do, if only indirectly, for him.

Camilla watched the lovely home, crawling now with strangers. The house that someday—soon?—would belong to Chaz and Sydney Cullen.

The rental car slowed to a crawl. Before it came to a stop behind her, Camilla was out of her car. She saw Chaz pull up on the brake and both doors opened at once, the engine still running. He started forward. "Charlie!" Sydney hung a step behind.

"He's in the hospital," said Camilla. She started to reach out and take his hand or perhaps touch his arm or shoulder. But she did not.

Their faces looked as though the bones and muscles had melted. Their eyes were blank.

On the thirty-minute drive to Panama City she told them what, at that point, was known. Chaz sat in back, wild-eyed, asking questions. Sydney asked only one or two. Otherwise, she did not speak. Twice, she half-turned and reached her hand back between the seats to hold Chaz's hand. Several times she put her fingers to the corners of her brimming eyes as she stared, seemingly numb, out the window.

◇◇◇

The bullet had hit Charlie just right of his sternum. He had probably just raised up and turned toward the man.

He went into surgery early in the afternoon. When the surgeon came out three hours later, the best he could muster for Hudson and Libby was a tight-lipped compassion. He spoke softly. "*That* went well. We were able to do what we most needed to do. But we don't know at this point. The prognosis is uncertain. Your friend sustained an enormously traumatic injury."

One lung was collapsed, they'd removed bone splinters from his severely bruised upper stomach wall, he was on a respirator and hooked to a complex system of IVs. His heart was uninjured but functioning erratically, throwing dangerously high v-tach waves. If the medication didn't level the rate, stroke was an imminent risk.

Chaz took the next three-minute visit and, an hour later, Sydney the next. They sat in the waiting room tentatively, spent most of their time pacing the halls and going for coffee.

Hudson, Libby, and Camilla looked up from their books and magazines to one another and back. For most of that evening and throughout the night, they stayed close by one another, reading or trying to. When the particularly disagreeable family that occasionally dominated the waiting room became too oppressive, they, too, walked. On these occasions they grappled with their inability to believe what had happened.

And the shared feeling that Chaz and Sydney, for some reason, didn't deserve turns in the ICU. That the three of them should have those additional little windows of time, to hold Charlie's hand, to tell him to come back.

Once, around four in the morning, the three of them went into the small chapel on the floor above. It was dim and quiet and they sat without talking for several minutes.

Hudson felt the current of their fear and their questions.

And an uneasy sense of jealous, outraged vigilance.

# Chapter 35

At noon Sydney leaned into the pay phone stall in the food court of the huge outlet mall in Destin. She picked up on the first ring.

Terry's voice. "*Marcia?*"

"Hi," said Sydney, keeping an eye and an ear on the two stalls to her right. "I've just dropped the guys off at J. Crew. Got us a twelve-forty-five tee time."

"How are things?"

"No change. Hanging by a thread."

"Well, I'll see you there at twelve-forty-five. You remember the directions?"

"Yes."

◇◇◇

Forty minutes later, in the busy parking lot of a supermarket in Fort Walton, Terry left his vehicle, walked over, and got into Sydney's.

"I have to be back in Laurel half an hour ago," she said, her voice threatening to break in fury. "I can't be missing in action." She paused. "So, now what?"

"We have to finish the job."

"Your job."

"I'm telling you there was no pulse, no breath."

"Well, there may not be one for long—but the point is, there still *is!*"

Terry spoke with forceful calm, giving each word equal weight. "We are in this together. We were, we are, and we always will be. And you know we want to get it right."

She nodded, even calmer now than he. "Yes. Can you be absolutely certain that he didn't see you?"

"Don't you think that's what's keeping me awake? But, no, he couldn't have. For all intents and purposes he was dead."

"Well, he came to enough to pick up the telephone and drag it to his mouth."

"For the ninety seconds I was in that room he wasn't conscious. I know he wasn't."

"You'd better hope so."

"So had you. What chance are they giving him?"

"They don't know or won't say."

"We have to make sure he doesn't come out of the coma."

"We've thought about that. I'm sure you have. We know who has to do it. The most you can do is pay a visit or two. We're the ones who are there on a regular basis." She looked at him dismissively. "You fucked it up but you'll still get your five million. As you say, there's no turning back now." She looked into the rearview mirror. The skin around her eyes was puffy and ashen from lack of sleep, but the eyes were bright.

"We'll do it all right. And we'll do it soon. He'll simply stop breathing. They have a shunt in his esophagus. Nobody'll think twice about it."

◇◇◇

The next day he was moved to a private room in the intensive care unit. There was no major change. The vital signs had improved slightly. The medication was helping his heart rate. But not enough.

Hudson, Libby, Camilla, Sydney, and Chaz were on a rotation of four hours, with Fentry and Victor each taking two-hour shifts. Each of them was now allowed to sit beside him for fifteen minutes of every hour.

◇◇◇

In the late afternoon, Chaz and Sydney talked quietly in the guestroom at Hudson's cottage. Moon had apparently decided that if it was okay with Hudson that these people had been here twice now when Hudson was not, and without acknowledging him with even a cursory pat on the head, it must be okay, and had sauntered off for a nap.

Hudson was at the hospital. They were trying, futilely, to rest.

"We're going to split an Ambien," said Sydney, reaching for the glass of water by the lamp. "We *have* to get a few hours of sleep. We *have* to be able to think." Chaz looked her and reached out to put his hand on her thigh, as if to make sure she was really there. There had never been any question which of them would do it, but he asked, "Are you sure you're okay with it?"

"Yes. I have to be. For us." She fished the pill from her bag. "Now take this and let me sleep. He's due back around eleven or twelve. I'll get you up."

◇◇◇

Moon, too, had been unable to rest. He wagged slowly back up the hall, looked into Hudson's empty bedroom, and then at the closed door down the passageway. He approached it slowly, nosing the air, his eyes quizzical. He turned and went halfway back to Hudson's room. As if confused and not knowing what else to do, he lowered himself to the floor. He lay his head on his paws for a few minutes, watching the closed door. Then he roused himself again.

For some time he wandered circuitously, down the long hall, around the great room to the front door, and then back again.

# Chapter 36

Hudson sat and stared, one hand idling along Moon's head and neck, the other holding a scotch. The small lamp beside him gave the only light in the room and without really seeing it he looked at the wan reflection of his head and upper body in the black windows. He wore only an old thin pair of gym shorts; his hair was still damp from the shower.

When he had come in a half-hour before, he had been hot and tired, covered with that layer of clammy film that is the unique memento of airplanes and hospitals. He was glad to have the cottage and its middle-of-the-night cool quietness to himself. Even Olive had given a rare indication that this was the preferred state of affairs, choosing the ottoman instead of the sofa, dozing close to his feet.

They had, as before, left a note. Sydney had written:

*10:45*
*We're leaving now. Victor came by and so did Susie, so we're well-stocked. And Fentry must have spread the word to friends—the phone didn't ring and no one came by. We slept nearly six hours!*

*Please eat something. And please get as much sleep as you can.*
*S & C*

Below, Chaz had added:

*Susie gave us her number so we can get to you if we
need you.*
*Why not take the phone off the hook?*

At seven-thirty, Charlie had been taken off the respirator by
the physician in charge and seemed to be breathing peacefully.
But he had not regained consciousness and with every hour
that he did not the odds that he ever would were ebbing. The
doctors still weren't committing themselves to much. "His vital
signs continue to strengthen, there's no apparent brain damage,
and those are good signs…but we just can't know. The situation
is grave. We can only wait."

He didn't know whether to interpret the day's other new
development as positive or simply innocuous: they were now
allowed to sit beside him around the clock. When he'd arrived
for his shift, before he had even entered the room, he'd heard
the low tones of Libby's marvelous voice, tinged with fatigue
but still vibrant by most standards. She sat as close to Charlie
as possible. Awkwardly, probably very uncomfortably, she balanced a large book against the edge of the bed with one hand
and with the other held Charlie's hand. As he came in Hudson
could see that she was gently squeezing for emphasis. She looked
up over her reading glasses and tilted the book. *The Wind in the
Willows.* She smiled. "I really didn't know what to bring. But I
always liked it."

◇◇◇

Hudson *did* need to get as much sleep as he could. The shapeless
present tense, like some dull mysterious pain, kept expanding
unpredictably. He'd probably had a total of about six or seven
hours in the last seventy-two. His concentration hadn't been
reliable on the drive home.

There had been no time for sleep. The drive time to the
hospital was nearly an hour each way, and when he hadn't been
at the hospital, he'd been interviewed and re-interviewed by the
ATF people and the local investigators.

They all had. Actually, it had given him and Libby and Camilla something do in the endless agonizing hours. They compared notes. It seemed no more real than Charlie lying near death, but it provided at least some focus and at least the illusion that they weren't merely drowning in helplessness.

The investigators seemed increasingly accepting of the fact that Charlie had been shot by Mark DeWayne Lukerson, a twisted venomous zealot who was wanted for bombing a family planning clinic in South Carolina. He had been renting a room in a boarding house in Pensacola for several months and working as a painter. The letter at the scene seemed to fit his m.o. and the handwriting was a match.

They knew from Terry Main that he had done a small painting job almost five months earlier at the Blue Bar. He was a replacement for the regulars who had just moved away and he came with references. Main suggested they also talk with the Alburtys on Potero. He'd done their garage. They were away and had only had one five-minute conversation with him. Main had been busy at the time and spoken to him only twice, ten minutes if that. The guy had certainly given no indication of knowing Charlie, but he did make one or two weird comments about politics and the big revival in Pensacola which, Terry said, would be reason enough not to have hired him again.

But that was more than four months ago and he hadn't been heard of since. Why he had the idea that Charlie was a hard-core porno producer was still anyone's guess, but then why did people like Lukerson think that the Holocaust never happened or that Oprah Winfrey was the Anti-Christ?

Charlie had either heard Lukerson coming down the hall, had his gun ready, lain still, and tried to shoot first, or, more likely, heard something only in time to get it out of the drawer. In either case, both men apparently fired at the exact same moment. Libby was just a bit surprised that Charlie had kept a gun, an unregistered one. But it really wasn't very unusual in the area. Between them, she and Camilla knew three or four other people who did, including Brad, who had remembered to bother with the paperwork only to avoid even the slightest chance of embarrassment when a cousin had been elected to the state legislature.

◇◇◇

But instead of taking any satisfaction from the official satisfaction, Hudson felt that things were hurtling out of control. Something was wrong and he didn't know what it was and every step forward seemed less like progress than a frustration, adding up to nothing, leading nowhere.

He needed to sleep but he couldn't let go of some unformed idea that he needed to sit up and stay awake until he got a handle on something. Knew something. They had worked out this schedule so that they could each get at least some rest. That made sense, was necessary. Fentry, along with Camilla's assistant, was covering the 26-A. Other than some reading, Hudson hadn't thought about work. But he was uneasy with the other result of the rotation. If you weren't with Charlie, you were trying to sleep. They were passing like ships in the night. Out of touch. The circle broken.

It was eleven-fifty. If he got to bed before one, he could still get a good night's sleep.

He sat in a stupor of weariness so profound that he couldn't feel his body, but his mind paced like a wild beast. Utterly still, his breath even and light, he grew more and more detached from the reflection of the man in the window and imagined as a beast indeed whatever it was that comprised the invisible self, out in the night beyond, ranging farther and faster, now beside Charlie's inert form, now at the dinner party, Camilla across the table, silver gleaming in candlelight and Sydney and Chaz gleaming from their ends of the table, now running on the beach toward a vague and lowering horizon in the hot milk-white morning. Running. Running.

Just at the moment the beast circled back to lift him by his guts on a gorge of anger, he fell asleep.

◇◇◇

He was watching a preview of a film, as he sometimes did, on a Saturday morning. He sat near the back of the theatre, alone in the dark. He had stopped at a Starbucks on the way and held a large cup of black coffee.

In the scene in the film, a teacher was talking with a high school class about *The Great Gatsby*. The teacher was animated, intense, and the students were enthralled, questioning her and one another in vigorous discussion. She had voguishly short, spiky, red hair and wore thin wire-rimmed glasses. Her voice, however, was Libby's voice, throaty, rich, burnished. And Hudson recognized what she was saying about the novel, the lines that came out in Libby's voice, as exact phrases *he* had spoken.

But the teacher was Sydney Cullen.

Something at the back of the classroom caught her eye and she stopped talking. The principal and her associate had entered the room. Kate and Camilla. The students turned as the associate came forward along the outer row of desks. The principal spoke calmly but authoritatively from the back. "I'm sorry, but we're having something like a practice fire drill and we need to move quickly and silently to the front hallway downstairs. We're in no danger, but I want you to come now. Don't worry with your things. You can get them later. Quickly now." She gestured to those students nearest her and they began to filing out.

The teacher remained composed. She and the associate principal followed the last students to the back.

The principal put her hand on the teacher's upper arm. "There's been an accident."

As though in a seizure, the teacher bent nearly double toward the floor. The two women reached down to support her as her limp body jolted with shuddering sobs.

The camera moved in for a close-up. A grimace dissolving in tears. Strands of red hair plastered on the cheek. Glasses dangling madly from one ear.

The screen went black and the sound system sputtered into silence.

He turned to look up at the projection booth but apparently there was no one there.

◇◇◇

Though it felt as if he'd been asleep for hours, it had only been minutes. His legs were like cement when he stood up, but he got his bearings and headed over to the kitchen where he poured out a second small scotch and grabbed an ice cube.

He walked down the hall and into the guestroom. He turned on the bedside lamp. He looked first in the waste can near the desk and then in the one in the bathroom. There were several wadded tissues in each. He opened the closet door and looked at the few things they had brought. He opened the overnight case and the shoulder bag they'd had with them when they'd come back from Tallahassee. In the bathroom again he went through her small beaded cosmetics bag and his Moroccan leather dop kit.

He looked in the mirror. It was that haggard man in the middle of the night again. The brow furrowed, green eyes streaked with red and sagging in pinched sacks of bruised-looking skin, the hair a tangle of reddish brown and grey. The man he'd thought had gone away.

He leaned forward, his arms on either side of the sink. His face was only inches from the glass but he was blind with the old upsurge of dank emotions. What seemed an inescapable pain that kept compounding. With all the not-knowing of life. The not being able ever to do enough. With everyone going away and leaving him. With Kate. With Charlie. With fearing that that he would never want to reach out to anyone ever again and knowing that if he ever did he would be afraid to.

◇◇◇

The mirror receded even farther and for the millionth time he saw Kate's face. That early spring morning more than two years before that had become a fixed and eternal moment. Sitting beside him on the loveseat that flanked the small round table in the breakfast room. Talking idly about something in the paper.

Laughing a low morning laugh. He had gotten up for more coffee. Only steps away. When he turned back, she had a look of astonishment on her face. She opened her lips as if to speak but instead suddenly sagged and fell forward heavily. Kneeling beside her, he looked up into her face. All in a handful of seconds.

But, already, she was no longer there. A small rivulet of blood inched from the crevice of her lip. Her jaw had hit the edge of the table. He called 911 and while he waited, rocking her, looking into her sightless eyes he had said over and over and over, Oh, sweetie, you've hurt your lip, your beautiful lip, your lip, your lip....

The paramedics were probably on the scene within eight or nine minutes, but those minutes had already become eternity. He propped her gently against the sofa to let them in and told her he would be back in a second. But he knew that when they reentered that room she would not be there. An aneurysm, he would later learn. No pain, the doctor assured him. Immediate. It didn't matter. Her beautiful lip was bleeding, Kate's lip was bleeding. The doctor. Aneurysm. Immediate. All that would come and go. Come and go.

But her beautiful lip was bleeding. Her lip would always be bleeding...

◇◇◇

His face slowly swam back into view.

When it did he no longer saw a face of grief but one of rage. Just as the tears welled suddenly from his staring eyes, toppled over the red bottom lids, and coursed down to the corners of his lips, he thought suddenly of Sydney, of how, on entering Charlie's room during the past few days, he had often found her with her eyes glistening with tears. Never actually in the act of crying. Never an obvious show, never an overtly manipulative performance—but, frequently, the suggestion of *having* cried.

That strained, reddish look in the whites of eyes that have been staring, held open, for awhile. Without blinking.

In an instant he was crouching beside the waste can. He couldn't believe it—and neither could Moon, who had awakened and now joined him—but he was pulling out the tissues, examining each one closely. There were seven or eight. Most of them were still slightly damp. But there was no sign of anything like makeup. Or mucus. He lifted each one close to his nostrils and breathed deeply, over and over again.

He went out to the waste can by the desk and did the same thing.

Of course he couldn't be sure.

But he knew something about tears. And in the slight, rather uniform moistness that remained in the wadded tissues there didn't seem to be the faintest trace of salt.

He set the alarm for six.

# Chapter 37

"We need to talk," he said to Libby. "Now. I wanted to call last night but knew you needed the sleep."

"Same here, I'm just pouring coffee and was about to reach for the phone."

"They'll be here within the hour. I'm calling Camilla and will be right over."

◇◇◇

By seven-thirty they had been through one pot of strong coffee, and were working on another of decaffeinated, along with an assortment of fruit, Susie's oatmeal cookies, and Victor's cold quiche Lorraine. They sat in various chairs, they moved around, they went onto the screened porch and came back in. Their few hours of rest had only fueled their sense of frustration, and they fell onto the food and coffee as though girding for a fight.

They had been impressed and rather amazed at Hudson's account of his odd late-night search but not, in the end, surprised.

"I have tried over and over to tell myself that they're just shallow and that *that's* why we just don't like them," said Libby. "At first I found myself fighting some feeling of prejudice about Chaz. I thought it was an unfair expectation. Peter Cullen was such a lovely man and he and Charlie cared deeply for one another."

"All I can tell you," said Hudson, "is that I think she is a rare actress, but that she *is* an actress, and that she's acting now."

*But why? For what reason?*

"They have their lives before them, shallow or not," he reasoned aloud. "Chaz has kicked his addiction problems, they apparently love one another, have decent incomes, have some decent sort of inheritance no doubt from Chaz's father, and were just given some substantial monetary gift by Charlie and the promise of one of the best houses on the Gulf Coast."

◇◇◇

In the course of their conversation, Camilla seemed to Hudson to have become somewhat withdrawn and, more than simply fatigued, preoccupied. When she finally spoke again, she reminded him of himself at midnight, her thoughts and her voice disconnected from her body. She was oblivious of the coffee cup she had been holding poised before her for the past three or four minutes.

"There's just the one computer in the office," she said quietly. I'm about to order a new one. Charlie took the old one home." She smiled. "You know he went hi-tech kicking and screaming. He got competent at what he needed most but had become fond over the past year of joking, 'Hey, I'm retired, I don't have to learn that.' He'd been disking the hard drive files he wanted to take home.

"Three or four weeks ago, I was doing some bills and correspondence. I wanted to check something in a note I'd trashed. Instead I pulled up a letter Charlie had trashed but not yet emptied. It was brief and I suppose I sort of took it in before I realized that it wasn't what I was looking for, and possibly not for my eyes. I put it on a disk with a couple of other documents he seemed to have missed on the desktop and put it aside for him. I remembered it for the first time this morning when I was dressing to come over."

She paused, finally taking a sip from her cup and putting it down. "I decided that, now, it *was* for my eyes. I stopped by the office on my way over and read it again. It's only a couple of paragraphs, a few lines each, to his attorney, Daniel Gardiner, who's been in London for six months on an exchange program with a firm his own does business with. It simply says that he hopes it's been interesting and fun."

She looked at Hudson and then at Libby. "And that as soon as he gets back in a few weeks he wants to get together and go over some changes to his will."

"The house? Maybe something else along with what we all assumed was a nice check the other night," said Libby. "I wondered if Charlie might not be setting up some sort of trust to supplement whatever Chaz may have from his parents."

"That was my first thought," said Camilla, but her tone sounded unconvinced.

Libby sat down on the sofa heavily. A suddenly old woman, thought Hudson, weary to the bone, the sides of her mouth drooping. She looked out through the tall floor-to-ceiling windows into her garden.

"None of which can possibly have anything to do with this Lukerson nut," said Hudson.

Camilla nodded. "That was my second thought."

Libby turned back to them, as though she had just remembered they were there.

"I know that Peter Cullen was in Charlie's will. He mentioned something once. But I have no idea in what way. And I don't know what he would've done about that since Peter's death four months ago. And the only other thing I know is that he's made a passing reference or two to the fact that he's making really sizeable endowments to a couple of the organizations he's worked with. The child abuse shelter and the literacy council. And to the outreach programs of the diocese."

"And we know Chaz and Sydney are well provided for," said Hudson. "And that you," he said to Camilla, "and your group are buying the 26-A and the Blue Bar."

"Yes. I'll be the majority partner, Fentry and Victor together will hold thirty-five percent, and Charlie's keeping five. Charlie's been edging toward the door these past few months. We talked about it again just a couple of weeks ago and were planning to do the paperwork as soon as his attorney gets back."

"Could any of that be in jeopardy now?"

"Certainly."

"Was anyone unhappy about the plan?"

"I think Terry Main's nose may have been a little out of joint when Charlie first told him. They'd never discussed it but I had the feeling that Terry may have had some notion that he'd have a chance at it. Charlie asked me if he could assure him that he could continue as manager."

"And you said...?"

"I said yes. It might not have been my first choice. Oh, he's a fine manager. I've just never, well, warmed to him."

"Why?"

"I don't know. Perhaps that I never know what he's thinking. Of course I haven't had that much reason to get over to the bar very often. If he was disappointed, though, he seems to have gotten over it. When we are together, I don't sense any personal resentment. It's a perfectly *all right* professional relationship."

They sat for a long while in silence.

Finally, Hudson got up and walked slowly to the end of the room and back.

"What about that land?" he asked.

"No idea," said Camilla.

"No," said Libby. "I suppose Brad and I have assumed for some time that that's why he's really retiring now. To make sure that it's handled exactly the way he wants it. Something respectful and low-key. A small lodge, or a few really nice cottages, maybe. He wants people to enjoy it, but he doesn't want it ruined. It wouldn't surprise me if he didn't leave it as a conservancy or something like that."

"And it's worth millions?" asked Hudson.

"Brad has guessed the land could bring forty to sixty, but that if you had a major stake in some sort of heavy development that would easily increase to as high as a hundred."

"Have you told Brad about Charlie?" asked Camilla.

"No," said Libby. "No I haven't. I wish he were here. But..." she shook her head, "you have no idea what these three weeks in Montana with his old buddies mean to him. I go gallivanting around all the time and he's so wonderful about it. I want him to have this time. I just don't have the heart to tell him. He'll have to know soon enough."

The three of them sat staring at one another for a very long time.

"So until Charlie made whatever changes he was planning for his will—who would inherit the property?" Hudson asked.

"Some of it, at least, would have gone to Peter," said Libby. "For all we know, he may even have owned parcels of it or held some of it jointly. And Charlie very well may have already designated all or some of it as a preserve or wilderness trust or whatever."

"We just can't know, can we?" asked Camilla.

Libby rose from the sofa, slowly, leaning for support on the arm. Hudson noticed, however, that the glint was back in her eye.

"Let's not say that *just yet.*"

She went over to her old burled walnut writing desk, situated herself in the chair, put on her half-glasses, and pulled a small book out of the drawer.

"Dan Gardiner's mother was my best friend. He's probably just about you all's age and I can see him sitting right where you two are now about thirty-some years ago eating my peanut butter cookies."

She called his firm in Destin and got a number. "There's attorney-client confidentiality, of course," she muttered to herself as she hung up the phone. Then she looked over her glasses at them. "But when Danny hears what's happened to Charlie, he'll tell his Aunt Libby what we want to know."

"What time is it in London?"

# Chapter 38

When Hudson arrived at the hospital he found the usually unemotive Victor in a virtually unrecognizable state. He kept watch over Charlie like a gentle giant, his large, muscular frame leaning ardently forward from the edge of the small armchair, Charlie's hand completely covered in both of his own. As Hudson approached, he could hear the sonorous voice with its Aussie syllables approaching something like fervor.

"At's it, my man, c'mon Charlie, c'mon, we're waitin' on ya."

Hearing Hudson, his head turned quickly, the short blond pony tail swinging nearly horizontal for a moment. Almost always unrelievedly deadpan, Victor's face was now ablaze like a six-year-old finding his heart's desire on Christmas morning.

"He moved his hand!" he grinned. "About twenty minutes ago. I was reading the newspaper to him and I thought I saw something out of the corner of my eye. It was this hand—his left. It moved and then a few seconds later it moved again. It wasn't a tremor. He moved his fingers and flexed a bit." He leaned closer. "You *moved* it, right, Charlie?"

They talked for a few minutes until Victor rather reluctantly stood. Without ever having released it, he bent over and placed Charlie's hand in Hudson's as he might a small injured bird.

"Well, here you go."

◇◇◇

For the next four hours, Hudson held Charlie's hand. Or rubbed it, or squeezed it, or gently manipulated the fingers. He stood from time to time and went to the other side of the bed to do the same with his right hand. Very lightly he massaged his forearms and shoulders, as much as the IVs and tubes and bandages allowed. He talked to him. He read to him. He read from magazines. An old *U.S. News and World Report*, the current *New Yorker*. He read some homework, Waugh's *A Handful of Dust*. He read some poetry that he selected from an anthology, including one he'd never read before by Jorge Luis Borges titled "Plainness."

When his voice became hoarse, he placed the lightweight headset on Charlie's ears and played a couple of his favorite CDs.

As he watched his friend's face, his arms and hands, hoping for the slightest sign, he went over and over again both the frustrations and the frightening progress of the morning's conversations.

Just before he'd had to leave for the hospital, Dan Gardiner had returned Libby's call. He was stunned to hear her news but wasted no time in telling her what he could.

He had received Charlie's letter about a month before and had made a calendar note to call as soon as he got back. He had no idea what changes he intended to the will. As it currently stood, the entire tract of eighty-five acres east of Seagrove would accrue to the estate of his cousin Peter Cullen and, unless the will were altered before Charlie's death, would pass to his heirs.

"He has one son, Charlie's namesake, I believe?"

"Yes," Libby had said. She had thanked him and cut short his baffled questions. "You know that you can trust me with this information, Dan. I won't abuse your confidence and you can trust that Charlie would want me to know this. I promise I'll be in touch soon. Thank you again."

◇◇◇

Camilla was to come at two, and Hudson grew anxious for her arrival.

He felt as though he might rip apart. Part of him seemed connected at least as directly to Charlie as any one of the tubes that webbed his upper body and pierced his wrists. But another part of him wanted to be out doing something. Exactly what, he wasn't yet certain, but in his gut, he knew that this nightmare wasn't over.

It had expanded.

How could Sydney and Chaz possibly know, if his own attorney didn't, that Charlie intended any changes to his will beyond leaving them his house and some extremely generous financial settlement? People didn't casually murder their relatives on the possibility that they might inherit quite substantially but not entirely. And even if they could, indeed, somehow know that he was planning to dispose of the land otherwise, perhaps, as Libby posed, as a low-development resort or even a wilderness preserve, what possible connection could the svelte young Cullens have to somebody like Lukerson?

◇◇◇

When Camilla got there, he didn't leave.

At 2:25, Hudson moistened Charlie's lips with some crushed ice in a paper towel and then rubbed a little Carmex on them. Camilla sat holding his left hand, lightly scratching the palm with her fingertips.

Hudson walked across the room to throw the towel away and as soon as he turned back Charlie opened his eyes.

He looked first at the ceiling, then to the side at Camilla, and then over her shoulder, at him.

"*Charlie,*" she said, gripping his hand.

Hudson stood beside her. "We're right here, Charlie."

The lips trembled, not quite parting.

"Don't try to talk right now," Camilla said. "Just rest. You're doing fine, now, okay? You can talk to us soon. Just rest and let your strength keep coming back."

The eyelids drooped, closed, opened again.

But before they closed again, Hudson saw the sort of abject confusion and fear in them that he had not seen since the aneurysm had stunned them at the breakfast table and Kate had slumped toward him, and in four or five infinite seconds, away from him, forever.

He had been helpless, of course, to do anything then.

A sudden prayer shook him with the conviction that he wouldn't be now.

◇◇◇

Chaz called around three. He'd just heard from Victor about the morning's breakthrough.

When Hudson hung up the phone, Camilla said quietly, "You didn't tell him about…just now."

"No," he said, almost to himself. "No, I didn't."

◇◇◇

They talked for nearly an hour, alternating between fits and starts of suppositions and silences. They took turns holding Charlie's hands and, uncertain as to whether he might somehow hear them from his still, twilit space, they tried to keep the urgency from their voices.

They called Libby, who was ecstatic with the news and talked with them in turns to savor every possible detail and nuance.

The joy subsided quickly enough, however, and there was a long, heavily shadowed pause.

Hudson had the phone, and he finally heard Libby sigh, "Well, I have thought and thought and thought until my head feels like it's just gonna come unglued…and I get absolutely nowhere. Have you come up with anything other than our instincts?"

"No. But I think we may just have to work with that for now."

"But work *how*? *Where*?"

"Right here. We're not budging. I don't know what else to do." He turned his back to the bed. "I don't know why or how, but there's a connection. I don't know if there's some bizarre link to some crazed right-wing organization or if it's just as unbelievably personal. But there's a connection."

"What's the plan? They'll be there from ten till six."

"So will you." He lowered his voice even more. "Whoever or whatever wants Charlie not to come back has to make their move soon because he's getting better. That's all I know. It means you'll have to be here from your regular gig at six until six in the morning and we hate that because we know how worn out you are already."

"Oh, you know old people don't need much sleep. So I just keep my eye on him?"

"Exactly. Nothing's going to happen so long as one of us is there. All you have to tell them is that you just don't want to leave. There's nothing they can do about it. Can you play a willful old lady?"

"Ask Brad. What if nothing happens?"

"Then Charlie keeps improving and gets well and we figure the rest out as we can."

"Have you talked with the ATF folks about what we know?"

"Not yet. Camilla and I are torn between alerting them or not right now. We don't want to alert *them*. We'll keep thinking about that. We're going to my house from here and we may decide to call them tonight. I don't know. I don't know much. I just know I believe that if somebody's going to try something it's going to have to be in the next twenty-four to forty-eight hours."

"I'll be there before six." She paused. "Put Camilla on, sweetie, before I go."

Camilla took the phone and listened, looking across the bed at Hudson. "I think you must be right," she said. "See you soon."

She hung the phone up and Hudson lifted his eyes in question.

"Don't be embarrassed," Camilla smiled. "She said 'I told you he's not just a pretty face.'"

◇◇◇

The doctor came by at four-thirty. He was guardedly optimistic.

Then, their waiting resumed. Camilla read a magazine while holding Charlie's hand. Hudson stretched and paced. His eyes roved the walls of the room, fitted with various and sundry metal plates and extensions and wires, as if looking for a means of escape. He distractedly examined the impersonal hardware, the monitors, machines, equipment, and tubes, what whirred and clicked, and invaded the body of their beloved friend, holding him back from the edge.

◇◇◇

And then, just before five, as Hudson was mopping Charlie's forehead with a damp cloth and Camilla was finishing up a bit of business with Fentry on the phone, a man they did not know knocked on the door and, with a modest smile, entered.

"My name's Tim Faraday. I'm the administrator here at St. Andrews."

He shook hands with Camilla and then Hudson as they introduced themselves. "Now, you're not Charlie's cousins, the newlyweds?"

"No," said Camilla. "Old friends."

"So am I."

He walked to the bed and very gently touched Charlie's cheek, and then stood for a moment, holding his hand. He was an attractive man. His very deep, husky voice seemed not to match his tall, thin frame. He was perhaps fifty, wore round wire-rimmed glasses, and had thick sandy hair that kept falling in a slant across his high brow.

He turned to them. "May I sit with you for a few minutes?" he asked, indicating the sofa. "Please," said Hudson. Camilla sat beside him and Hudson drew over the chair.

"I've been at a conference in Richmond. Got back last night. I just learned today that Charlie was here." He paused. "I've spoken with his doctors. They tell me he may be turning a corner."

"We hope so," said Hudson.

"I don't get to the 26-A as often as I'd like, but haven't I seen you there?" Faraday asked Camilla.

"Yes, you have. And now that you mention it, I believe I recognize you, too." Over the next few minutes, she and Hudson reviewed their histories with, and their fondness for, Charlie.

Faraday nodded often, smiling. Occasionally they even allowed themselves to share a discreet laugh.

"I moved down here twelve years ago. A native of St. Louis. Didn't know a soul. I met Charlie at a fundraiser for our new pediatric cancer unit. An interfaith tennis tournament sort of thing, actually. We played each other in the first round. July. Hot as hell. I remember him saying to me when I won that I hadn't played too badly for a Yankee Lutheran.

"He invited us to be his guests at the restaurant. Introduced us to some very nice folks. Really took us under his wing."

"Sounds like Charlie," Hudson said.

Faraday's face fell suddenly as he looked toward the bed. "Why?"

"Well…" Camilla began.

"No, no, sorry. That was rhetorical. I know you've been living with this for days now. Don't repeat it for me. I think I know the basic outline." He looked at the long brown suede oxford at the end of his long crossed leg. "Sick bastard."

Hudson said, "There are official and unofficial theories."

"Was he acting alone?"

"That's the official theory."

"But it's never completely true, is it?" Faraday spoke with a soft intensity. He seemed to be making an effort to keep his resonant bass voice carefully leashed but it rushed ahead of his intention like a fierce rumble. "There are always people behind them aren't there? They take all that ignorance and fear and twist it into hatred. And then when some poor idiot goes off, they're nowhere in sight."

Hudson nodded. "They're safe behind their vitriolic patriotism and their pulpits and their radio stations and their websites and their well-stocked bunkers."

"People like this are pawns."

At this, Hudson froze. He seemed so lost to the conversation for a moment that Camilla looked at him as if he had physically left the room. When he reconcentrated his focus on them, Faraday was saying "…and he was there when my partner had a serious car accident later in that first year. It was a long recuperation and Charlie was a regular, driving all the way over here, always bringing food. He knew I'd just begun my job. Knew what my schedule was like. Knew that we didn't have an extensive network of friends.…"

"I'm sorry," said Hudson. "What you just said about pawns. It made me realize something. There's a lot we don't know about this." He nodded toward Charlie. "But in just the past day or two, some of us have begun to put some things together and…"

"Do the authorities have other leads?"

"Well, no. We don't think so."

Faraday sat his lanky frame straight up and brushed the hair from his brow. His eyes glimmered in their round glasses with a sort of adventurous intelligence. "But you do, don't you?"

Hudson and Camilla looked at one another without speaking.

"Is there something I can do?"

Neither of them quite knew what to say.

"Sam and I have always felt that we'll never be able to repay Charlie. In our lives he has defined the word 'friend.' We haven't seen enough of him lately, and that's our fault. Couples get in their own ruts. But I want to have the opportunity to correct that. I want him up and out of here. He's one of the finest men I know. I respect him and I love him."

He eyed them both.

"Short of breaking the law, I will do absolutely anything to help him—and you. Tell me there *is* something. I'll do it."

Hudson spoke slowly and softly, continuing to find his way as he went.

"Actually, yes. Yes, Tim. I think there is."

◇◇◇

When Libby arrived at five-forty-five they brought her up to date.

And an hour later, Faraday had rearranged schedules in order to double-shift two nurses whom he knew particularly well and trusted implicitly. He swore them to secrecy and promised them he would fill them in as soon as he could.

Libby would keep the door open as much as possible.

The woman in the room across the hall from Charlie's had improved sufficiently to be moved off the intensive care floor at noon.

The new admission, a surprisingly healthy-looking man of forty, would lie as quietly as he could during the early evening, passing the hours watching television, and then, through the long early morning, he would simply rest in the darkness with half-opened lids. An older man who might be the patient's father would be in evidence throughout the night, his chair facing the open door, working crossword puzzles, stretching from time to time in the hall. Never more than a matter of feet from the door to Charlie's room.

They were Faraday's best security people.

# Chapter 39

As evening closed around the cottage, Hudson and Camilla grew silent, exhausted from talking, from thinking, from feeling. Camilla had stopped at her house in Seagrove on their way back and picked up some things, and walked now down the long hall toward the great room in loose cotton pants and shirt, drying her hair. Hudson stood at the butcher block table, tossing a salad.

"I just can't believe it," she said. "They can get back in the house day after tomorrow?"

"Saturday. That's what Fentry said he'd heard when I talked with him just now."

He had called to let Fentry and Victor know that he would be going back at six in the morning. Perhaps they'd like to skip a shift and get some more sleep. Both declined.

"Apparently they plan to have finished doing all those forensic, fingerprinting, whatever things they do."

"It's been four days," Camilla murmured. "It seems like it could be four hours, or maybe even four years. But, somehow, not four days."

"No."

"I hate it. Their going into that house."

"Yeah, I know, although I also hate having them here."

They drank a little wine. In near silence, they poked at the salad and the tenderloin that one of the 26-A waiters had dropped off on his way home.

◇◇◇

At eight-forty-five, they decided to call Rogers, their burly, jocular ATF contact and coordinator with the local investigators. He arrived in less than an hour with South Walton County homicide detective Fields, a slim, muscular, very beautiful African-American woman.

"How's Mr. Brompton?" Rogers asked. Since he'd first shown up at the house, Hudson had admired Rogers' ability to juggle punctilious shrewdness and down-home warmth.

"We think we have more reason for hope."

Thirty minutes later, they had laid out their concerns, and waited watchfully as Rogers sipped his coffee and then balanced it in the saucer on his very solid thigh with the exacting care of a large and muscular man who does sometimes risky work that calls for delicacy. As if in keeping with the relentless torrent of unlikely events, Olive lay draped over one of his shoes. "Oh, yeah, they see me coming. We have two at home." It was a picture, Hudson thought, of grace under pressure.

"Interesting. Very, very. Anything we can call evidence? Something we can see, touch, taste, smell?" He interrupted himself, "…not that this doesn't smell."

"Nothing," said Hudson.

"That's one of the reasons we debated whether to call you," said Camilla.

"And the other?" asked Fields.

"We think they'll make their move on their shift tomorrow night," said Hudson. "Charlie's improving by the hour. If they can't finish the job tomorrow night they may never have a feasible chance. And we, we have…"

He couldn't believe he was saying this. How would they? "We have a plan. And we're afraid that if you were to call them in for questioning, we'd never get proof."

Rogers reared back, putting his coffee aside on the table, and clasped his hands together almost in glee. He rocked on the edge of the chair, looking as though Hudson had just shared a good joke, and let out a little snort of a laugh. "You two are pretty resourceful."

He looked over at Fields. "This is good, you know?"

Fields tried to sustain a note of cool professionalism. "Do you think your friend, Ms. Lee, is in any danger tonight? Or Mr. Brompton himself?"

"No," said Hudson. "They may be desperate to finish the job but these people are very far from uncontrollably crazy."

"We've made a point of letting them think that they'll be alone with him tomorrow night," said Camilla. "That Hudson and Libby and I all have conflicts we can't do anything about."

"Tonight," said Hudson, "we have someone else keeping a discreet eye on Libby and on the room."

Rogers stood, gingerly lifting Olive to the sofa. She looked at him with disgruntlement but surprisingly little outrage. He walked over toward the door, his hand rubbing the back of his football player's neck. He came back and sat on the ottoman, his huge knees bulging in his khakis.

"Boy, oh boy! This is something. I don't know, I just don't know...." He shook his head slowly, looking at the floor.

"Well, neither do we, but we feel we know enough to trust our instincts."

Rogers looked at his colleague. "Officer Fields, what do you think about all this?"

"I think we're both going to have to pass this information on, of course. But I also think that, as of this moment, we have absolutely nothing concrete to work with, nothing but supposition, and no evident tie to Lukerson or any other party or parties." She sipped her coffee, looking at Hudson and Camilla. She turned to Rogers.

"And I also see two smart people here who want a friend who may have been lucky once not be put to the test twice. Let's hear this plan."

◇◇◇

Rogers and Fields left just before eleven.

Hudson and Camilla sat facing one another in the chairs by the hearth. Moon lay not nearby but sprawled in front of the door in a well-mannered indication that he hoped no more strangers would come and go, at least for awhile.

"I guess we can trust them?" she asked.

"Yeah. They want to see what happens tomorrow night as much as we do. I believe they'll do what they said. File a cursory report on our conversation tonight but not do anything about interviewing them again until day after tomorrow. Even if we're wrong and nothing happens tomorrow night, they're not going to jump to conclusions or show their hand. They're not suppressing information, much less evidence."

The phone rang. It was Libby calling to report that Charlie had regained consciousness for about thirty seconds around eight o'clock and for nearly a minute two hours later.

Chaz got on the phone briefly to second the good news and then gave it back to Libby.

◇◇◇

"He sounds excited," said Hudson.

"Oh, yes."

"But there's a very fine line between sounding excited and sounding scared."

"I think so, too." He could see Libby smiling at Chaz and Sydney. "Yes, he seems to be…more and more."

"Are you okay? Are the guys there across the hall?"

"They sure are. Chaz just went down to get a bite to eat, and Sydney's watching Nightline and I just gave Charlie a shave and think I'll do some more reading. We're all just fine. How about you?"

"You'll be there 'til they leave around five-thirty?"

"Sure will."

"Then if we don't hear otherwise from you we'll be there at six. I'm meeting Tim Faraday in his office. I tried to talk Victor and Fentry out of their shifts but they want to be there. Camilla's going to let them in on what's going on."

"Sounds great. Good night, Hudson."

◇◇◇

Hudson poured some wine and asked, "How about a little quiet music?"

"Please. I think there's nothing else we can really do right now. And my brain is shutting down."

"Mine's trying to. But part of it's there, you know? With Charlie."

She nodded. "That's something I've had to work on. For years. And every time I think I'm making progress something comes along to cause me to wonder."

"A divided mind?"

"Or spirit, or whatever the case may be. I believed I was doing the right thing, but now I think I lived too long in my marriage after it had already died. I became too adept at compartmentalizing my thoughts and feelings."

"I know." He paused and smiled at her. "But I don't think we should beat ourselves up about it too much. Sometimes we have to do that to survive."

"I would think you've had to."

"Oh, yes."

"But you're going to survive."

"So it would seem. I mean *yes*."

They sat and sipped their wine and listened for awhile to the faint, comforting sounds of Stephane Grapelli's jazz violin.

"Does this make you *angry*?" she asked. "I mean—beyond Charlie—does this make you angry somehow about your own life?"

"How would you know that?"

"Because *I* am. I find that I'm suddenly very angry not only about Charlie but about being distracted by this nightmare from my own life. It reminds me too much of the old days. And feeling angry makes me feel selfish."

"About what?"

"About not letting my life fragment again. About being afraid that life is something that's going on somewhere else, over there, not…"

"Not here?"

"Yes."

She paused and smiled wearily at him. "Sorry. It's the exhaustion talking. I think we're just so saturated right now with a lack of trust that I'm afraid even to trust myself."

"I think you *should* trust yourself. You like truth even when it's not easy. If what you mean is that you feel you don't have time for sorrow and for death, then, yes, you're absolutely right. I'm angry, too. I don't want to be forced to realize, to consider on a recurring basis, that I'm fragile, vulnerable, hanging by a thread. I want to be able to believe that I'm not really a dead man trying to fool himself and other people."

He paused. "Yeah, I'm angry, too. I want to do my work and enjoy my friends. And if part of what you meant is that we seem to have begun a new friendship and now all this has gotten in the way…"

They both leaned forward and reached out their hands to one another. It felt awkward to him at first, but because they had all been holding Charlie's hands so much among themselves these past few days, not as awkward as it might have.

"We'll just have to keep a place…clear."

After a minute or so, they let go, and settled back in their respective chairs.

But the air felt somewhat lighter.

◇◇◇

They could hardly hold their eyes open but, like children on a parents' night out, were determined to savor for as long as they could their sense of space, their impromptu moment of independence. The small oasis of music and wine and affection they had created.

Hudson had worked away at a crossword puzzle and Camilla had leafed through a *Gourmet* at a leisurely pace. When she put it aside, she asked, "Would you mind letting me read one of your reviews?"

"No. Not if you'd like."

"I would like."

He went to the desk and flipped through some hard copies, his brow furrowed, trying to decide what to offer.

She could see what he was doing. "You mean they aren't all perfect?"

He laughed. "Of course they are, but some are more perfect than others."

"And this is an example of your releasing yourself from rigidity, of relaxing fully into the here and now?"

"Oh, all right. *Here.* Just take one." He went over to her with a review in each hand.

She closed her eyes. "Caution to the winds," she said, and pointed to one.

She looked more relaxed than he seen her in a week. Hudson looked down, and a shadow of hesitancy crossed his face.

"In a way, you've already heard some of this one earlier today...."

## Us vs. Them
### *American History X* tries to reveal the enemy within

Tony Kaye's feature film debut earns a large A for Effort. *American History X* seeks to give a human face to a momentous issue, the renascence of white supremacist hatred, by approaching its subject not on an abstract socio-political level, but as psychological drama. Like the startling black swastika tattooed on his chest, the character of young Derek Vinyard (played beautifully by Edward Norton) is an emblematic embodiment of the causes and effects of neo-Nazism. The film follows the arc of his attraction to the movement and the consequences for his family, particularly his younger brother Danny (Edward Furlong).

*American History X* is Kaye's and screenwriter David McKenna's attempt, a much-needed and honorable one, to bring large audiences face to face with what they may perceive on a daily basis as marginal, unconnected news stories. In the end, *American History X* is somewhat oversimplified and superficial, but not to the degree that it should be avoided; it is thoughtful, provocative, and moving, and Norton's performance is further indication of a considerable screen talent in the making. Kaye, most famously a director of commercials, is also cinematographer, and the film's opening sequence is one of the most evocative of the year thus far, a gray, monochromatic vista of ragged clouds and surf along a deserted beach. The tone of the film is immediately, almost viscerally established; the seductive, haunting beauty is pervaded with a sinister foreboding (and the troubled strings of Anne Dudley's score). At the end of the sequence, Kaye's deep-focus longshots zoom in toward a few structures perched uneasily under the lowering sky at the far end of the shore, and the sense that we may have just looked from the window of Matthew Arnold's "Dover Beach," where "ignorant armies clash by night," suddenly gives way, and we find ourselves in southern California. It is a southern California not of the sun and oranges, of surfboards and movie star enclaves like Malibu, but of Venice Beach, an ethnically mixed community of Los Angeles; other than the boardwalk, it could be an urban neighborhood of almost any American city. An adolescent boy, in voiceover, observes: "It used to be really cool, a great place to live. Then the Hispanics and the black gangs started moving in from South Central, and everything went to hell…"

Kaye employs an interesting narrative frame for the story. Danny's principal (Avery Brooks), alarmed by Danny's evolving ideology, has forced him to write a paper tracing the impacts of his older brother Derek's attitudes and activities on his life. With the use of flashbacks that eventually come abreast of the story's present tense, Danny relates the salient points of the family history, its decline from the middle-middle to lower-middle class, of Derek's adoption of skinhead values and his emergent leadership, and of the night when Derek kills two black men outside the Vinyard home. Derek goes to prison for three years. Danny

becomes fully involved in the skinhead scene. As
he begins his paper, his brother is released. Danny
is deeply conflicted when Derek tells him that he
is leaving "all that hate bullshit" behind, that
he disavows his previous beliefs, and that he
wants Danny out, too. The cautionary denouement
of *American History X* is tragic and chilling.

Edward Norton is one of our more intriguing
new film actors. As he showed in the 1996 thriller
*Primal Fear*, he is as adroit at purveying eccen-
tricity and extremity as he is the ordinariness
of the guy-next-door. His relation to the camera
is of the rare sort that can make a good actor a
star. He can project the modest, gee-whiz, Everyman
quality of a Jimmy Stewart or a Tom Hanks, and in
the next moment, his face can take on the veiled,
troubled intensity of Montgomery Clift, or the
galvanizing intensity of the young Peter O'Toole.
Though thwarted by the character's underscripted
transformation, his work here is memorable. Furlong is effective, too, evoking the adolescent
Danny's drifting, yearning search for something
in which to believe; and Beverly D'Angelo has a
few very powerful scenes as their mother.

The film's reach far exceeds its grasp. The very
best aspects of this psychological investigation
of right-wing domestic terrorism happen also to
be its very worst aspects. Expectations are raised
with heady frequency only to languish unfulfilled.
This film wants essentially to examine the banality
of evil and the effects of paranoia, but certain
elements of the story are jarringly contrived,
and we are never taken below the surface of the
breeding grounds of hatred. As a character study of
Derek as an individual, *American History X* doesn't
go deep enough, nor is it quite emblematic enough
as an investigation of how Dereks—intelligently
articulate, sensitive, murderous—are formed. (His
father, a fireman, was killed in the line of duty
in a drug-ridden tenement in a black neighborhood.
Not all of the folks turning to anti-government
militias, skinhead rallies, and Internet-nurtured
hate groups are propelled there by such highly

specific events.) The film's glancing treatment is maddeningly equal opportunity: NRAers can leave the theatre thinking it was about the evils of "big government" and liberal civil libertarians will feel assured it was about the dangerous organizational and psychological links between ultra-rightist religious demagogues, politicians, media, militias, and domestic terrorists. The only message the film purports to get across is that we should get over being so chronically quick to content ourselves with the idea of the single shooter, the lone ranger, the "mad" man—which message it then spends two hours neutralizing with its own ironic demographics appeasement policy.

Of course, the rumors of "vast right-wing conspiracies" are, as any sentient and objectively informed citizen knows, truer now than ever, but for all its good intentions of shedding light, *American History X,* like Mark Pellington's recent suspense effort, *Arlington Road,* starring Jeff Bridges, and so many others before it, simply proves instead that there's another conspiracy also in need of exposure: that of Hollywood producers who keep insisting that Americans are incapable of watching a movie and thinking at the same time.

Films remain to be made that force us finally to confront the frighteningly demoralizing complexities of race in America and the fact that much of the Us vs. Them fear and hatred in our society—whether racial, anti-woman, anti-gay, anti-intellectual—is engendered, or at least abetted for political purposes, not by the more obvious fringe dwellers, but by those in church pulpits and legislatures, and, more recently and perhaps most frighteningly, even by major news networks, who wrap themselves loud and long in the most insidious forms of demagogic religion and patriotism.

It was after midnight before Hudson made Camilla at home in his bedroom and went off to sleep in the loft.

# Chapter 40

By early afternoon the job was nearly completed.

Hudson had met with Tim Faraday in his office at six to go over things again, and half an hour later they had met the carpenter, electrician, and technical consultant outside Charlie's room. The security guys across the hall were sent home.

Camilla, still whispering to an extremely wide-eyed Fentry, sat with Charlie while Hudson, Faraday, and the workmen went into the empty bay just west of Charlie's room.

It had been a multipurpose space for years, most recently a temporary coffee and food service room while the new wing was being built. It was soon to be reincarnated as a medical records storage office, but for now it was merely an empty room with an adjoining bath, half-fitted with terminals and crates and coiled wire.

After Faraday's appearance with the crew that morning, none of the staff thought much about the sounds of minor construction that came from the room throughout the day or the men who came in and out of it and, occasionally, quietly, Charlie's.

The physician in charge came in and was pleased. The heart rate had steadied and the neurology reports from the tests the day before were encouraging.

Victor traded places with Fentry at eight, and Hudson sat with Charlie while Camilla went through the story again down in the coffee shop. When they came back up, Victor still looked flustered, and Hudson could tell from the way Camilla frequently touched his arm and the soothing tone of her voice that the big man didn't want to leave and go to work. As he held Charlie's hand in his and looked at the two of them, Hudson could sense his free-floating bewilderment giving way to something tightly focused and coiled, as if, given a signal from Camilla, he would throw Charlie's own team of doctors to the ground one by one. Finally, Camilla walked him down the hall as far as the elevators, reassuring him that they would be in touch. Soon.

Whether anything happened or not.

As the day wore on, Hudson and Camilla looked and listened as the work went on. They watched the clock. They took turns by the head of Charlie's bed, reading to him. When the men had to use their drills, Camilla put the headset over his ears and played favorite music.

He was coming to, though only for a minute or two at a time, with some regularity now. He clearly recognized them both. And though they debated whether it was wishful thinking or not, they thought they discerned just a faraway hint of the old glitter in his eye. Even when he lapsed away from them again, it seemed less an utter absence and more like sleep.

At two, Rogers and Fields arrived. At two-thirty, the men thought they had it finished. Hudson called Tim Faraday and he came up immediately.

They went next door. They came back into Charlie's room. They tested. Re-tested. Made adjustments and readjustments.

At three-thirty it was as right as they could make it. Faraday left for a meeting. Rogers and Fields disappeared.

Libby called at four-thirty. She had gotten some decent sleep despite a constant nagging that she was out of the loop.

When they had told her first about Charlie and then the preparations, Hudson said, "You know you're right here with us."

"Call me."

"We will."

They waited.

◇◇◇

At five-fifty, when Chaz and Sydney walked in, Charlie's eyes were open again and he was steadily returning Hudson's pressure on his hand. Chaz put down some papers and magazines and a small bag on the sofa. Sydney came straight to the bed.

Camilla and Hudson moved slightly, and when Charlie's eyes swam weakly over to Sydney they saw something like the faint light of pleased recognition again, which seemed to delight Sydney. She reached out her hand excitedly. "Chaz!" She leaned down and kissed Charlie's forehead. "You're doing so well, Charlie. We're right here."

Chaz went around to the other side of the bed. He seemed to Hudson out of breath and a bit edgy, nearly snagging the catheter meter with his foot and then catching his watchband momentarily on the IV as he took Charlie's other hand.

"Hey, guy. You're looking really good."

Charlie dozed off again and for a moment, they stood there, looking at one another, one of Charlie's hands in Hudson's, the other in Chaz's.

"There's more good news," said Camilla, smiling evenly. "The cardiovascular surgeon was just in and said that the slight tear in the esophagus should be mended and that he wants to dissolve the shunt tomorrow morning. Charlie will be able to start taking liquids by mouth and in a day or so soft food."

"He wanted to talk today, we're sure." Hudson smiled as well.

Sydney looked over Charlie's bandaged chest at Chaz. Her widened eyes began to fill with tears, but she lifted her chin just perceptibly and smiled at him.

While Hudson and Camilla gathered up a few things, Sydney asked a number of questions. All intelligent, all earnest. Was it important now to keep talking and reading to him? To play music? What if he tried to speak? Did he need just to sleep?

Hudson thought the solicitude as genuine and normal as anyone might expect in the circumstances and as he and Camilla went down on the elevator he wondered aloud for a moment if they weren't perhaps desperately wrong after all.

"I don't think so," said Camilla as they walked down the long front hall. At the doors, she stopped and turned to him, her hand gripping his upper arm for a moment. "And if we are? If we had to live this over again, knowing what we know and what we don't know, are you saying you wouldn't try it again?"

"No."

◇◇◇

St. Andrews is a moderate-sized hospital. Its one large parking lot wraps around the front and down one side of the building, both flanks of which were visible from Charlie's room.

As Hudson first walked Camilla to her car and then went several aisles over to the Highlander, he imagined he could feel their eyes on his back. They would be able to see him leave through the gate and drive down the street as far as the access road that would take him west to Highway 98, back to Laurel.

They wouldn't be able to see him when he circled two long blocks over and returned to the hospital from the south, entered the small underground lot for physicians and senior staff, and parked in a taped-off slot beside the administrator's.

# Chapter 41

Sydney was worried more about Chaz than any other variable. He was like a sick cat, alternating between anxious testiness and a distanced morose sulk.

The latter had seemed preferable for awhile.

Their first five hours in the room had become almost unbearable. It was as though some time-warp synapse had fired and he had been transported back to the throes of some very bad coke rush. Manic, he stalked the small room one side to the other, over and over and over again. She sent him out to walk the halls when she couldn't stand it anymore, telling him to slow down as much as he possibly could and to try to look encouraged, relatively happy. She knew that fatigue from anxiety was expected, a helpful cover, but she didn't want him drawing attention by running up and down the halls half-crazed.

Neither of them looked often at Charlie, and they went to the bed even less.

Chaz got juice and coffee and water and saltine crackers and anything else he could find down the hall in the small service room. He went down to the cafeteria twice and came back. He rattled three papers and read two magazines cover to cover. He stood. He reclined tentatively on the sofa with a pillow behind his head. He sat on the sofa, he sat in the chair. He held the remote control as if it were some hold on a fleeting reality, channel-surfing wildly, repeatedly, watching perhaps one entire sitcom and probably three hours of fragmented snippets as brief as seconds and no longer than a few minutes.

He talked back to the screen, indirectly to her, muttered to himself. With the remote still in his hand and clicking away, he would walk over and pick up something from the pile of reading materials, look at it, mouth out disparate snatches.

But now it seemed, as the clock inched toward midnight, that he was even worse. He had sunk into an unreachable chasm, sitting in the armchair and scarcely moving, watching a talk-show at low volume on the tilted screen above without giving the slightest indication that he was seeing or hearing it. He didn't go out into the hall, he didn't go for juice or crackers, he didn't look for something new to read, he didn't respond to her suggestions, he didn't respond well when she had attempted, twice, to kiss him, to tell him it would be over soon, it would be all right.

She understood his nerves and knew what to do about them. She knew less well what to do about his dangerously imploding fear. It had descended an hour before.

Chaz was in the john and she had control of the remote long enough to stay focused on Angelica Huston's final scene in *The Grifters*. It seemed fortuitous that she had happened on this scene of this film, on this night, at this moment. She'd always liked the way the mother's body dropped into a hopeless hunch over her dead son and the heaving guttural animal sounds of stunned grief. She watched now utterly transfixed.

Chaz came out just as it ended.

And just as Charlie's eyes suddenly flew wide open.

Sydney saw the sick terror in Chaz's eyes and turned toward the bed. Charlie was smiling at them and slowly, with obvious effort, was lifting his left hand from its usual resting place at his side.

It was a salute. He nodded his head slightly. Proud that he'd accomplished it. That he reached them.

He drifted off again.

Chaz reached blindly behind himself, flailing for a moment, before his hand closed tightly on the edge of the bathroom door. She got up and went toward him. But she touched nothing. He had ducked, almost falling backward, into the harsh fluorescence. The door slammed in her face.

She whispered. "Chaz!"

The sounds of him being sick went on for two or three minutes that seemed like hours.

Other than a couple of monosyllabic replies to questions she tried to shape as comforts to him, he hadn't spoken for the past forty-five minutes. Only in the past ten did she seem to be making the crucial contact with him that would let her know she could get him through it. She had taken her chair over beside his and held his hand. She fed him crackers and cold water. After awhile, he rested his head on her shoulder for a minute. When he raised it again, he smiled sheepishly, pale, his eyes gorgeous and dark. "I'm fine."

"I know you are. I count on you," she said.

It was going to be fine.

She did something like pray.

For her poor, dear, weak, beautiful husband whom she really did love. He was the only person she had ever met who seemed emptier than herself, and that made her feel things she had never felt. Strong. Useful. Loved. She prayed for herself. She prayed for it to be over, for them to be away. She prayed for a hundred million dollars.

She prayed that she would be strong enough not to look at her watch or the clock every two minutes.

She prayed most of all that Charlie would not waken again to disturb them.

She prayed that less than two hours from now they could know for certain that they would never have to worry about that again.

She passed the remaining time by considering her reactions over and over again, matching specific reactions, or a repertoire of ready possibilities, to specific individuals and groups. When the time came, like any good actor, she had to believe it.

Chaz never looked at Charlie again. He worked a crossword puzzle with unrelenting concentration, his mournful mounting hysteria confined to the circumference of the pencil.

◇◇◇

They would now have seemed, to anyone who might have seen them, nothing out of the ordinary, nothing more or less than what they were—a handsome young couple keeping a late-night vigil by the bed of their loved one.

An expanse of hardware and fixtures and sockets and equipment rose before them, along the wall behind the bed, staring down impersonally on the figure in the bed, a cluttered mass of harsh necessities.

They sat amid the wires and tubes and monitors that blinked or dripped or clicked or whirred, each according to its function. They sat silently amid the seamless, inscrutable, almost submarine, sounds.

They could never have distinguished, among this confused but authoritative welter, three new sets of very small holes in the wall that had not been there before, one pair nearly six feet up from the floor, another a few inches lower to the right, and a single metal-collared aperture set in the bank of control panels and armatures just over the head of the bed.

# Chapter 42

Hour by hour, the hall had slowly subsided from its usual daytime demeanor—charged, hurried, clamorous—into the suspended twilight that passes for night in a hospital.

By 12:30, the two nurses had made their rounds and were doing charts at their station, and a young man from housekeeping had swabbed the floor from side to side and moved on with a slow hypnotic rhythm and a faint diffusion of disinfectant.

◇◇◇

At 1:30, Sydney got up from her chair, laying aside a recent issue of *Architectural Digest*. She murmured something to Chaz.

The blood left his face, but he nodded slightly.

He went to the door, opened it, and looked up and down the hall. He shook his head, and a few seconds later a med assistant pushed a cart by and gave him a wan, tired smile.

Seconds later he looked at Sydney, who stood near the bed, and nodded.

She leaned in over the edge of the bed, both her hands rising quickly toward Charlie's face. Simultaneously and without hesitation she gripped his nostrils shut with one hand and clamped her hand over his mouth.

◇◇◇

At the same moment Chaz let out an odd, strangled "No!" and her hands jerked to her sides.

A large man in a uniform was twisting him around and jamming his arms into his back.

A uniformed woman had hurtled past them and crossed four yards in three time-lapsed lunges and now gripped her own arms.

◇◇◇

As they were escorted quickly down the hall, Sydney saw, incongruously, Hudson DeForest standing off to one side.

She didn't look at him.

She was trying to silence Chaz with a look.

She was trying to think, but she could not.

She had never given a bad performance.

She always made everyone believe because she only played what she believed. But she found herself unprepared for failure. She had no script, no lines. No motivation.

Where was the truth?

She was aware of the stares and could only listen, passively, to the people around her talking. Remote external details.

◇◇◇

When they emerged from the cool gray unreality and were taken through the harsh sodium vapor lights to a waiting police car, she suddenly recoiled. She heard, from somewhere far away, what sounded like gunfire.

"They *always* have to start early," chuckled the big man to the woman and another officer who sat behind the wheel.

It was one week before the Fourth of July.

The window between the front and the back seats was like a cage. The woman's sharply creased uniform smelled faintly of starch.

# September

He had only three days, not enough time to use sixteen hours of it driving.

Camilla and Libby were to meet his plane. He looked through the glass panel of the long walkway that steered the Labor Day weekend passengers from the gangway into the small waiting area.

He saw neither of them. Perhaps they were late.

He came to the end of the glassed walkway and stood to one side. As he resituated his shoulder bag and searched the atrium crowded with holiday travelers, he heard through the clutter a soft voice from somewhere behind him.

"Hudson."

It was Charlie, sitting on a short bench. He had put on a few more pounds in the past month. His color had continued to improve and the smile was almost back at full tilt. But he still looked frail, shrunken.

"Well, what are *you* doing here?" said Hudson. He gripped the outstretched hand and leaned down for the only sort of hug the recent wound could tolerate. "Did Nurse Ratched give her permission?"

"Nurse Ratched and Camilla are waiting for us out front." As they slowly negotiated the swarm he said, "I just wanted to meet you myself, under my own sail. To prove I could." He grinned. "That's what I do these days, you know. Eat fatty foods four times a day and try to prove things to myself."

◇◇◇

The three of them, together, had told Charlie what had happened to him.

They'd had to get it over with only days after he regained consciousness. They delayed as long as they could, fearful of a relapse, but finally they'd had to group themselves around his bed and tell him. They trusted Rogers and Fields to keep their final questions to a minimum and to be as gentle as possible, but there was no gentle way to tell Charlie that his only living relative and his bride had conspired with one of his employees to encourage an unbalanced fanatic to kill him.

◇◇◇

Libby had insisted on being the day nurse since Charlie had come home after three weeks.

"He's not going back into that house alone or with just a hired nurse," she said. "We can't have him getting depressed."

They had moved Charlie into the downstairs bedroom. Before Hudson had to leave for Memphis in early August, to get back for a week of settling in before school, he and Brad had taken turns spelling her for a few hours every day, and Camilla came when she could. Fentry and Victor checked in regularly, and a night nurse, carefully vetted against Libby's burgeoning set of criteria, came on from eight to six.

They also took charge of the new, seven-week-old chocolate Lab puppy—whom Charlie dubbed Ruth and who slept nightly on his bed without once interfering with his bandages—exhorting Charlie, as they dealt with the rigors of housebreaking and tripped over chew toys on a regular basis, to hurry up and get strong enough to assume more of his appropriate paternal functions.

Libby became infuriated, as no one had ever seen her, to find, one morning, a crudely scrawled note about *getting rid of faggots* on the front walk. The police were later able to reassure them that, ironically, it was the wholly unconnected, fairly generic work of a Seagrove boy who'd been up to other similar mischief in the neighborhood for a couple of months, including a particularly obscene bit of graffiti mailed to a nearby Methodist minister's wife. The reminder that such virulent hatred could have been bred and was already seething in an eleven-year-old was an especially bleak sort of reassurance.

They kept Charlie engaged with reading and television and movies and music, with trying to eat, with the physical therapist's first assignments. And to keep his disbelief and sorrow from swallowing him back into a mute darkness, they talked with him about *it.*

A little here, a little there, letting him take the lead but trying not to let him brood hopelessly on the nightmare he had wakened to. They kept him on task. Getting stronger. Getting well. They were all they could be to him. The people who had always been there. The ones who loved him and wanted him back.

They themselves had learned, in grisly pieces, the full scope of the outrage soon after that night in the hospital, and they took encouragement from the mercifully quick closure. Cold solace that it was, at least it was something, and they hoped they might somehow pass that solace on, a positive current of energy, to Charlie.

Sydney had apparently been prepared to fight despite the damning videotape and eyewitnesses, but she gave up after Chaz shakily emitted a lengthy, detailed confession and Terry Main was intercepted at the Puerto Vallarta airport carrying a fake ID and twenty-eight thousand in cash.

◇◇◇

By the time Hudson had to go, there was some abatement in Charlie's physical pain. And, characteristically, as the only gift of gratitude he could offer them, he was working hard at doing what he could about his emotional pain.

On the day Hudson left for Memphis he had come by just as Libby was helping Charlie negotiate his fork over a mashed-up baked potato. Still ashen and wraith thin, he was propped in the winged armchair near his bed.

Suddenly he noticed his reflection in the full-length mirror inside the closet door which Libby must have left open. He gestured feebly with his fork, and when he was sure they were looking, he smiled.

"Guess she was wrong," he rasped.

"Who was wrong?" Hudson asked.

"Duchess of Windsor. You *can* be too rich and too thin."

◇◇◇

Charlie proved something else that night. With Hudson on one side, Libby on the other, and Brad just behind, he walked very slowly but steadily not only into the 26-A but up the stairs, even more slowly, one at a time, to his regular table overlooking the main room.

Camilla finished up a few things and then joined them, carrying a bouquet of native hawthorn and early chrysanthemums that had just arrived with a note from Susie, now on staff with a magazine in New Orleans. They had two bottles of Chateau de Mareuil sur Ay. Victor served the meal. The soup was of chilled pumpkin, shallots and nutmeg, followed by a salad of romaine hearts in a light vinaigrette with kalamata olives, mint, tomatoes, and feta, followed by a terrine of fresh corn, peas, crab, and peppers in tarragon aspic, followed by Gulf red snapper grilled with a tapenade of garlic chutney, and apple tart with cream for dessert.

They were well aware that he rankled under having been the center of attention for too long. He was back in his element now, deflecting that attention, enlivened by his connection to others, to the world. He listened with a kind of boyish elation to Hudson's first anecdotes of the school year, and asked about the book, and Brad's golf game, and Camilla's son who had been with her for two weeks before going back to school.

They talked and laughed and ate and made toasts and drank. They watched the diners below. They repeatedly told Charlie not to tire himself but were elated at seeing him very nearly back to being Charlie.

He proposed the final toast. He looked very deliberately around the table at each of them in turn and lifted his glass.

"Thank you."

In all the sum total of their years of knowing him, and through all the unimaginable horrors of the past ten weeks, they had never seen Charlie cry. For a moment they thought their mutual history was about to transform itself once more.

But he swallowed hard, smiled, and tried again, testing each word like a man on a high wire.

"*You* are the finest family I could ever have imagined. Or ever been blessed to have."

◇◇◇

On Sunday afternoon, Hudson and Camilla walked the beach to Seaside and back. They had told him the night before that August had gone out like a roaring furnace, but this day had dawned in a cool drizzle.

There was no particular destination, no particular reason for going to Seaside. They walked barefoot, along the surf, with lightweight ponchos over their shorts and shirts, enjoying the wet freshness and the light whipping wind.

In the village, they passed some indeterminate period of time browsing through books at the Sundog, had a salad at Bud & Alley's, sat for awhile with hot chocolate on the wide steps of the market, and drifted aimlessly through the shops and galleries.

"I thought you weren't a shopper," she said as he scrutinized an awful piece of pottery.

"I'm not," Hudson said. "Loathe it. This isn't shopping. This is wandering. It's good for the soul, I hear. Particularly the souls of teachers for whom the year has just begun like a huge boulder rolling down a steep hill."

"Do you remember what we talked about that night in the cottage, the night just before..."

"The part about 'keeping a place cleared'?"

"That part."

"Yes," he said.

◇◇◇

When they headed back, the skies had cleared for an unimaginably spectacular sunset. They tried just to let it happen, managing silence for minutes at a time, but it was too much to bear. Like children, they burst with exclamations, they oohed and aahed and pointed, so overpowered as they walked toward the west that they occasionally wheeled in little circles or fell into a silly skip.

By the time they approached Laurel they had forgotten themselves.

The summer.

Time.

They moved silently now, slowly, a part of the land and the seascape, as the saturated colors glowed, then vibrated, and finally muted to a jagged wash of infinite pastels seeping into the Gulf.

They waded through the shallow breach of the lagoon where it meandered across the beach and suddenly felt the wind from the northwest pick up against their faces.

They stopped for a moment and turned to look through the gathering twilight for the roof of Charlie's house, for the end of the upper porch, discernible from only one particular perspective over the high dunes and the tangle of scrub oaks.

They reached out for one another's hands.

To receive a free catalog of other Poisoned Pen Press titles, please contact us in one of the following ways:

Phone: 1-800-421-3976
Facsimile: 1-480-949-1707
Email: info@poisonedpenpress.com
Website: www.poisonedpenpress.com

Poisoned Pen Press
6962 E. First Ave. Ste 103
Scottsdale, AZ 85251